Radical Notes 9

In a Future April

A Novel

Series Editors

Pratyush Chandra

Pothik Ghosh

Other Titles Published in the Series

1. Akhtaruzzman Elias: Beyond the Lived Time of Nationhood
2. Neoliberalism and Hindutva: Fascism, Free Markets and the Restructuring of Indian Capitalism
3. The US Financial Crisis
4. The Sri Lankan Crisis and the Search for Solution
5. Neoliberalism, Primitive Accumulation and Politics in India
6. Loss as Resistance: Towards a Hemeneutic of Revolution
7. The First Global Economic Crisis
8. Notes from Tomorrow: On Reason, Negation and Certainity

Radical Notes 9

In a Future April

(A Novel)

Paramita Ghosh

AAKAR

In a Future April (A Novel)
Paramita Ghosh

First Published, 2017

ISBN 978-93-5002-510-9

Published by
AAKAR BOOKS
28 E Pocket IV, Mayur Vihar Phase I
Delhi 110 091, INDIA
aakarbooks@gmail.com

Typeset at
Arpit Printographers, Delhi 110 032

Printed at
Mudrak, 30 A, Patparganj, Delhi 110 091

A movement in a sense is a struggle over the definition of reality—how reality is constituted. It is this struggle that builds the focus and targets of the movement, informing the praxes towards social transformation. Inherent in this struggle is the act of reclaiming—sense and sensibility, words and meaning...

The word "radical", which in this post-Cold War phase of Global Capitalism or globaloney has been reduced to a general notion characterizing all kinds of extremism and deviance, is one such word that has been time and again reclaimed by the practitioners of social transformation. "Radical" derived from the Latin word, 'radix' meaning 'root' = 'basic' = 'fundamental' is a concept that aptly defines a transformatory practice as an endeavour to reveal and target the essence of what is given to us in appearance. Radicalism in this sense is nothing but fundamental transformation rather than politicking in appearances. Further, and foremost, it is the all-round critique of the status quo and its genealogies, rather than accepting the disciplinary divide/boundaries that the capitalist system perpetuates in order to control labour-power and labour, our efforts and their fruits.

Radical Notes is an endeavour to coordinate the radical voices around the globe, with special focus on South Asia. In our view such focus (which could have been anything) is not just for convenience, given the facilitators' cultural and intellectual comfort, but is also needed to concretise any 'radical' pursuit. In our view South Asia provides us the opportunity to visualise the reproduction of 'global' capitalism and struggle against it in a regional setting. But we must remember such focus is always fluid with the ever-dynamic radical needs of the humanity.

Radical Notes booklets are contributions on social, cultural, political or economic issues from counter-hegemonic perspectives, which need not be confined to any established socialist and communist current of thought (though these approaches are most welcome).

Series Editors
Radical Notes

To
P & P

Foreword

"An operation carried out in the written language"
–Italo Calvino

This foreword is not an apologia. It is not an attempt to provide justifications for publishing a work of fiction in a series of booklets and books that belong to the essayistic genre of critical theory and/or political analysis. The readers can themselves determine whether or not this novel, or other creative works that we intend to publish in the near future, fit into the dynamic politics of this series. Nevertheless, the question remains whether these literary-creative engagements replicate what political essays do, whether they provide insights that these essays cannot even think through.

We are not formalists who study the specificities of forms in order to see them as their own justification. In fact, there is no such formal autonomy. If you find one, rest assured it is the poverty of form that the essence generates and productivises to generate illusions of such autonomy.

"Essence must appear or shine forth. The essence is thus not behind or beyond the appearance; instead, by virtue of the fact that it is the essence that exists concretely, concrete existence is appearance." (Hegel:197) We consider the identification and study of the practice of form very crucial to access specific levels of reality—the *structural* dynamics that *appear* through this form.

A literary work accesses aspects of reality that only a literary form can reveal. Not very long ago, Italo Calvino approached a literary work "as an operation carried out in the written language." Literature involves "several levels of reality" and it is the awareness of the distinction between these levels that makes a literary work possible. Calvino further elaborates: "In a work of literature, various levels of reality may meet while remaining distinct and separate, or else they may melt and mingle and knit together, achieving a harmony among their contradictions or else forming an explosive mixture." (Calvino: 101)

Hence, a literary work emerges as a methodological *operation* demythologising Reality into levels of reality. It is through this operation that we access these specific levels. As Spinoza's "extension" and Marx's "sensuous activity", literary practice is intrinsic to those levels of reality of which it is an awareness. Calvino, however, cautions against the tendency to overgeneralise, to forget the form's immanence to its own levels of reality—in the case of literature, these levels are part of the "written world". Calvino while "distinguishing the various levels of reality within the work of art considered as a world of its own", and, therefore, avoiding the sirens of historicism, is emphatic in considering "the work as a product, in its relation to the outside world in the age when it was created and the age when we received it". In fact, this historicisation is what is termed as self-awareness—when literary works "turn around on themselves, look at themselves in the act of coming into being, and become aware of the materials they are made of". (Calvino: 103)

Almost a century ago, Hungarian Marxist Georg Lukacs had expressed very eloquently the dialectical problematic of form and content in literature and its historicity. He understood a literary genre as intrinsic to an "age". "The novel is the epic of an age in which the extensive totality of life is no longer directly given, in which the immanence of meaning in life has become a problem, yet which still thinks in terms of totality." (Lukacs: 56) The novel is born in an epoch characterised by the separation of labour from labour-power. In such circumstances, the totality cannot be accessed in its immediacy because forms of labour are dualised: the concrete becomes discrete, and gets individuated and differentiated from its meaning in totality. In other words, the concrete is rendered an undifferentiated mass of particular appearances. Thus we need "the force of abstraction" to access and to reproduce the totality in thought.

The "form-giving intention" (or, what Marx in *Grundrisse*, of which Lukacs must have not been aware of at the time of writing this work, termed "living, form-giving, fire") of a novelist reconstructs or systematises the totality abstractly. The totality is not immediately and organically accessed, rather it emerges in the creation of the novel through "abstract systematisation" that exposes and distances from the conventionality of "concrete life", the "objective world". It emerges in the process of a critique of this concrete, objective life and world, revealing "the interiority of the subjective" world, the "political unconscious".

The living labour of a novelist creates totality in a "socially symbolic act". (Jameson) It is a critical operation that in its Utopianism creates a crisis for subsumption—providing a glimpse of real totality beyond the swamps of false totality—of capital and state (the conventionality and its everydayness).

"To see the world in a grain of sand"—William Blake

Till recently a slice of reality was considered sufficient to grasp the truth of reality—to see the universe in a grain of sand. This Blakean radical vision originally was a reminder of metaphysical holism, that was losing its grip in the nineteenth century. It was restricted to those who saw the future as a doom or a dawn—the judgement day or a world revolution. You could make out the total sense of a particularity.

The processes of "infinite regression of quibbling and calculating" (Badiou: 40)—a continuous discretising and recombining, the so-called "creative destruction", was effectuated by the generalised commodity economy and industrialism, which led to the perpetuation of analytics, analytical philosophies and positivism. Eventually, the Blakean vision was reduced "to see the world *of* a grain of sand," so that the elements of these grains could be identified, discretised and recombined—isn't this what production is all about?

But still you could imagine a universe of many universes —a meta was still there but as an aggregate of atomic individualities or as a forced universality. Hence, national revolutions, national socialisms, socialism in one country, national development—however, the vision of national liberation still had an international tenor as it grasped liberation in terms of "liberation from". The collective dream that politics embodied was condensed in the *possibility* to empower the dethroned subjectivity, bypass the developmental pains and still catch up or even divert.

But as the economy got more and more integrated, the humanity and sociality were further analysed and discretised—to be invested in the social factory. It is the digital recombining of anything and everything as mere numbers. As the world increasingly became a global village, we were transformed into villagers—"formed by simple accretion, much as potatoes in a sack form a sack of potatoes." (Marx) As we were increasingly reduced, and reduced to sameness, we militantly asserted our difference. The postmodern assertion of relativities was nothing but the other side of modernist absolutism. They mutually energised one another. We assert our differences, and in an instant they are equalised, accumulated and turned into gold-and we are reduced to "packets of time, separated from their interchangeable and occasional bearers." (Bifo: 95)

In a Future April is a novel about revolutions in this age—but being of this age, it is truly a "monstrous abbreviation" of all times, even of those revolutionary periods which were inaugurated exactly a century ago. All revolutionaries of those times were aware of the elements of passive counter-revolution in these revolutions, but the passage to the decline was always considered a struggle. Revolution and its systemic subsumption could still be compositionally, spatially and temporally differentiated. But today in late-st capitalism they are both the same. If this is a novel about precariats and cognitarians as vanguards, it is also about vanguards as precariats and cognitarians. But was this not true for all revolutions? *In a Future April* narrates and operates the stories of revolutions to abbreviate them into the pregnant dialectic of hope and dismay.

November 23, 2016 **Pratyush Chandra**

References

Alain Badiou (2005). "Philosophy and Desire." *Infinite Thought.* Trans. and ed. Oliver Feltham and Justin Clemens. New York: Continuum. 29-42.

Franco "Bifo" Berardi (2009). *The Soul at Work.* Trans. Francesca Cadel and Giuseppina Mecchia. Semiotext(e). Massachusetts: The MIT Press.

Italo Calvino (1997). "Levels of Reality in Literature."*The Literature Machine.* Trans. Patrick Creagh. London: Vintage Books. 101-121.

GWF Hegel (2010). *Encyclopedia of the Philosophical Sciences in Basic Outline Part I: Science of Logic.* Trans. and ed. by Klaus Brinkmann and Daniel O. Dahlstrom. Cambridge: Cambridge University Press.

Georg Lukacs (1971). *The Theory of the Novel.* Trans. Anna Bostock. Massachusetts: The MIT Press.

Karl Marx ([1852] 2002). "The Eighteenth Brumaire of Louis Bonaparte." (Trans. Terrell Carver) *Marx's Eighteenth Brumaire: (Post)modern Interpretations.* Ed. Mark Cowling and James Martin. London: Pluto Press. 19-109.

Contents

"...We survive, in the confusion
Of a life reborn beyond reason.

I beg you, ah, I beg you, don't desire death!
I'm here, alone, with you, in a future April..."
(Pier Paolo Pasolini, 'Prayer To My Mother')

Revolution is not an answer. It is that which makes life an open question.
–An unnamed militant

CHARACTERS

The Partisans

Mir, Biran, Lavni, Hog, Soli, J Babu, Uma, Kanhu, Guli, Danish, Jiro

The Dongs

Baba Lala, Commissioner Hall, Kuberos, Polo, Mangu

The Fairlanders

Cliff and Penny McGowan, Caelian Dado, Colonel Saunders, Woegore, Hardy Screw

The In-Betweeners

Aristu Argot, Jallar, Mr Darius, Kirit

1

One Day, I'll Become What I Want

At the other side of The Gate, a car. A couple was crossing and uncrossing their limbs around each other inside it. The windows were up. After sometime, with a touch of a nail, it rolled down. No one looked up to The Bus, where H Hog, seated inside, was thinking about the one or two thoughts he had about love in his time. Men and women are dead, but love can be made to appear, he said to himself looking away from the car in front. Years ago, or was it a few hours ago, he had seen himself vanish as a pair of immovable dark eyes had opened next to him in bed, and he had waited for a sign when Lavni would release the sun held down under her tongue in a big orange bubble.

Elsewhere in The Frontier, people were waking up in batches. The day, fancy that, was here again, let's see what today will make us do. Hog had combed his hair at seven in the morning, he had his tea minutes later and had been at the bus stop by nine. By nine, every hair on his head was disciplined, every thought that would pull him down, erased. He was not successful but he was not a failure. He did not have a desk but when there was work, he had a chair. He was not included but he was not excluded. He was not about to be saved but he was not about to be killed. What was keeping him alive and what was keeping him safe was his sense of office and the feeling for discipline, that made him eat an egg at ten past seven and reach the bus stop at nine, clock-time. The bus stop, not The Bus, *had* to be reached at nine. At some point, the driver, a man of honour, would keep his word and bring the bus around, and Hog would take his place in it. If two people were waiting for each other, he believed, they would find each other.

In The Bus, rode a people for whom solitude is both baggage

and common property. You could turn to your neighbour and have a long conversation and then be silent again. Some doors are never locked. There is no greater silence than the sky noiselessly spotting itself with stars and the stars are for everybody, said Hog, half-aloud. The man sitting next to him turned to look at him. It *was* a rather long sentence. But Hog was comforted. Nobody should mind if a neighbour notices one's silence and deepens it with his, he said to himself. In The City where they were all headed, he felt all this did not happen, as a window suddenly clapped itself open onto the street. The dust in its corners fell in loose sheets, the half-open eyes of a woman met his over the curtains. "But... I will always leave towards The City," thought Hog, and perhaps in some of the heads in The Bus, the same thought was the first thought of the day.

They filled The Bus from The Frontier with forty men and women and disgorged them at The City gate. One creaky bus. Eighty people. Each day, twice a day. Once for going, once for coming. Sometimes, The Bus appeared the day before—when there were more men to be carried to The City to build a temple, build a bell, pull up a bridge, polish a few hundred shoes, water the begonias in record time. Then The Bus became a jet. On other days it moved like a duck not because it was over-full but because the road had to be imagined.

"Which son of man says it is my business to repair roads too?" growled Gorora, the driver, over the din and shot a look at an overhead box on the bus's roof in which he stored picks and shovels to fill in the cracks made by cheap coal tar on the ground, and also knock a few heads down when he felt like it.

The Bus was a test of optimism and sublime torture. On the days it picked up people all through the night, they had people who sang all through the night. They brought their drums and they sang; when they forgot their drums, they banged their feet on the floor of the bus as a heavily whiskered old man who unfailingly managed a place by the window wept out ballads of impossible loves and longings, of courtship between the mountain and the moon, of marriage between a pigeon and fox. But the old man knew how to keep things light. As the sky changed colour, mauve to purple, purple to black, white on white, and a few children climbed on his lap, it was, for him, a sign—as if he needed one—that he could begin the silly season.

*Sirraras, good mararras,**
Madhu's brother I
Madhu coming, monkey going
Monkey thought, Madhu had
Tiffin in his cloth
Monkey bite, Madhu fight,
Pain do, sir, pain do.

Once or twice, Gorora had mentioned to his bosses the festive atmosphere in The Bus. The bosses had looked at each other, alarmed. No singing, they said, and especially no singing together. So Gorora had tried to get the old man on his side. He had offered him a seat beside his, a cup from his flask of tea.

"Why sing? Don't sing," he had gruffly begged during a bus ride home. It didn't work, so he had offered him money.

"At the end of the day it's about money, isn't it? Take it. Just don't make so much noise," he had insisted.

The old man hadn't agreed. He wiped his face with his shirt, cleared his throat and opened his mouth to sing. "See, the beginning of the day, it's about money. The end of the day it should be about art. If we are noisy, our art will be noisy," he said.

The queue for a place in The Bus was serpentine. If you missed The Bus, you lost a day. Three hundred would return home and go to bed early to return to the spot where The Bus that had seats for eighty, caught them by surprise daily. But it should not be assumed that the bones of men, by nature, are at ease standing in queue just because they know that standing is a habit they must not break. Where the bus stops, there is the bus stop. There are poles dug here and there to hold on to. But there is no shade. Hog stood every day holding onto a pole till The Bus arrived. Then he would sit. As an employee of *The Meat,* and a man of mixed blood, he looked Fairlander enough to be guaranteed a seat. But standing is a condition and a habit he must not break. But in the morning shining with generous sunshine, he does not want to think of all that. In the morning, as the wheels of the bus scraped the ground and dragged the loose loamy earth of The Frontier over the neat shiny street of The City, the two provinces of The Lambda, Hog told himself anything was possible. Mixed up was good.

MEN SCHOOLED as managers from The City came to the dusty Frontier, the frantic Frontier, the Frontier of the Factories. They shouted through microphones from every corner of this undulating land in which the lives of people as seen from the top seemed of a smaller scale. On every elevation, they pulled down a hut, rolled their bulldozers over every curve and trough and they did so with such rattle that the souls of trees that can think of one or two things only, that is, to multiply and smell the air above the ground, decided to give the land, a barrenness. One day, a manager wired back from a one-window post office, a hovel roughly put together at the end of a nameless corner in The Frontier: "No green, fit for steel." Sitting on its steps, he suddenly felt upon him, the bulbous eye of an owl and the quiet eye of man, many men, that the wooden ships that were landing in the Frontier's northern coast, were throwing on shore. And the ships were bringing in all sorts of people. They had heard of the Plebiscite and the promise that The Lambda would one day be a nation, and if they were joined to its beginning, they felt, it would give them what they wanted. One day, we will become what we want* ...

"Hut-hut-hut," said the manager but the people would not move, neither would they blink. Every wrinkle on the horizon turned out to be a ship full of them. They looked in his direction from the shore, then at the metallic sky, then at the chests of their children torn by the ropes on which they had jumped, and disappeared quietly down the troughs to build their homes. Some climbed up to the post-office and squatted at his feet. So he decided to tell them a story of building a nation of Cities, brightly lit Cities, so bright that if they were willing to pay, they could do away with night. He was a bad raconteur, they did not believe him. Big mistake.

The next day, the front page of The City's papers announced the decision to build a warehouse to manufacture gigantic glass orbs that would be filled with five hundred sodium vapour bulbs. On the second day, a few who had travelled on The Bus and had got hold of a few papers, read aloud at the Frontier's square, the decision to hang them from 800-foot steel rods. The first batch of rods and bulbs would line The Gates to The City was the news on the third. On the fifth day, *The Meat* said– the newspaper that had all the dtails–their light would illuminate, every hidden feature, every mole, any unspoken thought, any mess, every mole, any unspoken thought, any mess, of all the people who entered The City. It was necessary, said *The Meat* on the sixth. On the seventh, the paper wrote an editorial on the benefits of steel. Steel was an example of what a man can do, it said. And what men can build, in the days that followed, they built.

2

The House of Freedom

Eleven. Hog got down from The Bus and started walking towards the office of *The Meat* two kilometres away. The man who sold peanuts at its gate had travelled by The Bus too—on the roof—and as it stopped, he began to sprint to take his place by the newspaper's gate that was now his after he edged out an elderly peanut seller last summer. He should be settling down now, Hog thought, with his handcart under a streetlight, and would be looking up cursing the sun after every few minutes; his little boy, his face burnt like a nut, would screw his face and cry noiselessly wary of his father's fist; his hungry eyes would watch young men hurrying past with heavy parcels. Further down the road, the plangent call of a hawker would sound and spread over the entire street. It would dry the hawker's throat but leave the street undisturbed, it was too early in the day for a sale.

They used to call *The Gentleman* (in moments of nostalgia, Hog would refer to *The Meat* by its earlier name), the barometer of The City, an institution that set the morality of the people living in it. "And this was the mistake," thought Hog as he watched the building's first white pillar come into view. "If The City dies, where will *The Gentleman* be?" At eleven, this was the tableau of Hog's life. Calamities did not claim it or interrupt the passing of this procession. At eleven, this was also the tableau of the peanut vendor's life, and Hog, his brother in tedium, appeared in it every morning without fail.

There were two ways of entering *The Meat* just like there are two ways of entering any building. Hog avoided the front—the glassy entrance, the burst of marble, the impersonal salute and most of all, the mercantile clamour of the advertisement section of a newspaper office.... From the back, he always said, you were who you are at that time of the day.

An old rusty olive jeep, cranked out a moan as it halted in the shadowy back entrance of the building stacked with bundles of unsold newspaper, cellotape, packing material, some broken flower pots, odd bits and ends. It had just brought in Billie, the telephone operator. Young girls, from whom The City had not yet taken everything, called Billie "The Voice". A hundred calls were made to the paper just to hear him say in his low rumble, "Good morning. *The Meat*...."

Still ten or twenty minutes later, the guard at *The Meat* wiped his hand on his trousers and began his day's work. He was a different man at the front entrance. At the back, he no longer stood in attention. The babus rarely passed this way. He squatted in the bright sunshine, showing his back to the passing hours. Hog didn't know his name. The guard knew his but confirmed it each day.

There must be something comical about my walk into office thought Hog. "The guard sees the comedy, which is why he salutes me. He salutes me only on some days. Those days I must be more comical than the other days."

"H Hog, editorial?" the guard asks him every day. Hog involuntarily presses down his hand over his hair and runs his fingers over the head of the pen peeping out of his shirt-pocket. "What—does he expect me to deny it?" thinks Hog as he signs the register in front of him. Hog had seen him reading *The Meat* at various corners of the office and wondered what the paper could offer him. His children could not attend the schools whose admission policies the paper discussed. The roads, the municipality was spending thousands of mukkas on to repair, were not for him. The advertisements of soaps and shoes heaped on *The Meat* were not for him. The projects the government had flagged off would not benefit The Frontier where he stayed.

"No man takes more than is in his fate," Hog decided as he hauled himself up the grubby stairs stained with spit and snot. *"But children don't know these stairs. These stairs tell the history of this house. I have memories beside these stairs, of waiting on them, of being pushed down them, of making way on these stairs.... But the* *children just see these stairs,**" Hog, grateful and surprised, mumbled to himself at the kind turn somebody else's poem should do him by returning him to poetry. But in the flickering light of the bulb, he was finally forced to see the stairs as an absence of sympathy for those who moved up and down it.

A brown pail at the top of the stairs stopped Hog's ruminations. To his surprise, the curly head of a junior reporter was seen next to it.

"Soli—what's up?"

Soli nods. "Aristu had asked me for feedback on his editorial. He had said 'Show some spirit'."

"And?" asks Hog.

"'Just don't tell the truth', Boss had said under his breath."

"Didn't catch it?" asks Hog bending to help him drag the pail.

"I didn't catch that," says Soli and dipped his hand inside the pail and took out a rag to give the floor a good hard scrub. How the marble shone!

3

Street Theatre, Crime City

Argot Aristu was no professor of psychology but he understood that men and women wanted to be in business. He had begun a career in The Frontier in gum and cigarettes in a market short of them during the war and had realised that greed put in the service of chance could become good friends in the great game. He always acknowledged the part they had played in his life and never held formal schooling against those who turned up for jobs as journalists if they had not been to the right one. Grown into manhood in the back alleys, on his broad bare body, he used to hang a holster—in which he stored bullets on the top-that was connected to another leather case hanging sideways from a trouser-belt. Aristu kept his M1 Girond, a semi-automatic, close to him. It slapped against his thighs as he moved around The Frontier in search of an unsentimental education. By all accounts, he was a good shot. Since the change in his station of life, in *The Meat*, except for the one instance at the beginning, he had not had to use force to make people listen to him. A poor parish priest he had befriended and from whom he had picked up a manner of Fairlanderese, regularly blamed himself at confession, over his friend's excesses.

"If a man can fire a bullet that smokes for seven days, he has done well," Aristu liked to say. "Correct me if you think I have done badly. I had no background in running a newspaper but I run one. I had no connection with the cigarette trade except that I knew how to smoke. Schools don't teach you to take risks. They teach you to sit and stand, and then confuse you with moral science."

The native obsession with education, he felt was a character flaw, the conspiracy of educated gentlemen and their continued thrill at having grabbed the best jobs, as clerks, under the Fairlanders. The qualities he looked for in his staff were different. He asked them about their strengths and weighed them as if they were onions and potatoes. "If you want a job, say that. Don't say you can write well—what if I need you to sing well, as well?" Interviewing staff journalists, he would ask them to show him a portfolio of their best articles. Those who brought them along, didn't always get the job. He didn't want the staff reading his mind. There should be, he thought, no difference between a man and his shoe. He studied people with the same interest that he studied buildings. Both needed paint, upkeep. Both cracked, and he could wait for them. If a building was demolished, you could replace it. You could also re-wire men with new ideas if you could show them it was to their benefit. History was full of them and he was on its side.

When the news of the Plebiscite first broke out in The Frontier, he was settling a dispute in one of the units of his factory. One of his senior managers returning to the factory after a drunken fight at the bar had thrown the shoes of workers in boilers for piling them at the door.

"If you have whisky in your stomach, you do not take action," he told the manager and told his staff he would sack him. He didn't. The workers, who were baying for his blood, were calmed into better thoughts by promises of jobs to their relatives at his newest venture—the newspaper. Gum. Cigarette. Newspaper. For Argot Aristu, it was all the same thing.

It is said Aristu heard of *The Gentleman* when a young reporter from the paper landed outside his factory one day during the labour trouble. He had his guards break his left hand in warning to the right one and then had him brought into his office. He made him drink his tea with six spoons of sugar and then told them he had the highest regard for the profession.

"Unlike philosophers, journalists like specifics. I'm learning, so, what is your name?"

Soli said his name was Soli.

"Son, in a few months, I will be running *The Gentleman* that stands at The Hollow. Thought you should know if you are around next time we meet in that office."

That evening, Aristu went to meet his friend, a mercenary, who had jumped off his ship to protest the distribution of bad rum along with inhuman cabin conditions. With Heaney in the middle, they met a man, the stockbroker, Marianoos, a former employee of *The Meat*, who nursed a grudge against the owners and wanted them to lose it. So, Aristu set out to outline his big plan. He had decided to have faith in the young stockbroker as he had faith in all self-made men and their thirst to make something of themselves, and self-madeness was what Aristu was after. He told Marianoos about meeting the new banks and its directors agreeing to put up the cash for a hostile takeover. He told him how he had had to scold, bribe and supply whisky, cigarettes and well-endowed women in private consignments to their houses to convince them.

"When it comes to being self-made, you will see I will not be found wanting," he told Marianoos, who by now had started dialling and smiling into his telephone.

"Find the value of *The Gentleman's* scrip and buy the shares at a higher value. You know how it can be done. After that, I know what I have to do."

There are no witnesses to how the takeover actually happened but stories of successful men are usually formed like this—they first land as myths, then live as metaphors and then pass onto everyday language. One rainy afternoon, Aristu took twenty of his toughs to ride The Bus from The Frontier into The City and got down at The Gate. His advance party bribed the guards of the offices in the buildings surrounding *The Gentleman* and then to make it look that they had given them trouble, gagged them and locked them in the lifts. Some of his men slipped into the guards' uniforms; the others took position on the terrace. His best snipers took aim at a window on the third floor. Then they waited for Aristu.

The hours rolled by and the sun became a blip of light. Argot Aristu got down from a rickshaw and walked to the newspaper office. He looked up at the building and his bootlegging heart skipped a beat. It could have been a trick of the eye but the building seemed to him like a Roman stadium built for epic battles. He sent in a slip to Penny McGowan—a girl who being the director's daughter needed no one's permission to take stupid decisions—and was handling for a day the paper of her father, Cliff McGowan, a man who had made his fortune transforming the farmers of The Frontier, into labourers at the tea estates of his fellow Fairlanders.

Even though all the guards had been replaced by his men, Aristu decided that she should be allowed the ritual of calling him in. He would wait for her call. So, he beckoned a passing staff member and handed him a slip to give the director. Meanwhile, a waiting lackey, who had run along with the rickshaw while he rode it to *The Gentleman*, waited with a change of clothes. Aristu adjusted his trousers, put on a new boiled shirt and the cap of his dead friend, Heaney, knotted a tie and thought about what he had written on the slip.

In a line, it was simply this. He, Argot Aristu, the owner of the Highway Cigarette and Gum Factory and since this day, the majority shareowner of *The Gentleman*, was here to give her economic advice and that she should take it.

Penny McGowan sat behind her desk and examined the content of the slip. Its implication was a catastrophe. But, she girdled her gown remembering that her father had a benign notion of them. His paper announced one each day. Catastrophes even if they come in a chain, he said, could be turned around with a good headline and if you don't panic in the first ten minutes. Penny decided to give herself those minutes to hatch a plan. She told herself that she had much to lose if she admitted Aristu into her room in haste. As for the bullets pinging her room, she let them fly. The first bullet knocked the nose off the marble Queen Luna figurine standing on her father's table lined with the finest Macassar ebony. As she was no fan of Queen Luna, Penny did not mind. But when a bullet singed the whiskers of the grey rosette cat on her lap that her father had got her and which she had, with her characterestic overstatement named, Miaow, she realised she had better be up on her game.

She sent for Argot Aristu. And was quick, too quick, in making a move on him.

Said Aristu: "Before there were newspapers, there was

gossip. Priests gossiped about God—if He was in His temple or he was not. Whether God who gave health, food and children was the same as the one who brought fever, pestilence and death to mothers. News destroyed God. And good or bad, news is our business. But I'd say it is the same thing. The business of God and the business of newspapers is the same business. It is the responsibility of editors not to put out news that make people sick, but what makes them healthy... I believe, Miss, you are having a fit."

Miss McGowan was not having a fit. She was struggling with deep emotions. The day had been a nasty surprise. She had offered to stand in for her father that day because she had gone to the zoo in the morning and found it closed. The cinema she had sailed into after that, had been bogus.

"At last I thought 'let me go to *The Gentleman*," she told Aristu with dewy eyes. "It would be open. As far as I knew, no one was planning to shut it.... How old do you think I am?"

"Thirty."

"No. Nineteen."

"You don't look that young."

"It's makeup."

On behalf of her father, she said she would sign partnership papers with Aristu so that Plebsiscite—a word that actually made her curl her lip and disturb her stomach—when it came, and if it came, he would find her by his side.

Aristu who discovered nationalism at around the same time he got his hold on capital, spurned the offer. White women, he said, had been the inspiration for *Paradise Lost*. He had known, he said, better women than Eve.

The next day, the body of the daughter of Cliff McGowan was taken all around The City in the latest scientific import, a refrigerated car, meant for transporting fresh lobsters. People milled around the hearse and whispered. Fairlandermen wondered at the silence of the government. A few youths, who had partnered the little lady at the Fairlanders-only club, raised a few confused slogans unsure of how to protest against a government run by men of the same colour. Elderly Fairlanders, great believers in the colony's bureaucratic machinery, demanded a response from its bureaucrats. They had immense faith in commissions, enquiries and reports. A stiff statement should be issued and a panel discussion should at least be held, they said. Justice and Fairness, were not just Christian miracles; they should be part of life and not just delivered by court, they said. Finally, the crowd went home saying public servants were a harried lot in these changing times. There were too many secrets to pass on or too many mouths to seal that they could not be bothered with young women who lost their heads from falling down office buildings in red applique underwear.

"This is getting worse than dangerous," said a bystander suddenly. "These days, none of us know what we don't know."

In a year's time, Argot Aristu, changed the mast and renamed the paper *The Meat*—not to appear cavalier but to tell journalists that they need not take journalism that seriously. He commissioned artists to work on his likeness in black marble and had his busts installed at key work areas in the office—the printing press, the reporters' cabin, the newsroom, the accounts section. His staff never forgot who they worked for. The lackeys who had accompanied him on that fateful day when a Fairlander miss thought she would give less and take more, swore he had moved into the office and no one had seen him leave.

The journalists most prone to spine-bending, the men and women most prone in their story-telling to take the side of the strong against the weak, those who only looked to project the times of celebrations as a state of permanence, those who saw in conflict, a disruption of life and not a moment ripe for transformation, those who saw in the possibility of transition, no opportunity to demolish old structures and reject them, those who were waiting to sign up with the new elite, those who aligned their interests only to the top and wore their colours, waved their flags, and were ready to join the church of Aristu—those, he, Aristu Argot, sought to encourage, fete and promote. He would catch them during office hours and offer his friendship.

The newspaper, he said, while walking around his office, was a job of magic. "As journalists, there are only two things to think of when filing a story or while pitching it to your bosses.

First, that life is sad and second, people want miracles. They do not expect you to be a hero. There is disease. There are earthquakes. And pillars fall. If a pillar falls in the middle of the night, they will not expect you to rush and prop it up. But next day, they must find it in the newspaper otherwise they will take it personally. Is the life of the man dead under the pillar valuable? Some of you will say yes, some no. What would I have you do? Just this—Do not show that you are detached about what other people are attached to. If it makes the reader happy to see his broken life in a newspaper, show his broken life. Life is sad—give people what they want. In our business nothing is false news, you simply have to find it. But if you think, the work of *The Meat* requires you to go and talk to people on the streets and once out there, it is your job to lead crusades, I will break your leg. Now, tell me, do you smoke? Do you drink? You don't drink! Drink up! Otherwise how will you grow up?"

4

Confessional Literature

The place where we go to work has a lot to do with living and thinking. That is, it is connected to the way we live our life and the way we think about it. So it also says something about the way we are getting ready to die. Giving up on life is not easy and giving up on death makes it the same. From our place of work we carry home one or two questions that usually kill us, messes our sleep, disrupts our streets, muddies our friendships, shows the lies in our truths, our incapacity for hardness towards ourselves and others whom we see as extensions of ourselves, but most of all, ourselves. When we think, we think with the best part of us, when we live, we are indefensible.

"Sometimes, I can't string two sentences together," thought an old man sitting at his desk. J Babu found himself unable to move beyond it. He had sat behind this wooden desk for forty years. The wood had aged, he should get another desk, give his room a paint, but he wouldn't change a thing. These little allowances, the liberty to have ideas, to be able to decide the fate of his space and what flowed from it, and in a sense, decide that his little world could exist in a separateness from the dominant architecture, made him feel masterly—like someone who had been given ownership and a stake in the office's systems, its overall symmetry. All these, he now admitted to himself, had spoilt him, given him illusions. But in these forty years, he felt he had earned his spurs, faced many storms in the course of work.

"But did I face them or did I manage them? I certainly arranged things to my benefit. No, wait, I did face them," he mumbled, surprised at his indecisiveness, a handicap he had never had at work. If you read J Babu's editorials in *The Meat*, as The City always did in the morning, you felt reassured. The sun was climbing the east, the housemaid was out walking the dog, the cook was marinating the mutton for lunch, A was a letter of the alphabet, 5 was a number, wars were being fought Elsewhere—this morning, the world was at just the place it should be and where you had left it last night.

For forty years, J Babu had done the moral thing; he had produced order and balance in the universe, and also at his office. To his juniors, especially the very young and the very restless, he had been part priest and part football coach, privy to their afternoon whispers, their little suppressed struggles, their flexing of muscles, their doomed protests against shadowy structures. He would correct their opening sentences, school them on editorial policy and cushion the nastiest cuts (the "unfreedoms of a free press" he liked to say with such a laugh that it was difficult not to feel that this greying man was on your side) by telling them how you could still be the good guy who fights and be accepted, recognised and unfailingly promoted, with the gentlest of anecdotes drawn from his personal life.

What he had learnt from his bureau chief, a Mr Morin, he channelised without break or adaptation as if without that continuity with his past, he would be like a broken pipe standing knee deep in dirty water. Who, what, when and where, are the pillars of reportage would say Mr Morin, was the first line of any peroration. "The reader", he said, "depends on the paper to tell him these things about the article on which he has spent two seconds of his time. And the reader wants to know all this without prejudice and bias. In the beginning, said Mr Morin, he may not trust what he reads but once he gives you that trust, or in other words, gives the paper that trust, he will then adopt your attitudes as his or her own so be careful of your 'truth' which should not be too different from the general truths. And from that moment onwards, things were crystal clear."

J Babu's anecdotes, it is true, were enigmatic. You could read them in any kind of way. They didn't lead you down this or that path, but left you in the middle. He didn't believe in brinksmanship and he would always argue for not taking things too far. Perhaps the lesson he seemed to be teaching was simply this—here is the road, and if you so wish, dance here. But he wouldn't show you the way to his home, take off your coat, help you to a chair and let you prick his infinite peace. He had his pangs, he had his moments when he felt he had not been true to his profession but his bosses could always depend on him to resolve them in his head. He stayed with his demons for a day, or, gave it a week if he was feeling really transgressive. But in the end he would pipe it down and read aloud from some poem and prose on about the verse: "To save your world you asked this man to die/Would this man, could he see you now, ask why?"

It was in between a bout of Auden and tea that Aristu came to visit J Babu, his seniormost editor on the Statement page, one evening, tapping his silk umbrella.

"What is this talk of revolution I hear, J Babu? If it is true, we must have a revolution against the revolution."

Born in the month of April in The Lambda, a place blanketed by a slow-spreading, disagreeable heat, J Babu was prone to untimely chills. He moved close to the window that had a wide view of The Frontier to catch a bit of air even though he realised Aristu's eye was on him. The hand on his shoulder reminding him "to do the job" was an order, clearly an order, that he could not call by any other name. But for some reason, today, he was taking the risk of turning his back to it if only to postpone, by searching for something as he scanned the horizon. The Bus was readying to leave for The Frontier. It was the time to unlock The Gates it seemed.

The Gate, which acted as a barrier between The Lambda's City and The Frontier, was cranking open with the exertions of the guards working on a motor that had begun to rust. (The gossips at the marketplace had talked of little else that week.) It remained closed through the day opening once in the morning at eight for the bus bringing employees attached to various city establishments, to enter it. But it was not a straightforward passage. It couldn't be. The vehicle had to stand in queue for the managers of the factories to get their cars in first, roaring into The Frontier. After these cars moved, it moved. Picking passengers all over The Frontier, some who had waited all night for a seat, it would then hobble its way through the broken-down roads carrying clerks, peons, the petty trader, the postman, the constable, to The Gate, and then, if allowed to pass, to some of the offices in The City. A seat in The Bus was no guarantee for an entry to The City. To enter it, you needed to have a purpose and an acceptable one. Last year, the civil administration had earned fines in thousands of mukkas from people who had somehow slipped in and loitered around, squatted on the squares, placed their dirty fingers on shop windows, sung unknown and therefore dangerous songs, and had asked terribly insolent questions.

"You must take charge of this business, J," said Aristu with a smile joining him at the window. With his cane, he tapped the window pane. "Just look—who knows the place could be crawling with troublemakers. Guards grow old, the eye could fail. Whichever way The Plebiscite goes, trouble is trouble and we must take a strong line against it. After that, of course, you can write a piece on....I mean, let's see which way it goes. Why is no one following what I say these days? Create an opinion. Spread it on all our pages."

By evening, J Babu had perfectly worded and headlined his editorial calling for a new law to limit the number of people from The Frontier working in The City. He adjusted his spectacles on the bridge of his nose and finally took them off. An odd restlessness had taken hold of him. He looked closely at the proofs and got up from his desk to switch on all the lights in his room.

"That was it," he thought with relief, "it was the lack of light!" and went over to his bookshelf hung on the wall. He appraised it with pride. It was a fine collection of books. He had maintained them well, lined them up as troops. He fumbled for the key to open the case and then saw it lying next to his tea kettle. He fitted the key in the hole with some difficulty and opened the case. He looked for his glasses and found he had taken them off his nose. He was misplacing too many things but he did not want to blame everything on advancing age. Forgetting had nothing to do with growing old; what you wanted to preserve, you remembered. He picked up a book and turned its pages. In the cold Russian winter, many men and women were renewing the faith of their youth, choosing insecurity consciously to side with the revolution against all sorts of official gods – even the ones they had erected. "Of what have I to be afraid? I did not kill anyone...," said J Babu aloud, almost speaking to himself. The charge of insincerity can be raised by no man against another, he told himself. On some day or the other when a man has been made to feel he is nothing, every man compromises, he muttered.

He felt he was at the brink of another life even though the calculations of this one were holding him back. Something in his unconscious stirred, an old spirit of dissatisfaction which would earlier make him call things, people, by the names they deserved. But as he was out of habit, he did not feel confident taking such a stand. How would he topple his own school, his own statue? Over the years he had sought culture, built professional success and acquired things he had learnt to guard. Being a senior in office was not enough, what he had, he had, not just out of ambition but out of greed. He had sought knowledge not for clarity, but for power. His wanting to know had meant getting to know ahead of others and then keeping it from other people. His conversations had become more and more sophisticated; his likes and dislikes, timely. He tried to steady the hands that held the book. His eyes grew moist, his spirit mocked him. He went around the table to take his seat behind the desk and wasted himself in sighs.

Who will save the rights of journalists? Journalists can protect the rights of journalists, wrote the senior editor after a while in a thick roughly stitched diary. Then scratched it out, then put it back again. Accustomed to living on the side of the norm, he was finding the choice difficult. Choosing truth while living is difficult. To be able to speak the truth the conditions around him must change, he felt. He began again. "For in the end," he wrote looking at each piece in the sentence as if it were a fresco, "if a journalist speaks the truth and he is doing it consistently, he cannot be saved. So in these times, should a journalist speak the truth? When should he speak the truth?

Should truth leave everything as it is? Should it break anything, change anything in a future April? Can truth mess with my friends? Should I keep the truth for myself and grow old with it?"

The pen dried out at the end of these rolling sentences. "At my age, I should be having the answers to some of the questions, not discovering them," he thought. A tap on his door made him close the diary. He took the sheets of the next day's editorials and shuffled the proofs. It was Hog. Tonight, I will tell Hog about my brother, Lohar, he thought.

Fairly early, J Babu told Hog, Lohar, decided he was not going to be a gentleman. In his seventh month, he began to shit in his mother's womb. As a result, he had to be brought out early and he let everybody know he was angry about it. Father, who turned to God on a daily basis on questions of faith, wealth and family, called the neighbourhood priest. He said he had never been so embarrassed in his life. For twenty kiseta of rice, the holy man said he would take care of it. You would think the matter rested there. It didn't. Each time a member of the extended family came for an inspection of the newborn, father dusted out the story of his second son's entry into the world. He said he had never been so embarrassed in his life.

"From this one, no love and respect ever came my way," Father would say years later.

For my brother Lohar, love, respect and security were conditions that were to be fought for and delivered by politics. "When there is a revolution it will change the family—it will take everything along. Mother will no longer have to be the one getting up in the morning to serve us tea."

When Lohar was twelve, they laughed about it. "Embarassing our parents comes naturally to us I think," said Lohar. "Our parents think we do not deserve them. I think they do not deserve us. What they do not expect from the State, they expect from their children."

Lohar's hands were gentle. His words were not. They were blunt and sharp. He spoke much but was not careful. "Unlike me", said J Babu, "he wouldn't waste his time waiting for the perfectly formed sentence. There were days, and let's be frank, even nights, when he would keep me up talking. His dreams included many people. He would help you build the stamina for your dreams and fight for them as if they were his own. But he had no time for refined rebellions."

"I will never be sure if he was or was not a good boy. His goodness, I saw, was a problem for everybody. One morning, father discovered he had written an article for a paper calling two of the Lambda's great dead leaders, "a fascist pup" and the other, "a man who believed that by calling people sons of God it made it all alright." So, father wanted to throw him out of the house. He caught my youngest brother, who was edging towards the stairs to slip away into the street outside our house where his friends were playing, and said: "Do not copy him. Do not look for him. I will make you grow up like me. I will be your brother."

With his youngest son by his side, father turned vicious. One day, hell broke over the breakfast table. "Rude! Callous! Ungrateful!" father spat behind a newspaper he found lying on the table. "You will not understand this now my boy," he said to Lohar, "but a son is not an award, one can give up. You are my son and I am your father whether you like it or not and that is how things will be as long as we live."

Father congratulated himself thinking he had won with a quick knockout. Lohar wanted to kill father at least in a poem. "All our sons feel their mother is The Virgin. I am, of course, a villain," father railed to his cronies who came to our house every evening ten minutes before tea time without fail. "My second son is ashamed that he is born to a father who draws a regular income. That has gone against me! But if I had not had a regular income, he would not have been able to study, but where did all the studying go? Into the reading of the Communist Manifesto. And the more he studied, the more difficult he became...."

The consensus reached at these tea parties was to tame Lohar with a job. Working at The Buckle was a big deal. Father knew its PRO; he got mother to coax Lohar to take a job as the floor manager with the shoe company.

Thomas J Leather came to the office during his annual visit

a few months later. The first thing he did was send for Lohar. He had intelligence from someone on the office staff, who had acted only in the interests of business, about our brother giving funds to a "Communist paper" run from a little alley behind *The Meat.*

"If Communists wear your shoes do you have a problem?" asked Lohar. Thomas J Leather went home to the Fair Ises. Lohar returned home without a job. Father announced that from then on he would prefer being called the father of two sons, not three".

HOG IS A PROOF-READER. He is an appendage to the editorial. He is marked by his time in the newsroom—that is, there is a diary that makes him note his coming and going. The success of the procedure of course depends on the honesty of his pen, but not entirely. There are other eyes keeping a check on the clock. And there are as many kinds of clocks as there are people whose job at *The Meat* is just to ensure, that a person whose time in the paper is over, goes over. Hog comes in before the others do. It is required that he should be present and available not emotionally, but skilfully, so that young sub-editors on the desk may try out their newfangled words on him or ping pong him with questions.

"When you hit someone, Mr Hog, if he sees red, why does his eye turn blue?"

"If a handicapped person is seated, is he sitting in his wheelchair or sitting on the wheelchair?"

"*On* the wheelchair would make it a matter of preference. *In* the wheelchair makes it a matter of compulsion. At least that's what my gut says." When he has something sensible to say, he says it. And this is how it continues through the day.

"An astronaut has died. His ashes are to be scattered over the sea. What sort of heading could work?"

"From the man on the moon to the bottom of the sea—maybe?"

The pity is, he always had to have a response in his pocket. Not having an answer would bring him to the attention of Aristu. Sometimes, he dropped a zero off an employee's paycheque on that score.

The young ones anyway kept him on his toes. They take up all his day. How animated ...how untroubled...how young.... Hog would marvel at them. But after eight hours of work side by side, he did not know them. Sometimes their paths would cross in the corridor and they would nod. Most often they would not, their eyes criss-crossing, then darting at a space above his head rendering him invisible. Grabbing a cup of tea from the workers' canteen, Hog would remind himself—he was not successful but he was not a failure. He was not about to be saved but he was not about to be killed. He did not have a desk but when there was work he had a chair. He was not included but he was not excluded.

One day, returning to his cabin which he shares with some stenographers and the editorial assistants of senior editors, he found a bundle of paper lying on his chair. They were the practice sheets of trainee journalists. Hog daily notes with care their grammar. Commas and semi-colons rule their lives. They watch over the syntax of sentences as if they were romantic commitments. They are crushed if they do not know the intransitive verb of see and smell but of history, he noted in mild protest, they had not the slightest need of, it had come to mean what was the day before. Aristu was hiring children and putting them to work because they were not at play.

"Someday," Hog says to himself as he wraps his muffler around his neck getting ready to leave for the day, "there will be one among them who will have other questions. And he or she will want to know who else was here and what they were doing in the year of the death of Lounis." He takes out from his pocket the ticket of the bus he travels on every day.

For the past one month, he has been saving it—one each day, up and down. He plans to do this till the day he retires, which is a year away. In this biography of a year, he will note what he considered important in a day. So at the back of the ticket, he is writing a list of events, an ordinary worker's news-list of stories his paper left out. His friend, an editorial assistant, had been supplying him the daily newslists of the morning and evening meetings to get a sense of the reporters' collection and compare it with the editors'. He had started to check what came out in the paper the next morning—what was in, what was out. Kept under wraps, the protest of the people, however fragmented, was nevertheless a reality. This work of documentation, to Hog's surprise, had begun to make him feel purposeful. He pitied himself a lot less, he had begun to see the connections in the plight of other workers everywhere. "Our facts against their facts. Our language versus their language," that is how he had begun to see it. And so he longs to reach home soon. But home was still many hours away. The Bus had not turned up at The City gate yet.

5

Can We Break Everything?

It was nearly ten when Hog reached home. He had made it to The Bus in the nick of time before the gate of The City closed. He switched on the light. Two tea cups sat on the window seat, two on the floor. He took them to the sink and found its mouth blocked with cigarette butts. He dug them out and flicked them outside. They fell into the grounds of the church next door. The church looked like a museum whose keys had been lost. Lord! He had not been inside the church for a long time. He closed his eyes. He tried to contemplate heaven and hell and imagined himself walking on different floors of the same building, each floor manned by a guard putting him through the same questions for right to entry. A little laugh bubbled inside him like acid, he tried to divert his mind from the thought of office. He could do with some tea but could not find the kettle. Did they ever have one? But the house needed a kettle, he decided to tell Lavni, when she returned, so that she could buy one in the morning. But maybe he could buy it himself the next day.

During the day, the mobile court of vendors, outside the church's square compound, was one of the more lively corners of The Frontier. The loot from The City was to be found on the pavements outside it. The scraps thrown down The City's windows—handkerchiefs with frayed borders, discoloured apples, the forlorn picture frames left with half a picture, the long-stemmed wine bottles with dried up liquids, the chipped glass tumblers, rusty knives, cracked plates, the lot—ended in this market. The last cars, he now saw, were leaving with the factory managers and were moving in a line towards The Gates in the distance. They dappled the street in white rounds of light. If the Lambda becomes a nation, will we call The City, The City and The Frontier, The Frontier, thinks Hog. Names will always be important. What people remember is what people have themselves made or accepted. Or undone. From Saint Petersburg to Petersburg to Petrograd to Leningrad to Saint Petersburg—but which way would The Lambda go?

Who in his right mind would take rooms in a house next to a church or any place of worship, he remembered asking Lavni when he had met her for the first time. Someone who likes feeling sorry for himself, she had said laughing. He had watched her face sweat from the smoke rising up from the blackened kettle of boiling tea that she had been bending over all evening in her shack. A paraffin lamp at its entrance lit it up. The walls of hay blazed in reflected light. They had fallen jaggedly on her face as shadows. They added lines to her forehead, lit up her mouth, darkened her chin. The shadows added to her presence, it seemed as if there were two of her around. The shadow and she. Sometimes, they were one. Then she seemed almost monumental. Or like a boulder able to cause or influence events and disrupting traffic by simply lying in the middle of the road. He felt he was unable to describe her and by looking at her she would become familiar to him.

Men in twos and threes came into her shack from the factories over the troughs after crossing the railway line. They would come all through the night during breaks in their shifts and would drink their cups in silence. Sometimes they asked for more. Working in the factory can do that to people. You build it with your body, then it breaks your body.

Hog remembered telling Lavni one evening. "Would you stay in a house next to a church?"

"To what it is that you're really asking, I would say yes," she had said pushing her hair back into a coil. "How bad can it be?"

And that is how it was that he and Lavni went into a marriage registrar's office and began a life of struggle with the world and often, against the other. He, with his uncontrolled romanticism, the belief in personal goodness to change the world and a peculiar quality of not being encumbered even by his own ideals, however strongly he many have argued for them, beyond the moment. So with him, when it rained, it poured. After that, came a sniffling, stifling, muggy depression. And Lavni? She had her militancy, her views. If you empathised, you'd say they worked it out. Some giving, some yielding—that's what all marriages are, aren't they? If you did not see it that way, you'd see only its difficulties.

"I have not said many things, many womanly things to you," she said to him once as they set out for a meeting at the square, always at a canter ahead of him as he fell back from time to time to stop his feet from slipping out of the shoe. Another of his odd habits—even for a meeting at the square he would take out an ironed shirt, wear socks with shoes.

"If you are not able to kill the gentleman, you will find it difficult to understand what it means to be working class...."

"Coat-shirt-shoe! Now who's just looking at forms? What about what I feel?" he would say in protest.

"What you feel does not come from a vacuum, it comes from ideas attached to the shape and nature of things. From forms. What I feel expresses itself through what I do. Values or forms—same thing you know," she said to him repeatedly, not to put him down but because she was aware that for him, Communism was about Justice—a poor man will not have to go to the courts, Justice will be delivered to him the moment he is wronged—and that he had found his way to it by marriage and that he had not yet thought about what to do with it.

"But why is that such a bad thing?" she would say to attack his sense of inadequacy. "It's better than being Communist by birth. You hear about it all around so it becomes your Book. The son of a businessman, becoming a businessman, the son of a Marxist, becoming a Marxist—spare me. The son of a Marxist, becoming a Marxist—that can happen of course, but what if it didn't? Machines can give birth to machines, not human beings. Communism is not the private property of Marxist families, it belongs to everybody. To build it, we all have to be ready to lend flesh, sweat, blood and bone. Every moment demands this. And we have to do this for us and for all those who are not yet prepared. All the people who come to our meetings, don't come for socialism, some, I'm sure come to the songs at the end. So, just because they are clapping doesn't mean they are with us. You may feel I go on and on about this, but you know I also keep telling myself this, there's no immediate pleasure in all this. You've to keep throwing yourself at it.... Babu, we are not going to call our son or daughter Lenin or Rosa. Lenin! Rosa! Just imagine. All these Communist parents call their children, Lenin and Rosa. And then they grow up and are so disappointing. But let's hush, he speaks."

"Stop calling me Babu, haven't I...."

"Hush...."

"If you think...."

"Now hush..."

Dusk had encamped on the top of leafless trees. The sky, ashen. Men and women were sitting around heaps of broken stones. Their faces were turned towards a man, slightly over thirty. He had a good, generous face, but his words induced such a restlessness, that you would forget you had been startled by it.

Somebody called out to him—"Mir!" And he raised his hand. Waved. There was nothing singular about him, that is, if by a leader you mean a man of height or the owner of a voice that triggers that first jerk that makes men and women leave their homes to take part in the terror that is revolution and not watch it from their window. Mir spoke easily. Unheroically. He spoke in a manner that gave you time to think and form your own questions and if they did not agree with his view oh, he would defend them aggressively, of that you could be sure. So by example you would learn to sharpen your razor and defend your own positions. But you also learnt to listen. Not like a pet dog—he didn't want disciples or retainers—but to turn your mind to another in a way to take what was the best and the essence of a diverse view and build on it so that with every meeting you would have two people perhaps looking up at two different directions but with plans to meet to do the same things after the sun had set. Every encounter with Mir made you feel that you had only to walk with him and the world would change, you would live better, fight better and the Great Change, which everyone had begun to talk of these days, would come running towards you. And the people who made this comment were people who had walked with him so it seemed they meant this in the best possible way.

Night. And people still sat around him or got up to prepare the evening meal or join the last cussed shift at the factory. Lavni took Hog to sit closer to the group that sat around Mir. Sometimes that group broke up distracted by the activities of their children. A boy was running here and there daubing paint on tree trunks to serve as posters. To the slogans he had been asked to paint on the trees, he had added his own—'No work! No school!' 'My right to be useless! No school.' The few pamphlets he carried under his arm were snatched by boys younger than him for the privilege of sticking them at the factory gates. They would beat us for doing that, but they wouldn't beat our children for doing that, were their parents' hope. A dark, insolent wind rose out of nowhere and snapped at their heels. Voices, muffled and raised, cut through the air.

"...If we want freedom, let us first talk of what kind of freedom. If we leave it for later—later, that's a time that is never here. Or, who knows, we may not be here. So if we want freedom, let us now decide the kind we want. If we want the Lambda to be a nation, what kind of nation? To say we want to be free and in our own country, is useful because we can fight for that. When there is plebiscite, we will vote for freedom. But will we vote for freedom because we want to be free or we want to build a nation? So, see there are many things to be thought of and discussed. Let us not throw our hands up in joy at the mere mention of plebsicite. We need to think of the manner in which we want to be free."

"But if the Lambda can be a nation, Mir, should we not take it?" asked a voice to his right.

"Certainly. But in that Lambda, after it is free, will we have a part? Will we be consulted in its running? To take over a plant is not the same as having power. Every country is run like an organisation—so the important thing to know is who will be taking the decisions? I say, the building of a nation must go hand in hand with social revolution. Policies will decided by politics. In fact, let us be clear, that, that is why we will ask for a nation."

"Who will lead the nation?"

"The movement will throw up its own leader. In the fields, the farmhands will choose their man. In the factories, the workers will decide. In a newspaper office, the staff will decide. And we will decide and be part of each other's decisions. Knowing who the leader is, is an important information, only to gauge what direction a movement is taking."

"Will I see all this in my lifetime, son?" an old man raised his hand to ask.

"That depends entirely on you. Me. On us. How far do you want to go? Do we want it to change just your life or your son's life? Only so far to put rice on the table? For a wage hike of a few hundred mukkas? No. We are fighting to build a structure that will ensure that life for everyone, you, me, the welder, the teacher, the artist, the farmer, the doctor, the journalist, will be in harmony and in connection with the other. But if we think, I'm the artist so I will only live for that or I'm the teacher and just coursework is my job, then we will build a building all right but some of us or not all of us will be in the same building at the same time. Some of us then will be standing outside its doors just waiting to push ourselves in or pull somebody out. I'm not saying that we are in it to build families, but we can try to move together with the sense of being one, with the same tensions, the same instabilities, and discomfort that all real families share. Coming together for a purpose, moving on when that purpose is served, and then coming back again for a new purpose—all that is possible. And when even that is done, as must be done with all old buildings, we will take it down and build something else. Revolution is glorious and it is terrible. And it is not here. Make the Revolution where you are—not in jungles. If we want it, we have to work for it, create it, imagine it, pursue it, express it—each time we see its possibilities, and even more when we see it disappearing or failing."

"In the factory where I work," said Kanhu, the boy who had been managing the band sticking posters and who worked part time in a car factory, "we are not allowed to speak at work. We raised the issue and the managers said it is not possible. We ask for a half day's leave and 'it is not possible.' But it is possible to have salary cuts, a half a day's salary, if you punch in a second late. If you have fever, and one tablet is not enough, the doctor will insist you get well with one. 'Two isn't possible.' Lying down in the dispensary—it is not possible. At the slightest of our protests, they issue circulars, say we are being disobedient. Do not talk, they say. What do we do then when we detect faults in our goods? If men do not talk will cars talk to each other? Some days I feel like driving a nail through their heads...."

"Will there be violence?" asked Hog unable to quieten down an odd excitement that was washing over his spine. There were so many things he could think of that needed to be undone, they should begin tomorrow.

"This is panic talking. Yes, it may turn violent and it may be bloody. Independence will not come through goodwill. Please understand this: this revolution is not being fought for revenge, or to become the new elite. But in the shaking off there will be violence."

"Yesterday, I saw a film..." said Kanhu returning to the group taking the conversation elsewhere. Some of them tried to hush him but you couldn't shut this boy up. The last poster had been posted with some struggle at the factory gate. Mir asked him about it.

"Yes, they tried to stop us," he replied. "But I was there, wasn't I? I took care of everything."

"Well, they must have taken it down after you left. But you will then stick it elsewhere, won't you?" asked Mir.

"Yes, yes," he replied but his mind was clearly on his film.

"Hush boy, how you go on and on," cut in Mani, a welder, in mock protest. "Don't say things like that. You'll be accused of having culture. Listen to what people of culture think and how they shrink from standing in any kind of comparison with our own. My son works as a steno in that paper *The Meat*. Oh you sir, work there too, don't you?" he said, nodding at Hog. "Anyhow, one day an editor goes through the copy after he has finished typing it. The writing was illegible in parts, so my son had used his sense to type in the word 'worker' to describe a fellow who worked as a peon in a bank. My son thought my father works in a factory and he is a worker. So if a peon earns the same, the working conditions must be the same, the privations are the same, the questions in his mind have to be the same, his life too will be slipping through the same deadlocks and frustrations, the same inadequacies, the same empty shell and he thought the reporter did the right thing by identifying the condition and making the worker an adjective and a noun... but wait, his superior blanches at the word. He says he has introduced his bias. 'You have an agenda,' he shrieks. My son protests, as of course he must. In the end, the man says 'find another word—what do you get paid for?'"

"Don't let it crush you. It doesn't do to be depressed, be on strike," said Mir quoting from the *Coming Insurrection*, a work of The Invisible Committee, a group of young politicised anti-establishmentalists who were writing about the world as the world was writing about them. *The Meat* had tucked the news about the book in one of its inside pages.

"We have much work here too," said Mir. "There are many things to be built. Next time, we meet, let's talk more about all of this—when we have a factory, what kind of factory; if we are reading, why are we reading and the possibility of creating new literatures."

And so it went and the night slowly seemed to have shifted its plates. Words caught fire but the air was such that after many days, they breathed. The banality of the quotidian world disappeared; pillars moved; to the factory and the fields they promised a revolt; The City was as good as taken; and incantatory prose flowed out of years of impotent rage and unspoken desire. But imagination used to conjure up a new world only had meaning if good ideas were worked upon by others and not left alone. The day has the habit of rubbing out night as if it was a crease.

"I want a new toy," said Lavni's six-year-old neighbour's daughter who had been squirming in her lap. Managing to break free, she banged her doll's head on a boulder. "I want to break, break, break everything! Can I?" she asked looking around for her mother.

"I also don't want to get up early and cook for you. Can I?"

replied her mother, Uma, as everyone laughed. "Ask new questions, girl, change is coming. Eh, Lavni?"

Yet change is slow and history would be written and rewritten many times before a woman would be considered a worker head to head with a man. This would take time to change and the ground for it had to be laid, the work begun, with the cut-and-driedness of a de-worming project, not after the Revolution but much before it, in the years of despair and the year of self-congratulation, and also at its ebb. Revolutions come and go but they are begun at the convenience of men. But the questions she had been asking, or silencing, thought Uma, had been her mother's questions. She had carried them for years strapped to her body like a dead child. Her son, Kanhu, would not be asking these questions but with a beating he would.

Lotfi was watching his wife Uma with alarm. "All this mixing with that woman, Lavni, I knew would lead to no good. I knew this was coming," he muttered and chewed the sides of his mouth. He felt agitated. "First, she would want news of our meetings, and now she comes to each one of them. Hey, who is going to get me tea?" he barked. That's how anyone got a bit of respect around here. What's in a meeting, he wondered with some hurt. Didn't he take the family to the circus once in a while? But just his luck to have children and a woman who wouldn't laugh. Always going around the house with long faces. Was he dead? What's in a meeting he would like to know. People come and go, watch others, listen to talk, or talk themselves. But Uma said she had seen nothing like it.

"I know what I saw", he mumbles. "Eyes dropping with sleep, tired faces, smoke-filled voices, empty bellies, limbs stretched from working long nights at the factory. I saw a crowd. Too early to say if I saw solidarity." But he could be wrong, he admitted, what did he know?

But they were not rich. No one was getting paid for talking. Could he, a worker, really have the right to leisure? Decide when or how he would like to work? He had leave and he would have liked to ride the bus and visit The City, walk on its roads. It had fine roads, some of his neighbours who worked there as masons, had said. A house. A tree. And then a bit of road. A house. A tree. And then a bit of road—that's the way The City had been built. But he didn't really have leave—he couldn't take it. He must build stamina, his supervisor was constantly at him, telling him this. He must work, do more work, not watch the clock. And this stupid woman wanted to attend meetings! She could, if that's what she really wanted, but why should she?

It was a happy evening, recalled Hog. Five people had introduced themselves and asked him his name. He had made them promise to come home for tea.

"You were very quiet, Lavni," Hog remarked as they reached home noticing her silence on the way back. "I get paid to listen," she said and folded her clothes into the cupboard as Hog pulled a slab of wood he had beaten into a desk and began to write. Each day, he now wrote. If he had thrown away the bus ticket by mistake, he wrote at the back of his hand while in the bus the news that he was sure would not appear in the paper the next day. He had a sense of the story from the newslist and would on returning home write it up as an allegory in his diary.

The Untold Story of the People of Lambda as Children

Without Independence, The Lambda, people say, could be reduced to an example of political theory in history books. But in a year's time there will be Plebiscite. The people of Lambda, who are like children, will have to decide one way or the other which way they will go. Newspapers like *The Meat* aren't helping. When the people of Lambda say they want to be free, its reporters trust them, then doubt them. They are asked whether that is what they really want. But because they are like children and find it difficult to make up their minds, *The Meat* makes up their minds for them.

"This is the year of decisions," says Colonel Saunders to his gardener Olu while cleaning his gun one day.

"Decide my good fellow whether it will be yes or no, right or left."

Olu says he needs time to think and then thinks, what the heck, to go with neither right nor left, and decides to look down at his toes. By mistake, Colonel Saunders shoots him in the head.

Saunders' is the head of The City's special regiment, The Murkys; his mother belongs to one of The Fairland's first families and the sharp-shooting colonel is a decorated armyman. No newspaper, least of all *The Meat*, will pull down the pants of a patriot and hit him between the legs. The Soldier, the Police, The Army, are the pets of the State and it is unpardonable that if you cannot love them, you will not fear them.

6

Baba Lala and His Son

Polo watched himself getting off in the mirror placed on the wall opposite his bed and wondered why people thought him stiff. An access to Western education and its ideas had given him a different set of grids with which to plan his manhood. His boyhood, in fact, had been much the same. His education seemed to him like a family conspiracy. If he wasn't careful, his parents would have ended up finishing him off. He grew up wary and resentful. His mother had shouted down his father and had brought by ship at great cost, a Fairlander nanny. The joint efforts of the two women produced a child who learnt to pressure-cook his natural feelings, trained to release them only at long intervals. His mother's evocations of university debates, ashen skies spreading the rain equally over country homes and stately palaces in a Fairland she herself had never experienced, deepened his sense of strangeness. He had only known the relentless continuity of the sun, the adrenaline of privilege, the clannishness of people of the same blood and of equal wealth and believed they were right to distribute themselves and their enterprises in mutually watchful and self-contained neighbourhoods. He had watched his father beat his servants when they failed him and throw them silver at his pleasure. The order that was produced in a house full of faithful servants ruled by an iron hand are what, he felt, kept things in place.

"A society that has been produced for hundreds of years, needs no justification," he would tell his circle as he grew up. "People will vote Dong, you will see, just to ensure life continues. The factory owner's son inheriting the factory, the doctor's son becoming a doctor, the farmer's son becoming a farmer, the cobbler's son beating nails into the leather.... "

This morning, for some reason, he was not able to anchor his thoughts. He remembered how every evening, since the age of seven, he would sit in the Grand-Martin with the driver's son at the back as escort, and was sent to play with the son of Raya, the patron of The City's biggest temple, at his home. The driver Mangu, would rush out of his outhouse at the beating of the gong, and button his shirt with one hand and steer the wheel with the other, as the car would begin its glide out of their compound. He would take a circle around the neighbourhood, past the lawyers' chambers, the white gothic church and the red stucco post office, and bring the car to a screeching halt before the residence right next to their estate. Mangu would open the door for his master's son and watch Polo march out.

As a child, Polo had been welcomed, as the bioscope had been welcomed in days before the movie theatres, in most of the homes of Baba Lala's associates. Raya's son, Guru, would drink his milk only when he came along and recited with one hand to his chest, melancholic Fairlander poems from various centuries with one or two dead or dying in them. One evening, he let Polo lob him a string of no balls and beat him at the game just so as to have Polo insult his family goddess as Guru jumped up and down clapping his hands under a tree. It had been just a day that his personal servant, in strictest confidence, had revealed his father, Raya's intention of writing into his new will the condition that his son would inherit his wealth only if he proved beyond doubt his willingness to provide the goddess the finest muslin and peacock feathers to fan her with during the hot weather months, even after his death. If Polo was willing, they could hatch a plan to disown their parents.

These activities out of sight of his mother, created a set of ambivalences and conflicts Polo was unable to resolve. His mother, dissatisfied at the incompleteness of his education, was nevertheless happy at his progress in cricket. Books alone, she consoled herself, did not make a Fairlander. The effort to mould him, however, continued by indirect means.

Polo lost his mother at ten. A quiet child, he had suddenly started to bang his head whenever she would come near him. And then just as suddenly, the fits would stop and he would bolt out of her room and hide himself. His mother took this personally and her health, never robust, started to deteriorate. Her marriage to Baba Lala was a puzzle. She had brought him nothing. Her father's friendship with him was clearly the chief inducement. The two men talked to each over her head as the family sat for their meals.

By the time of Polo's birth, Hall had moved in and begun to occupy one of the huge rooms next to her husband's study. Hall found her dead on his return from a tour with his son-in-law to advertise the work of the newly formed Dong Party in The Frontier.

Polo recovered from his mother's death with ease. The gates had opened for him, as it were, to find his own place in a land which he could, till now, only guiltily embrace. As his grandfather led the funeral cortege out of their grounds, he drew the curtains of his room and latched his door to stand in front of the mirror. Black eyes. Black hair. The rest, he would leave to his father to manufacture. He had ideas, he believed, that would make people want to climb cliffs.

Unfortunately, his chief sponsor, his father, Baba Lala, had the attention span of a hare, to lavish it exclusively on a son. An early riser, he would girdle his dressing gown around him and set out for a walk, taptapping his immense grounds with a cane under the first rays of the sun and be persuaded by his gardener of the presence of underground oil. The afternoon would be spent drawing up, and then dismantling, areas of investment and expansion that would inevitably open up post extraction. By evening, his mood would be imperial. By night, funereal. But as he repeated this pattern days on end without any impact on the management of his assets, his competitors came to the conclusion he was no scatterbrain. His grumbles were meant for their ears. His absentmindedness and Hamletian self-doubts were carefully planned dinner performances aimed at throwing the scent off his main project before it was ready. Oil! Who could have thought of oil under the garden in the middle of the city? But the thought had been enough to unhinge all of them, risk the peace of their homes, hike the salary of their own gardeners, disembowel their gardens and massacre several flowerbeds.

When Baba Lala seemed to be doing nothing, he could be doing everything.

"We are champions of drinking and we are champions of thinking," he boomed at the gathering that sat around his table one night. "We, who have been friends for long, know our world is changing. But as a father, what do you do if your son is a fool?"

Kuberos, the most moneyed man of The City squirmed in his seat. Earlier in the evening, he had been surprised and honoured by having his seat close to his host. At present, he could only admire the trap. All eyes at the table seemed to be fixed on him, so he decided to look interested when Baba Lala opened his mouth to speak.

"This thing, my son, is half-Fairlander, as you know," he said taking the heat off Kuberos for the moment as all necks at the table turned towards the pale-looking boy clad in a darkish suit who had just come into the room and was quietly making his way towards his father. They had not noticed him. It was as if he had just tip-toed out of one of the dark shell cupboards of the room.

"From his grandfather, our well-wisher Commissioner Hall, he gets the love for doing the right thing. He may not look it, but he does. He lost his mother early but at 20, he now wants to fulfil her dream of becoming a poet. Before nature, we are helpless. But what future for a poet in a country that is not yet a country?" he said and signalled the head cook to beat the gong. Drinks were served. The table was cleared. Glasses filled. Napkins straightened. But he did not disperse the gathering. "Can you change nature? I know I speak among friends. Who among you will reject him because of his blood? Speak now or proclaim him your son as well."

Kuberos who was planning to open a park in the city square had been drawing a balancesheet of the pros and cons of just such a proposal. With Messrs Hall, Baba Lala, Raya, he had formed the Dong Party to draw the new professional classes into a fraternity with the old classes so that they could be the body that would challenge the Empire. So far, Baba Lala had given no indications that the syndicate would be an insurance for a dynasty. Hall, the liberal, had convinced them of the usefulness of being in touch and throwing open the doors of the association to the teacher, the owners of printing presses and even the postman. Baba Lala, his son-in-law, however, did not share his enthusiasm for the peasant.

Kuberos thought he would strengthen his host's position for the time being, and also acknowledge that he knew he had been attacked, with grace. "The farmer and the poet are our inheritance. One draws his labour from the wells of the earth, the other from his imagination. Both are our children and we will protect them."

"Goddamn it," thought Baba Lala, "that had been too easy...." And he nodded to the servant on standby to beat the gong. He missed Hall. The old cock always gave him a good fight. "Where's your big heart?" Hall would coax. "A newly single man *can* look forward to a friendship with a happily married woman. You have to open yourself up to all kinds of experiences."

"A hungry villager has no time for politics," Lala would insist with a laugh. The friendship between the aged, uptight Fairlander official and the brat of a landowning family had surprised society but most of all themselves. They had met one blistering summer in the Agriculture Department inside the imposing secretariat where Baba Lala had been sent by his father to seek official advice on their lands. The meeting had been brief but it had been illuminating. Baba Lala had expected professional expertise and he had not been disappointed. The Fairlander knew enough about seeds and livestock that would not be found in any book. But his passion for good governance, his ideas about the fundamental iniquities of the Empire, and the frankness with which he voiced such views sitting inside a government office, he had found startling. That visit would change their lives. The first meeting had been by appointment. Lala, who had gone home and reported the encounter to his father, found himself not unwilling to ensure that the next meeting would be by invitation. In time, Hall took the young man under his wing. At the fag end of his career, put in charge of a department as a punishment posting, that had little to do with agriculture and everything to do with revenue, he decided that very evening to stop issuing lackadaisical threats to his superiors that he would board a ship for Fairland with his daughter; and decided to stay put in The City.

Ever since, he became a regular visitor to Baba Lala's house. Every Wednesday, after work, he held the massive living room, choc-a-bloc with listeners, in thrall with his comparative analyses of the world's constitutions, questions of law and provoked the first thoughts about the need to form a political party for all the people of the Lambda—men and women, rich and poor—amid much eating and drinking, and his feet being stepped on by over-eager household servants. It was a magical time. No one understanding anybody, but all willing to add their voice to the happy mix of slogans amongst their own. The yellow rum cocktails came in salted and quick from the kitchen as the staff would bump against each other in their hurry to catch the line of arguments.

Baba Lala looked forward to these evenings but not without a little flutter in his stomach. After the guests departed he had Hall's undivided attention, which he dreaded. 'Are we making the most of the land?' 'Should The Lambda have a policy for industries?' 'Can land be owned by the government or should it belong to the people?' 'Can a government, any government, turn out to be expensive for its people?' 'When should the government go?' Now how on earth was he supposed to know!

Hall did not lose hope in him. In the beginning, Lala might resist his ideas but he was sure that in a few years' time he would stop wanting to play the propertied gentleman and be ready for greater things. When it was time to leave, he wanted to leave behind a nation run by professionals. Lala's reservoir of goodwill towards his teacher from the Fairland was full for many years. He was never stingy about acknowledging his debt to his senior friend, but when he made up his mind, he wasn't squeamish about how he would cut down the mighty oak. Nations, he decided, had to be enriched layer by layer. The poor would eventually catch up with the rich. He had had enough of comparative analyses of foreign constitutions and lectures by Cicero.

"If the Italians had the Roman Republic behind them, did the people of the Lambda have no one?" he remembered having said slapping the table at one of his last meetings with his father-in-law. His wife had bustled out of the room and barked instructions to the ticketing agent to book her father a passage to the Fairland, on a ridiculously expensive cabin next to the ship's captain. But he did not mind. He considered that his tuition fees. He had picked up what he wanted from Hall. The nanny's seat he would not pay. He had not insisted on her coming and he saw no reason why he should ensure her a comfortable departure.

"Nations are birthed by patriotism but the climate is decided by God, right Mangu?" he had asked his driver, cutting short his remembrances, who had blushed furiously with pride. Would his fool of a son, who spent all his mornings before the mirror, have the confidence to lead a country, he wondered as he instructed the driver to take a slow spin around The City. He didn't want to back the wrong arse. Sentiment had played no part in the amassing of his property and he, Baba Lala, was not going to be a fool and invest in his son for that reason. As he thought of the millions he had invested in unwise ventures across The City and even in The Frontier, he was waiting for exact information. To control the crisis, like all good businessmen, he needed to know more than its name. The City's premier newspaper, *The Meat*, was calling it the Plebsicite. Why then was The Frontier, calling it the Revolution?

7

Waiting for Rain

The morning after began late. The sweepress had only just swept the crumbs off the floor, when a shout rang out from inside the shrine. The Book had been stolen! Not just any ordinary book! Basil Master's book on Sarayu Dada! "Ignored that He has been by you sinners," said she taking up the shout and shaking the broom, "is it any wonder that Data would pick up His own book of life and walk out of the temple?"

And it was waiting to happen all summer. All night long, they had sat around His feet twittering like birds, cramming their stomachs with sweets, and singing praises for a new beast, a Party, that was promising freedom and opportunity as if they were fruits hanging from the trees, that not one of them had felt compelled to mention His name.

"Just as well. Sarayu Dada was an autocrat. He made obedience a matter of ethics. He was accountable to none; everyone is accountable to him," said a young clerk, a Fairlander-speaking youth who had got down from his cycle on hearing the commotion on his way to work in The City. "It is time to assert ourselves, if we keep silent and go by His book, it will always be Sarayu Dada talking, not us. With freedom, we will be free. No doubt about it."

But The Frontier had not been so easily convinced. They were surrounded by Gates—even though they kept only one open—and each of the eight gates were named after one of their gods. If they were named after their gods, they were under their protection. If the gods wanted to leave on their own to make way for the great change, which lads like this one was just saying was coming, they could. But the people would not push their gods out. They would not, they could not. Or, could they?

But it had to happen that summer. For, this seemed to be the season of losing books, forgetting them, burying them. If no one was reading, books may well be lost, which perhaps explains why they were being stolen. If Tulsi-dada's book was in every home, no thief would steal it. So it would mean that Tulsi-dada's book was not in every home. Losing books was almost like losing faith and faith can be lost or lived not suddenly but over a period of time. Gods were another matter, these days they were creating one every day.

"The real fight, wise men say, are not between gods," the lad jumped in again to say, "but about the right to build up one. But the real fight we know is for the street—so off I go." And so he went after casting a few reproachful glances at The Bus that had taken him by surprise and was squeezing him on one side of the road. It was dislodging its human load rather untimely that day.

If he had not brought his son Guli with him, a tired Mangu would have tarried awhile in The Bus. He did not want to get down. He loosened his shirt sticking to his sweating skin, straightened up and looked out gingerly. The sun blinded his eyes but there was no choice but to get off the bus. Now where was that boy? He had no idea the beating he had in store. Running off already to his aunt's house leaving him alone in the middle of the street to carry the suitcases!

He looked around. Accustomed to flatness, intentional symmetries, the mathematical certitudes of straight roads with cream-complexioned houses appearing and disappearing in his rear window as he drove the master around The City, the undulating landscape of The Frontier, its deep troughs and other physical abstractions filled him with nervousness. He was already fearful when a pack of dogs appeared suddenly from nowhere and hoofed the ground around him. He saw children with huge stomachs peering at him from the windows. The roofs of their houses stuffed with straw, brooms and old carrots, flew off as they coughed with an ancient cold. Mangu had not come home in five years—where on earth had the master sent him? But he corrected himself a few minutes later. He was determined not to miss a thing and that is why—as he would realise years later—he had missed the important things. He stood on one side of the road for hours but there was nothing all around on which a man's eye could rest and move on. As it was a long walk ahead, he moved. His feet, left asleep for long, shook with each step. He could not make sense of the geography. The land seemed to be in motion. His feet groped for firm ground and got stuck in cracks. The land, it seemed to him, was the workshop of strange forces; for miles, he would not see a soul and then suddenly he wouldn't be able to count them with his fingers. His head was beginning to feel heavy and he was hearing sounds. A few women with bricks on their head passed him by and he was just about to ask them the way, when he stumbled. The ground had given way here and there to reveal, it seemed to him and he wasn't sure, parts of broken ships hidden under huge stones. The sea was at his feet! When he had looked again, it was gone. His eyes sought out the muddy water ringing the Frontier's other extreme in the distance. The sun was playing tricks on him. This morning, he was not himself. Every little difference with The City disturbed him. He wanted to steady himself but his eyes refused to comply. He saw a thin crane edging close to the edge of an abandoned bridge near to where the waves were breaking then spreading like sheets of gelatine on the Frontier's northern shore. For some reason, the sight settled his soul.

But his sister Uma's house was still a long walk ahead, across a railway line that cut through two rows of squatter colonies, and Mangu had still not moved. The sun was peeling his skin. He began to walk. The outline of the ugly little engines standing on the railway tracks began to appear in the distance. He hugged his suitcase to his chest and trudged ahead. One day, he would take Guli and his mother on a long train journey—somewhere. His ruminations were cut short by a sharp jab at his side. He found himself suddenly in the middle of a crowd of factory workers going under a barrier to cross the railway tracks. The screaming engines passed by interrupting speech. The men closest to the barrier bore the brunt of the pressure of those at the back. The crowd was swelling by the minute. The factories were at least a half-an-hour walk away.

"Why push? You'll get there," said a worker to another. Their eyes blinded with soot, they nearly fell on the railway track. But the signal wouldn't lift. At a distance in between the criss-crossing tracks was a strip of uneven ground. A man stood with a bag, distributing newspapers to the hurrying workers exchanging with those who stopped in enquiry or curiosity, a word or two. Next to him, Mangu saw Guli.

"That is Mir," said a man next to him and hurried ahead. The signal had lifted. If Mangu had questions, he certainly had no time to reply. "Give the newspaper only to those who ask," said the man to Guli as his father walked up to him.

Mangu decided to be pleasant. He was in no mood for a quarrel even though his hands were itching. He looked at his son from the corner of his eye. Guli paid him no attention. He was dipping into the bag and taking out a fresh bunch of papers.

"I would like a copy. How much for it?" The paper, it turned out, was for free. He concealed his pleasure as he caught his son watching him. Wait, if this was for free, what was the lad getting paid? Getting mixed up in an upaid venture—why, of course, who else but that boy would think of doing such a thing! Acting big all the time and brains not even worth four mukkas. Why had he been chosen to have a son like this? He would speak to the master to hire him in one of his offices. Let him learn to make tea.

"What kind of newspaper is this? Employment news?" He found he was not the only one asking that question. A few men had gathered around the group. One of them had taken a copy of the paper from Guli and was going through it.

"No," said Mir. "It's about workers' lives. About our daily lives. Through this paper, we will tell everybody where we are, how we are doing, under what conditions we are working, our relations with each other as we work, what the masters are making us do, the illegitimacy of their demands, the extending long hours, its effect on our lives, our families...tell me which factory are you from?"

"Told you last time I passed, didn't I?"

The man was getting it good. Mangu felt pleased. It takes time to change the world and it doesn't happen by standing near railway tracks. Real change—now that was happening in The City. He looked stealthily at his son but the boy was busy talking to an old man who was patting him on the head.

"Next time, I see a union leader, trying to tell me things," said the man who had just attacked Mir, "I will take his head."

"Mir is not a union leader," protested Guli.

"Yes, yes, I know. We all know Mir," said the man with a growl. It seems he had something else on his mind. "This union leader I was talking of before this kid butted in, was a character. He harassed our owner, a fine gentleman from The City, with demands. A father of three, he has his own family to think of or not? But he harassed him with demands. If you have to demand, ask what can be given. No, but he wants this allowance and that allowance. And stupid me, I stood behind him in line and took up the shout. I lost my job. Now I have another job but it pays less. Was I a fool or was I not?"

And it was in the strangeness of this land, that Mangu saw to his amazement, that the man, and the man who had heckled him, should walk away together to go and sit on a stone slab across the railway line at a teashop. He wanted to set off for his sister's house but he was piqued. His throat was parched and well, there was no harm in tea. He could do with a cup. He didn't want to miss what the man was saying. And he was saying the strangest things.

"Brother, it might seem strange that on one hand we are talking of abolishing work and yet talking of wages. For it is true, if we abolish work what do we eat? So what are we saying? No work? Not quite. We are talking of redefinition of our needs. We will work only as much as is needed."

"It's fine for you to talk," said the worker with a snort. "I just want to know when will things get better. We have been hearing you talk for the past five years and things still haven't improved."

"Take it from me brother—it's going to get a lot worse. And don't waste your time and mine," said the man with a friendly slap on the other's back, "into turning me into a God. No divine intervention, no waiting for deliverance from above, we will do what we have to do ourselves. And we are not helpless. We will sit on strike tomorrow. Don't forget to bring your umbrella —I have a feeling it's going to rain."

That evening, a telegram reached Baba Lala: "Mutter serious. Come immediately." Mangu hadn't done too badly. In a week's time he had picked up enough bad English to confuse anyone who was following the exchange. But the packet that arrived from him a week later, had made him sharply draw his breath. The thin four-pager that called itself a newspaper had potential for harm. He scanned it for a few minutes, then angrily tossed it aside.

An editorial had covered its first page. Titled 'Important questions and the time to ask them', it exhorted workers everywhere to think of their labour not just in relation to wages and contracts but in terms of power. In the new nation, they were being asked what they would do. In the institutions of a free country they were being asked to think if they would have more say. What powers would they have to organise their work, defend fixed hours for work, enhance their skills and share in their organisations' profit? It asked them to consider who would represent them when they had demands, take part in negotiations, and whether they needed someone to represent them at all. The factory worker, the sweeper, the teacher, the press worker, the farmhand, the cook—they asked everyone to write to the address about their experiences at work tucked away at one corner of the paper. "These are important questions," and it repeated its obsessive last line, "the time has come to answer them." When the editorial ended, factory workers, he noted with satisfaction, had been the only people, to take up the offer.

When he looked closely at the paper, he saw the workers had not given their names but had mentioned the names of factories at the end of their witness. The bastards had even mentioned one of his. "Call Polo," he shouted out to one of his servants watering a vase. He looked at his face while the man looked at his feet. When had he hired this fellow? These days he could hardly recognise the people who worked for him. There were too many of them and he was convinced they looked alike. He held his hand out for his spectacles and decided to go through some of the entries.

They had called the paper, 'The Will.'*

Article 1: B.K. Lala Hooter Horn factory, Plot D-3, The Frontier

There are a hundred workers in this factory, all on contract. We get paid at the end of the day. Monthly pay is 11,500 mukka, the shift is of 12 hours. The horn marks the beginning and end of our shifts, lunch breaks. A few days ago, we learnt it will be sounded if there is fire. A meeting was called and officers from the administration brought fire cylinders and told us it had gas. They asked us if we knew what gas was inside. No one said a word. "It is carbon-dioxide. If cloth or rubber catches fire, you can douse it with this gas." A few days later, without telling us, they conducted a mock drill. We left our machines and rushed outside. We demanded our pay, we wanted to leave. They kept us inside for half an hour and they let us shout. After that, a senior manager told us it was just practice. Some were praised for keeping their cool. Those of us who had rushed out to the factory gates leaving the machines were punished with a 10-day delay in wages.

Article 2: Alert Factory Guards, Z Colony, The Frontier

They take us on the bus to The City very early in the morning to guard their houses. But they do not trust us. We stand for 12 hours outside their gates for Mukka 5,000 a month. We change into the uniform. We carry our own water. We do not go into their houses to ask for anything. The house servants slide us our pay through the door. One day I would like to see what is behind it. If it is beautiful, I would like to take it.

Besides work-reports, job news, there were news of labour unrest, dates and venues for labour to meet other labour to organise, political cartoons, songs, stories, house-and-board ads put up by small inn-keepers.

By the time he had finished reading, it was one at night. The house was quiet except for the buzz of bees on the vines outside. Sounds of laughter and unruly shouts broke through the thick walls of the hundred-year-old house. He recognised the heavy tread of one of his servants carrying the trays out of a room. A spoon spattered on the floor. Somebody was climbing down a tree—he heard a few branches break as their feet landed on the ground with a thud. One of them had to be present in the factory to take charge. They had better break it up and go home. He looked at a note that had just arrived. "Strike. They will be waiting for reporters at the gate tomorrow."

8

This is Odessa

But the trouble began closer home. From the ballroom of The South Malacca, it spread to its kitchens spilling onto the tea cabins outside where The City's plumber, the ill-paid teacher, the harried postman, the lumbering boxer, the cross-eyed clerk, the hard-up trader, the ambiguous house servant, in fact all sorts of workers, were to be found passing this street as an excuse to rest their feet and flip over the day's scandals.

Any matter at The Malacca was a reason for local excitement, so totemic had been the shape of this hotel, its ambition, and its emergence in the middle of The City. Its bricks and its labour had come from The Frontier, and one morning it had begun to pile up skyward from the pavement till its presence became irrefutable and the rest of the businesses on the street had to control its chaos and re-arrange itself so as not to seem out of place. So make no mistake, this was personal.

So from this street, the cry was taken up by the next street, the next alley, the little shops under the staircase, the barber's boy under the banyan tree, right up to the open windows of every dining establishment on every street where cooks were taking or refusing their last orders, till every serving man and woman began to look around for a can of petrol so angry and vulnerable they felt as the news flew all around them. They had not acted before—why had they not acted before, they began to ask. They did not have a reason, it had not threatened their bread. As they did not have a pretext for their inaction or an outlet for their impotent rage, they began to blame external factors. The new conditions were creeping in on them, they said—a strange position to take since it would mean that they were happy about the changes they had been told Plebiscite would bring and yet unsure if they had committed to change too soon.

Since the announcement of the Plebiscite the place had been on boil. Tongues were looser, hopes higher and routinely killed. A few of them, however, were taking a different line. They should stop howling about freedom—now. Let it take time. Let it come in a shape that was not a sham, when it would change their conditions and not turn out to be a ruse to bind them up in newer shackles, dry up their anger, divert their questions. To hurry it now because of the belief that any moment, every moment could bring a windfall, because those who were sure to benefit by it were in a hurry, would still mean having people at the bottom depending on leftovers from the top. Didn't they know what was happening in The Frontier? They have burnt our homes so that we flock to The City offering it our cheap labour, from clerks to scribes to masons, all of us. They have flattened our lands with their machines, impoverished our trees. They laugh at our lives and then give us a roof, throw us some food, take us in as servants. And so Brother Biran did the right thing, we will join our brother, they said. We will not join our voice to their lies. Are we fighting against the guns of the Fairlanders so as to live unprotestingly under those who would train the Lambda's guns at us? And for sure, old laws were being allowed to gather dust so that they could be dressed up with new names. The hounds were being washed and fed to run. And the guns, oh the guns were just changing hands.

Around five in the evening, Biran, a dishwasher at The Malacca, had entered the living quarters of Jaba, its nightingale. She had appeared at Kuberos's door some years ago and as she was discovered by one of his servants, the fool had turned her into one. Kuberos had seen the girl, tall as a shoot and dark as storm, as she emerged from behind the curtains one night after cleaning a window, and the sight had straightened his old bones. He would not bury her in a mansion, he told his friend Baba Lala. He would build a hotel, the Lambda's first hotel, a building taller than any other building shaped like a wedding candle, and she would queen over it. She would just sway and sing, sway and sing for him but would refuse no one a song. Paid for by Kuber, Jaba had eventually learnt language and grace from a Fairlander governess in transit, and the floosiest repertoire from another of her patron's mistresses, an Armenian girl with a big heart, to become the woman he now arched over once a fortnight. Now Jaba stood before the mirror brushing her hair curling down her back.

She looked at Biran but kept her hands busy in the making of a bun. But where was her jewelled pin? The gold-leafed petals were traced to its drawer and she gave them to him to hold while she organised her hairpin to hold hair and vanity together. She then stuck the coil high on her head. Biran saw she was wearing that dress again. Scarlet straps criss-crossed her breasts like lashes. But Jaba would not look at him. With one hand she held up a card on which she had scribbled the songs she was about to sing. She began to hum, tapping her foot to the slow thump of the drums as the drummer warmed up in the ballroom, but he knew her well enough to know that if he began to speak, she would be listening. "You are not singing tonight," he said to her. "Their Empire, kicking up or dying down, what is it to you Jaba?"

"The master has approved the song list. The Inspector-General is dining tonight, I would say it's a good time to sing," she said patting his cheek with her brush. But Biran would not be placated.

"Go ahead, scrape and bow. Don't take a stand. It's all right. Now that we know, there will never be any expectations from our end. But if you want to be part of an organisation, it cannot be at your pleasure or just because being part of an organisation answers some need of yours."

"All I want is to earn my living, you understand?" she said, her eyes flashing. "Each time before a performance, you have to spoil it and make me raise my voice—why?"

"This is not a career. No career needs to have you looking like this. Or singing praises of empires—have you forgotten why you are here? What were the conditions that were responsible for you to leave home and knock at that door? Tell me under what law was your father victimised? Tell me why should we agree to be ruled by a people who make such laws?

Will these laws go with the country's independence? You have forgotten, but your father was my friend. We have fought together. There will be a meeting tonight in his name. As his daughter, feel free to come."

"When will you leave for the meeting?"

"After the dishes are done," he said and was gone.

There was plenty of work left in the kitchen. But for the moment each eye was scaling up and down the gigantic square of ice in its middle as imposing as a cathedral. Pale white and greying, its edges had begun to smoke under the spicy vapours of the room. The boys who had begged off a day's work from their roadside eateries for a chance to hang around in the hotel's kitchens in the hope of a free meal on this grand occasion, were being made to pitch in. Even a free lunch has strings attached. They were shaving off thin shards of ice from the block. Another group was dropping them into huge vats to clot the cream for the soufflés. Little squares were plip-plopping into glasses of grape wine. In one corner, surrounded by at least twenty of the chef's underlings, stood William Hick, hands on his hips, the sailor of innumerable ships and the servant of none.

'Bhai William' to everyone, he arrived every summer, stories in one pocket and new recipes in the other, teaching them new words, cusswords, showing them photographs of new inventions, showing them the new cuts, sautés and fries. He worked in their midst thus earning his bread for the duration of his stay, which needless to say, he kept quite short. Sometimes you saw him at the beginning of a day and then saw him the next year. Hick was an enigma. The darling of The City's detectives, who tailed him relentlessly from the time his shadow fell across The Gates, his appearance meant they could take a break from writing reports on the reds and their impenetrable theorisations, and look forward to turning in good copy. His presence at The Malacca on the day of the Inspector-General's dinner, they were sure, was of significance. Usually attired in a combination of white and black, today he was all in blue. Around his neck he had knotted a navy scarf—to hide knife injuries or the wounds of libidinous nights no doubt—and his right hand was patting his left hip pocket too often. The stories he was telling his admirers this very minute, their sources said —and their sources were good—were mundane. Their plots were picked up from the dime novels found selling on their own streets!

Far from it. In the Far East, said Hick, the people were rising up not just with slogans but understanding. "It began with a waiter called Chou. One day while waiting at the counter, he smelt a chicken gone bad and refused to serve it to a guest. The master threatened to take his job but he wouldn't budge. As he was thrown out of the restaurant kicking and crying, the other waiters walked out and joined him outside. The cooks, took some persuading, being big bosses of the kitchen—not like our Gagan Bhai here," he said as Gagan Sardar passed by pointing them the clock, "but join the rest of the workers they did."

"Raise your voice, William, we can't hear you in the din," said a voice at the back. It was Biran.

"Hey, Biran, wash the dishes later. Listen. Yes, some secret abscess had been rubbed with the treatment meted out to Chou. The waiters at the next fancy restaurant where top officials met other top officials for dinner, decided to bunker down with their agitating brothers in the neighbourhood. They flung back their tips. By the end of the day, fifty establishments had put up a notice for strike and closed down. They had learnt to say no."

"We should do that too," someone muttered.

"Yes! Why don't you?" said Hick, "Say you don't want any favours. Say you want more wages! Otherwise you will stop work and march—say that!"

March! What a thought! They had never marched but they began to think, was it a difficult thing to do? They could try. The road is the only place we can walk together, shout together. If we march we will see who all are with us, with what purpose, with what common cause, and for how long. A march is speaking power to power. If we all march together we can walk under the big buildings and our shouts will reach their ears and we will shout that we are not simply against them but we are with the people who can shake big buildings. Come down and join us on the street, they would say, and we will also fight for you and if we shout together, we will...

"....everybody tell everybody to come along. We still have a lot of fight to fight," Hick was saying, hands still on the hip, when Gagan Sardar came bustling into the kitchen to drop the bomb.

"Jaba will not sing! Jaba wants to give a speech! The master is furious. So stop yakking and get the dinner on the tables on the double. Ply them with food. Cold cod—the first to go. Now everybody move it!"

If Baba Lala had not stopped him, Kuberos would have shot the lot. Jaba and now the kitchen staff—what was the matter with everybody? He had even had Jaba checked for flu refusing to believe that she was behaving in this fashion in full command of her senses. Hadn't they created the Dong Party as a platform for protest? If they had issues, they could have placed them at the party's table. What else was it for? They who knew how to take care of their own problems were here to take care of others. Those who had no one, the party would be their voice, their eyes, their ears. Today, in fact, was the very day they had planned to throw it open to all in The City and announce it in the presence of the Inspector-General, the man who would oversee the Plebiscite and deliver the Lambda back to its people. He, Kuber, had made money but he had also built roads, he had built motels, he ran trusts, but the ungrateful louts wanted more. He hoped he was not in the wrong place for he was beginning to have doubts of being part of any future government, if one had to constantly be seen doing things. "In socialism you don't have to do big things. Like idiots, you just had to share," he croaked as he wept and fumed in the hotel tower while debating how to deal with the blow. The velvet curtains that covered the wide windows of this room that he would urge Jaba to fling aside whenever he came visiting her now stayed closed. The night was windy, the curtains stirred. He trembled. He had not wanted to....

The evening had not yet abandoned him it seemed. He thought he heard guns booming from the head of the street—but he could be mistaken. He was! They were returning fire from inside his hotel! He rushed to the window—fearing to look out. A slow-mounting clamour had spread all around—he saw fires being lit at street corners, groups of men tugging then toppling electric poles, shadowy figures coming out of the gutters and then at a clap, the thud of a thousand boots approaching from a distance. Thin lines of the imperial police, who were big, who were blind and were boys dressed in black helmets and silvery bayonets, and were called the Murkys, were weaving their way through the lanes of The City. Crossing the bridge, they were now taking position on the entrances of the discreet bungalows of the Fairlanders' officers and The City's notables and moving towards the city centre, The Hollow. Their chief, Colonel Saunders—the only man in the regiment with eyes—disappeared in the office of *The Meat* for a good one hour which made the men fidgety. A few took aim at resting pigeons for practice but shot Kirit, a hawker, winding up the day's work in the boulevard. His wail, as he lay bleeding and alone in a street full of people and flash-fanatic photographers, crazed the Murkys. Without their chief around to give them exact directions where to shoot, they went berserk poking in their rifles through every open window, be they shops or government offices, and in the process massacred prized porcelain and engineers working late nights on stalled projects. It took five more hours to bring the situation under control. Meanwhile, The Malacca burnt. Refusing to return with his troops to the barracks, Saunders, when he finally appeared, led them at a quick trot towards Kuberos's hotel. He had set out with a thousand men; he lost fifty to open manholes. He lined up five hundred men, realigned the muzzles of their weapons, and positioned them at the head of the street. A row of twenty advanced in step towards the hotel dividing themselves up again to climb up the marble staircase and capture the lobby. In the lobby, they met Soli, the reporter from *The Meat*, dusting off an excess of ink from his pen.

Soli had express instructions from Aristu. He had been sent to cover the Dong conference and no more. He had arrived on dot to cover a routine story when he stumbled on the waiters' protest. By the time he had mustered up the courage to change his mind to cover the protest, the faces at its helm had changed. "That was Bhai William, this is Biran," a young boy helpfully whispered back to him.

"Friends, let us test ourselves," Biran was saying. "Let us no longer make excuses for kings, queens, masters—from within the land or outside. As we say in The Frontier, let us say it here. It's not about individuals, it's a regime. There, there are factories, here we have the hotel. First we take control of the factory! Then we say it is our factory! Then say destroy the factory!"

"Fine then—what do we eat?" asked Gagan Sardar resentful at the turn of events. But that question was drowned out by a shout from outside. A few tea-stall owners from outside were waving at them madly from the window. The dust from the stomp of a thousand boots was beginning to blow into the kitchen. The roll of armoured cars, the banging down of shutters, the sounds of the street emptying and crowding back—something was happening! Every man and woman found themselves holding knives and pickaxes that were being distributed by unknown friends. Children from the neighbouring terraces were heard screaming.

"The guns! The police! The Murkys are coming!"

At just that moment Soli's pen gave away. He had rushed to the lobby to get one. "A pen? You want a pen, Sir?" asked the manager with a bright smile.

"No, was planning to write with my blood." He was about to rush back when the frozen look of an armed sergeant stopped him in his tracks. In his hand was a rifle and his elbows were raised. Had he stood around to figure whether he would be shot or not, he could have seen the Murky bring down the seven-tiered chandelier crashing to the floor.

"Someone had called Saunders saying the Inspector-General had been shot by a Red inside the hotel... The Inspector General. At least a thousand guests. Staff. Someone was willing to sacrifice them all. It was middle of the week, a dull day. The Dongs were to throw the membership open and there hadn't been too many takers. So they made sure there would be a Bloody Wednesday and hid behind its back," said Soli to Mir on an assignment to The Frontier a week later. Biran had made the introductions between the two. Aristu, Soli had realised had handpicked him for the assignment with purpose. He could depend upon his disobedience to cover the revolt.

"They will now step up the effort to discredit us. Paint us as troublemakers," said Mir. "And Jaba. That silly girl—why? Did *you* give her the flag?"

Biran shook his head. He said she had got hold of it somehow. At the time they spread the lies about not wanting to sing, she was up on the tower rolling it down her window—but he did not want to think of Jaba now. If he began to think of Jaba he would begin to think of Holam the guard, a man who had never done anyone much harm and had never done anyone much good, because of what he did do in his final hours. He needed to find a safe house for Holam's wife in The City before they could take her to The Frontier. He had promised the man that. But if they were looking for him they were hunting for her. Biran saw Mir to the door and slipped on a shirt and started to walk north. It was eleven when he reached The Gates. A key was turned and he was let in. He shook a hand, embraced and sped ahead, his shadow touching the corners of the neatly laid squares even before he did. A cat mewling near the drain looked up at him. Biran picked it up and paused a while. His legs felt numb, he could go to sleep standing on his feet stroking the kitten when it jumped from his crook and hid behind a bin. Garbage lay spattered and unpicked in the back alleys of the grand mansions. It was a week since the revolt at The Malacca. The strike had spread throughout The City! On agitation for the last one year with various demands of dignity and a higher pay, the garbage workers had joined them it seemed. He hurried ahead with new energy. Just a hundred steps more and he would be in sight of *The Meat*.

The white columns of the building gleamed in the streetlight. A new moon appeared at its crown, then withdrew, leaving the corner in confusion. Biran stood before the gates but they were locked. There was not a soul around—he was not surprised. After eleven, the newspaper and the world outside mutually suspended their ties for a few hours. The phones in the newsroom rang less urgently, sleepy subs checking the wires stopped scanning the spilling paper, the low thrum of the printing press in the basement of the building could be heard—

if you were listening. Biran circled the building and stopped at its back. Since the incident at The Malacca, there were sentries watching every building of note but their backs were left unmanned. Propped up against the wall next to the library window on the second floor was a ladder. But Biran was feeling cold. His body wrecked by the long walk, was giving birth to Jaba through every open crevice of his being—an odd fear from his nostrils spoke her name, he thought he heard the sound of her feet turning the next street, his hands climbing the ladder were not his own—her dark arms were pushing him down. His feet missed a rung, if he wasn't careful he could break his neck. There would be plenty of time to think of Jaba—he had to reach the window.

9

The Revenge of the Mice

From his watch tower at The City's gates, Holam had been watching the day age over The Frontier. He had seen The Bus arrive, overseen the daily drama of the unsuitables evicted from the vehicle, the resultant rants and threats, the high drama, and given the order for the levers of the gate to be yanked back. This happened every day but the ordeal grew no lighter with experience. Every denial of passage was his responsibility, every entry, on his conscience. But sitting where he did, he had, over the past one year, tried to forget what was the law and what its violation. There were times when he had acted as if he didn't know the difference. No father of his had been involved in the making of law, he told himself and these days, he had seen enough to know that the law was actually opinions and opinion was formed according to the murmurs of every man's private self. But as the shouts for freedom grew, there were thoughts that he had not known himself to be capable of, that began to grow in him. If he wanted to remain in good health, they had to be spat out. What you do with cough, you should do with questions. He too wanted independence of one kind or the other, the freedom to be unambiguous, the freedom to be equal in spirit, the freedom to decide what he could be in relation to others, the opportunity to learn about himself through his relationship with others in society. Sometimes he felt like running away from these new confusions when he had not even resolved the older ones and the climbing down from that height of his watchtower felt longer, his legs leaden, unguided and dangerously close to taking a fall. Lately he had taken to wandering around the city at night after work and stand around listening at the night meetings of the city's disgruntled scum under a bridge, claimed a detective when the post-mortem examination of his role in the matter of The Malacca was done a month later. Holam, it is true, had started to change. Little by little, he had begun to throw away his glutinous depressions and self-doubts that seemed to clog the root of every thought from expressing itself. His wife had started to see the return of a different man after work. As he walked back home the stream of cars coming back into The City from The Frontier carrying the Lambda's babus, senior functionaries of the Dong Party, no longer impressed him or made him shrink into the shadows. They seemed to him part of the same formation demanding the same parade, the same ceremonies in which there would always be people, people like him, bringing up the rear. What change would Independence bring without a change in essences, in structure? When the Fairlanders left, who would they blame? He told his wife of the men he had begun to meet and their ideas. His wife, relieved to be living with a happier man, had but one consideration: if they set out soon enough for The Frontier they could still catch most of the first rain falling on their fields.

But Holam was in no hurry to go back. Once upon a time, he thought he had narrowed his desires to three. He longed for the freedom to decide the season when to work in the fields, the season to work on clay to make toys so that he may continue the art of his grandfather, and feed his family by these means. Holam talked little, but as his friends under the bridge realised, he had slowly begun to want the same things. Peace, security, a good life, were important things but there were other important things. Art need not take the *place* of Work but Work could abolish itself by becoming Art if a man could decide for himself the shape and direction of what he would do with his head, hands and feet, the way his muscle would turn every morning and this could only happen if men and women could stop Work altogether or rather the condition of having to work for somebody else and make way for a world where everybody got together with their creativity, producing what they could and only as much as was needed, and not reproduce the old malaise—the relations of Master and Subordinate. If Holam had the patience to stay with these feelings, with time, they were sure, he would begin to find the most important questions. And Holam had found them. The day this unassuming man with a giant's physique, who had started to turn up at every meeting in his green uniform, spoke with quiet understanding, he had given hope to the thousands shivering under the bridge, that the day was nigh when the movement could be tested by the power of words and the courage of imagination. If the new world had to be built—the next step was to build it. What were they waiting for? So, Holam was not in any hurry. The fields, he told his wife, had to wait and living with him, she too grew to realise that the freedom to be an artist or the desire to be a farmer could not be a matter of individual choice if it was at the expense of other people. 'When we make our toys, who will grow the food? Why should someone else have to take my place in the field? An intellectual's work is of the same value as those working in the factories or fields.' But as the call for revolution rumbled through the bowels of the Lambda, he found himself disturbed again. The old self-doubts returned: he felt hurried and duty-bound to be an insurgent. Was today the day to bring things down and had it not come too soon?

He heard the apprentice guard jangle the keys to turn the lock and decided to settle in for a doze when an owl smashed against the glass screen of the tower and fell to the ground. Holam was shaken.

The day had not begun well and by afternoon he was beginning to be troubled by a dull pain in his stomach. He got down from the tower to share a smoke with the other guard. Holam, in no mood for conversation though, said he was feeling short of breath. The guard nodded and gave him a look. Sitting on a high chair in that tower was the source of all that man's troubles, the guard thought. What work did he have to do but wave The Bus in and out? No question of being good or bad at that job. Those of them standing at The Gates faced all the heat. Short of breath—hrmph, for doing what?

"Trouble at The Malacca, I hear," he nevertheless said from the corner of his mouth. And after that, shut up. Holding his stomach, Holam climbed the stairs to the tower. The sun had lowered itself on The Frontier and had invaded each household. As a child, Holam remembered his grandmother beating him with a stick if he left the door of their house, cool and bare as a cemetery, ajar a second longer as he returned from school in the summer months. In the middle of their courtyard was the tree.

A shout broke up his thoughts. The fellow below had his hand stretched out, pointing towards The Frontier. Holam narrowed his eyes; the sun, too bright, created its own illusions. A group of men and women were moving all across the land in haphazard clusters as if they were going to a fair. They had tied their children on their back or were holding them up. Holam wasn't able to see but something in his guts told him what he saw. Sometimes he thought he recognised a familiar face but he couldn't be sure. Some words were carried to him by the wind; sometimes he recognised those voices. He stood glued to the sight, standing, when the cluster suddenly seemed to organise itself, took the shape of an advancing line, then fell out of line, and then broke into a run for The Gate. The thud of the approaching feet made his stomach knot. An old woman in the crowd he had seen years ago was looking up at him, her hands raised to her lips. He became immune to the cries of the guard below. He tried to look elsewhere but her eyes, those eyes... he had to hurry before she called out his name.... He leaned over and saw the dead owl. Its wings were singed. It was a *mar-chiraiya*. And he was transported to the courtyard at his grandmother's home—looking back the courtyard always seemed full of light. In its centre was the tree. He had seen the bird then on its upper branch as well on a sunny day like this. His grandmother had covered his eyes and driven him inside. A man may get killed by his own actions but the bird's arrival told you the date. For what reason had the *mar-chiraiya* of his childhood flown across The Frontier on a day like this?

Holam set aside his cap on the chair and shook off his uniform. He had to hurry. The sleeves of his khaki were well-worn, they slid off easily. He had cut a fine figure in his uniform; he had taken a minute to agree to wear it. But now he did not want time to think. When a man has plenty of time, it is not necessary that he will take the right decisions. He lit a match and dropped it on the crumpled pile at his feet. He watched it catch fire, sag and burn. He watched it turn into ash. A button had escaped the flames; it seemed to grin at him with the force of rotting tooth. He looked at it for a while, then kicked it aside. Climbing down the stairs, two at a time, he gave, what he knew would be his final orders, and walked back slowly to his quarters a few streets ahead. The old woman who ran past him pushed by the wave of humanity, turned back to give him one last look and surged ahead to burn down The Malacca.

Burning any structure down is not difficult, to offer its replacement is not easy. But people can, if they try, imagine an idea before it is there. If we do not try to demand evidence from our dreams, they can realised by the very act of remembrance, shared, talked about and fought for, first as theory, and then on the streets. Still, at present, they were not in a position to burn down anything. But you don't say that to new revolutionaries, so Mir and Biran did not say it. So they said: If they wanted to be known as arsonists, they had plenty of people on the other side to do that job for them. "They would surely shout The City down with this news. The government is not ours. The police was theirs. The judge, theirs. The newspapers were theirs," Mir shouted over the din as the insurgents gathered around a table in a school, a few lanes away from The Malacca, that they had occupied. They were anyway ill-prepared for the task. And Mir was not sure what could be gained by the spectacle. Storming the gates, he felt had set things in motion.

A line had been crossed, the barrier between The City and The Frontier breached. It was not enough. The people wanted more. Bring down The Gate! Burn down The Malacca! Not just a breach, the line had to be erased, they said. "For that we are ready to die," got up an old man to say. "All of you here give me a minute," said Mir. "You all want to die when every hand is needed...we are not in the business of trying to be heroes. History is made not by dying but by fighting. Let us fight!"

"Fight! We will fight!" the cry went around the room when Bali, a mechanic from the Zain factory, got up to say: "'Let us fight', 'let us fight!' What will fighting do? What do we do after tonight?" He said *he* knew what he was going to do tomorrow but he had come tonight thinking that they were going to be doing something together. Bali's words were ugly, his manner disrespectful, so a few people pulled him down, and then excluded him from their whispers. And as everybody was talking in little groups and joining in the conversation of other groups and generally shouting over other people's heads, someone or the other wanted water, someone wanted to use the toilet, someone got up to say if they could not provide their children water *now*, it would prove no one was in charge and they were free to run to The Malacca next door to ask for water since they weren't burning it down anyway—when the mechanic got up again to speak.

He squared his shoulders and looking straight at Mir, said, it was getting late. Late for what everyone wanted to know. Bali said if the night was to be spent talking—and everybody was very clear what he had in mind because that is what everyone else was thinking—they might as well try to get back to The Frontier before the sun went up. He said his muscles had grown taut under the strain of waiting, that he was tired of being led like sheep and have his programme decided for him and since he was quite sure very few would share his opinion, his leaving would disturb nothing and he would quietly slip out of the building and walk back home to The Frontier. This created an uproar. Everyone looked at Mir in alarm as it was easier to have the leader face the storm rather than face each other when they had the same questions. A few wanted to beat him up in deference to their leaders, a few said no one was sneaking back or sideways for anything and Mir and Biran smiled a tight smile at each other thinking they would always have to contend for, and take along as long as possible, all sorts of people till the time they could—people who would join in when a revolution was ripe, people who would encourage others to join in and then do nothing themselves, people who would work the hardest for it and then not turn up next morning. They nevertheless went across to Bali and persuaded him to stay.

The movement had just begun, they said, and like every

worker, they too, would learn from this struggle. "Should fear of making mistakes divide us?" they asked him. "Tonight," said Mir, facing the group, "give me your faith." If things went wrong, or if as a group, they were unable to achieve what they had set out to do, when they had set out from The Frontier, there would be someone else leading.

A pounding at the door made everyone in the room stiffen. The school, chosen for its proximity to the hotel so that they could mount a defence of their comrades still in The Malacca and retrieve Jaba's body, their refuge, they realised to their horror, had no back entrance. They had rushed into the building from the front under the cover of night and they would have to exit it the same way. Its location, deep inside a lane, meant that if a platoon was positioned at the head of the lane and at its end, on this street, their game would be up. Known as the Black Quarters, here were the fifty-bed dormitories of The City's servants, their bath houses, their teashops, grocers, their children's schools, their illegitimate women. Built back to back on one lane as if The City could bear their presence on no other, these dwellings supported a mass of individuals bonded by family ties to The Frontier by daily knowledge of their masters' dominance over their lives, by the same condition of humiliation, by the indisputable logic that it must end. They had spent half their lifetime in the fine houses of The City; after work, they returned to a room in which there was just enough space for a man to crawl back. At night, when sleep eluded their tired bodies, they listened to the rats come out from under their beds going about their daily forage in the shadows, unhindered, and they told themselves that if there was an art or a science in all of this, it was about knowing when to draw attention to oneself, when to be silent and when to lie in wait. Their fate, they knew, was sealed. As they would be hunted down like rats one day, they would behave like rats.

This is the place that Biran, after a recce, had chosen to spring their offensive from. As it turned out, it was thus the best place for a hideout—and the worst. The building, a school for the children of The City's servants, shared a wall with a police station. And for this reason, Biran was counting on the Murkys to count it out as a cover. If they could keep their voices down, they felt they would be able to go undetected and hold out for a few hours. But it was proving difficult. Disagreements over the operation broke out in the hall every two minutes. Differences of opinion led to wild accusations. Motives were being unearthed, when in reality, territories were being preserved. The moderates felt insulted being called moderates, the extremists, for being thus identified, as if it was a weakness of personality. So when unity between the two factions seemed impossible, a slight disturbance in the direction of the main road triggered a rush to the hole-like windows. Outside, the Murkys were on a rampage. Dogs and cats were being strung from branches of trees; women and children walloped for venturing out of their homes. In the Lambda, this night had been like no other night.

But the pounding started again though the fists seem to beat the door less forcefully this time. Men and women seized their sticks on Biran's signal and lined themselves up against the wall. The few rifles were quickly moved to the hands of the best shooters. They pushed the butts out and closed the windows from the inside. Fear and suffocation led to the rise of old habits. They remembered god, asked for his protection, pleaded with him to show a sign; when they tired of him, they turned on each other, pointed fingers, threw dirt, when a thin spindly child tugged Mir's hand and begged for the chance to be able to be let out of the door to investigate. A deathly quiet descended on the hall as his parents sobbed in fear. But they did not call him back. If he was killed, as parents they would grieve, but they had not joined the others on this day in order to discover or be restrained by personal attachments at a time of crisis. The door closed behind the child with a clap and almost immediately someone or something from outside began to push it. The pounding began—now should they open it? Then someone spoke in a slow, low voice: "Open the door, friends outside."

Mir had a split second to decide. Exchanging a glance with Biran at the other end of the hall he threw the door open and a crowd of thirty came in. On their shoulders, was Holam. Shot from the back, and then slashed with a knife from the front, he was leaking blood with every breath. His stomach, they saw, was hanging out, his eyes, the only sign of life left in his huge body, moved from face to face crowding over him. But there was no hope of getting a doctor at this time of night to visit this part of the city. Someone give the man water! Push back, give him air! Did no one have any bandages? But where would they get bandages—they were so far away from home. With one hand they had carried their sticks and guns, with the other hand, their children, when they came from The Frontier. They looked around the classroom—nothing, nothing that could be used was here. So shirts were ripped to stop the blood—but the man was dying and he knew it. Does his wife know? Send for his wife! Holam's wife was not at home, they found. With his last gasps, he told them she had gone to The City square to deliver under the cover of night, hundreds of bundles of the party's newspaper to Holam's contact in *The Meat*.

The Party! From the lips of a dying man thus fell a word they had not admitted to themselves—not in those days when they had first stopped bowing their heads and had run all together to jam the machines as the managers from The City came to mark out their land; nor on those days when their men had collapsed on the factory floor and the children had planned their own action and marched to rattle the factory gates till they felt they had been standing so long before them, they were actually in front of their own door and the factory belonged to them; they had not noticed it either when Mir, a boy from their midst, who ate the same worm-eaten rice as they did, began telling them of the possibility of creating a world with justice, and they had started dreaming with him thinking of themselves as poets, soldiers, missionaries and architects of that world, but not even then had they thought they could have their own party when for years they had been behaving as if they were in one. A Party! Their Own Party! Someone guard the horizon and call a priest, quick, so that he can give it a name before it vanishes or is taken away from us.

10

My Right to Contradict

A week had passed since Holam's death and Biran, standing on the last rung of the ladder climbed on the window sill and jumped into the room. The long walk took its toll, his head swam and his legs were beginning to cramp. He leaned against a wall to steady himself and thought of the things he had to do. After the business of the night was over, he would take back Holam's wife to The Frontier but first, he had to see the workings of the cell they had put in place to build the underground in *The Meat*. He put his hand out and shifted the ladder a little to the right—just the way it was. The façade of *The Meat* should still not bear their imprint. There was a time for showing the resistance to the people, for people did need to see others resisting, and a time for putting their heads together for work. With so much still to do, the time hadn't come to show themselves in full light. But as the evening proceeded, circumstances forced them to show their hand.

Biran looked around. For a library, the room was ill-lit. A single bulb, coated with the dust of years, illuminated the room in fragments. The walls, seemed barricaded with shelves filled with busts of Aristu Argot in black marble. Next to them were old maps curling around the nails from which they hung—Biran spread them out. They circled Aristu's new areas of business collaboration of a year back—the factories to build army trucks, the area to build new bungalows for the new bourgeoisie, the godown to store the best pieces of marble for The Malacca. A few tables and chairs, their legs broken, were also spread around the room. A few pen-stands stood on the table-tops. Pens were nailed to their cases or filled with vanished ink. Old editions of papers, *The Meat* included, however, were filed. They crumbled on touch. Those that did not, had fonts that were indecipherable. Books on any topic were clearly on exile. If *The Gentleman* under Cliff McGowan had been committed to a journalism that would justify the continuance of the Fairlanders' rule, *The Meat* under Aristu Argot was turning into a museum. Same difference actually. *The Gentleman* paid journalists to protect the owner's interests, behave as advertisers; *The Meat* was paying them to do nothing. Since Aristu's takeover, any attempts at a reporter's control over what he had seen and what he could report, had been effectively silenced. There were no more whispers about it—no one thought about it any more.

Senior editors, determined to retire with seniority, had been the first to fall in line. There was no voice in the organisation around whom the staff could gather, leave alone rally, to point out that it was plain wrong. A newspaper did itself the least amount of good if it undermined its own purpose and stopped being a newspaper and became a weather report of people in power. Truly, what difference was there going to be when the coming regime substituted the earlier one? The poor in the factory, the mine or the workshop under the Fairlanders' government would be poor in a Lambda under the Dong Party but *The Meat* would not ask why nothing should change. It would not consider it offensive. Or, they would look at the poverty but not question the structure that produced it. All this was external to their journalism. What politicians do in the name of the people, most of *The Meat*'s journalists did in the name of objectivity. Having an insect under a microscope and noting down their body plan cannot be the same as having human beings under scrutiny. It boiled down to having the right questions or deciding to be relaxed about not asking them at all. The people who prospered in *The Gentleman* had retained their jobs in *The Meat* under the same conditions—greater the complicity, more the pay.

Every system, however, produces its own death and they were of the firm belief that it should be helped towards its end. At the end of the day, a newspaper or a factory, or any institution for that matter, could not be about a few individuals, but whether it can break the inherent character of control of all institutions and bring into being a collective—to see their dreams, help forge a new society, put the existing one to constant questioning even if it is one they themselves had built, build collective confidence, collective action and in that churn new words, invent new meanings and set in motion new terms for relationships between human beings. "Not easily done," muttered Biran, grinding a half-smoked cigarette under his feet. Teething problems or not, there would be problems. Everyone had much to learn about everything. He tapped the door of a tall wooden cabinet, and waited for the return tap. Almost immediately, the entire cabinet slid to the right to open into a room.

Little more than a broom closet, it however had space for people to sit and stand around, even a window for looking out. Seated on a floor on a mat were faces that he knew. A chair propped up against the wall was empty. Hog and Soli came forward to say they were still waiting for someone. But as there need be no protocol to begin a conversation, Biran introduced himself, the work of The Party, his work in The Party, the goal of The Party to the few that had gathered. He was not put off by the lack of numbers, he was used to talking to empty rooms. When *The Meat* felt the need to join in the movement, and it was important that *The Meat* join in, this room would not be enough to hold all of them. What he needed to know was, was there yet a need from among the people in this newspaper to want to change things before they lost the handle yet again. Were there people who were willing to call the crisis a crisis? Did they believe there was an opportunity for its overcoming and were they willing to be agents of that change? Or would their politics be of acting under no circumstance? You could begin a revolution with two people but you couldn't sustain it with two. In that case, The Frontier, already insurgent, would raise the questions on its own till The City joined in. This is what he had come today to find out. He looked at the men who had gathered and saw they were all dividing their attention between the clock on the wall and him. He turned his attention towards the wall. It was a fine clock, two hands, a dial, just needed wounding up, he said to some laughter, so they stopped looking at the clock and decided, to focus on him. Perhaps because they saw each other every day, they would not look at each other. J Babu walked in a half hour later. He brought Holam's wife with him and that is how the strength of the meeting that night went up to eight.

"I am Soli, a city reporter".

"Dipu—guard".

"Danish—paster of bromides."

"Moron—printing press."

"Hog—I'm a proofreader."

"J Babu—well, I'm the editor of the Statement page, and Holam's wife, she is with me."

"Biran—of The Party," and so the introductions went and immediately struck a wall of silence. So Biran spoke.

He would be brief, he said. The meeting had been called to start a process of thinking about work, learn about each other's work, and the life they envisaged after the Plebsicite—and they could begin that work here as well by discussing which way they wanted it to go. Someone said the word 'politics' scared them and they had seen it betray and fail.

"Politics is the right of every human being," said Biran, "and the prospects of success and failure dogs every invention, every act of science does it not? So being scared is actually saying that you want to be closed to newness and be left to die without inconveniencing anybody, just in case any interaction with another person could become the nucleus of a group, which could lead to 'politics' which could lead you to becoming a person, like any other person, with the embarrassing potential of betrayal and failure. Come on now...."

They looked at the young man with piercing eyes with amazement. He had felt no hesitation coming into their office, he moved around the room as if he had grown up in it—with people he had just met, he used his words as if they were hammers. The only option was to listen or leave. No one did. "Politics is everywhere. If you and I come out of our houses by chance at around the same time while a policeman beats down a protester on the street, we could turn political by what we decide to do as we stand watching, if we stand watching, from the pavement. What is my stake in being here today? My freedom," he said, "depends on your being free," so wouldn't it make sense to struggle for it together instead of leaving it in the hands of other people? Their hopes of 'life afterwards', he urged, would be no different under The Dong, that believed in 'helping' people and robbing them of any agency, but now they had a window to change that if they were willing to commit to another vision.

"And that would be...", said Danish, the young paster, whom everyone else had been calling Dan. Dan, who had said nothing at all since the meeting started, raised his hand, asking Biran to elaborate. He was quite the mutterer. "Look I have stayed back tonight to try your new game. Let me know if you'd prefer me dead, quiet, or alive," he said when others hushed him down and told him not to disrupt the meeting. But they still would not open up to speak even as fear and excitement curdled their stomachs—how could they speak when J Babu himself was here in their midst? Let him speak first, they would first see what he would have to say. Biran seized the opportunity of the lull, and asked Dan to join them on the floor. "Come see if you like this poster J Babu and I'm spreading out on the floor." For a few meetings he realised he would have to be the doer till everyone involved started to punch with their own weight. The poster, for the moment, had been the glue. They crowded around it, they took it in their hands. It occupied everyone's attention. The message in it was formal, even simple. Finished with a few words, it was a call to open rebellion. It said:

"My
Right
to put up
a Poster"

—The Party

The goal was to plaster it on the director's door. To open up a front, Aristu, the source from which power flowed in their office, had to be challenged as visibly and as loudly as possible. It had to be a big shakeoff, a big shout of rebellion. But who would do it? It had to be someone from among them. Someone who had access, someone who had a reason to be around his office. Biran took heart—they had told him it was their matter, he could leave it upto them, they would decide among themselves who would be their man was for this job. What was left of the night was spent in deciding whether they would print the poster or write it like a dazibao* with strong, bold lettering and words or even paragraphs of provocation and on settling on the content of the next instalment of posters. The challenge had to be swift, sustained and continuous. No week should go without them not saying anything. Posters and pamphlets would be left in the newsrooms not surreptitiously but openly as the weeks would go by, mentioning the time of the next meeting and the agenda. The cell's men and women would share and learn from those who worked in the printing press, the executive canteen and the workers' canteen, try to force in reports about their experience into *The Meat*. If that failed, they would write about it in *The Will*, distribute it inside *The Meat*, throw it inside official vehicles, and helped by the packing department, slip *The Will* inside every newspaper that left the building in the trucks and get the drivers to scatter them at every square, every market, before every door in the city. They considered what they had written. Some of it was raw, no doubt, but they would refine it in the coming weeks and change it depending on how their onslaught was met at the top and among their peers. At the second meeting, it was decided not to sign each poster with the words, The Party. Instead, this is what they began to write—

"My
Right
to Contradict"
—The Workers

"I'm off for a piss.
Guard your own
gates, pig"
—The Workers

"Down! Down! Down!
We are taking the town.

We are at your door.
We are no longer sore.
We know your face.
We know your friends.
We know your foes.
Run! Run! Run!
We are cleaning our guns."

—The Workers

"We, the workers of your paper give you time to clear out with your men and women and leave the paper to us. This paper will be run like a Council. One day in a week, The Printer will go to work in the Canteen, Editors will learn to operate the Press, the Drivers will have say in deciding what makes news, the Proofreader will travel with the Driver to distribute the papers. We will learn about each other's work, be accountable for it, review it, and then decide who is to be deputed for what task, in which area do we need what kind of people. The guard need not be a guard for life, neither should the reporter. There is to be no difference, no extra value to be placed on journalistic work over mechanical work or vice versa. We will all work with machines, we will all decide what kind of newspaper this needs to be. Each work area will send a representative to the council, and the work of each representative is open for review. And now go."

—The Workers

Biran and Mir, who had joined them later after a few meetings had been held, had learnt much from the interaction. There was no question of coming to the newspaper to preach or lining people up for 'interviews'. As they had discussed with each other before setting the time and place for that first meeting, the organisation of work in a system that depended on profit had to be run on hierarchy and inequality—and it should make most workers militate.

In time, they had indeed begun to trickle into the meetings by themselves, then in twos and threes as if they needed someone else as well to be making, if this was a mistake, then the same mistake. There were among them the watchers, the scoffers, those sitting around looking glum, registering a holding back of allegiance with their monochrome silence. Sometimes their presence was reverential; it felt as if it they had come together for Mass when in reality it was the warm curiosity for murder—ever-watchful of new alliances, who was coming in, going out or who had stayed back a bit longer, who was being blood-let... But every meeting was a new day, sometimes the group did become a community, with each member trying to be agreeable or splendidly disagree after considering all lines of argument, appraising and re-engaging... and then there were days when just for a few hours each one of them moved as if they were joined to the other, unified in dreams, in speech and step, so that it seemed that they had come together if only to fall in love, as if love had been the agenda, and they felt so good with the other...and then one dull day, when the thrusts and jibes, the sizing-ups that men and women do so well were done, a few did make the leap. That number was few, but they kept their faith in love, the spirit behind all revolutions.

Because there are problems, there are revolutions and the people it puts in charge of leading them says something about the direction of those upsurges. To put the people with the most number of problems in charge would be like putting healthcare in the hands of the terminally ill. But to put it in the hands of those with the least bit of care, would be catastrophic. Journalists, no different from factory workers, also had problems, but they had to determine whether they wanted to be the bulwark against the economy that was at the root of the problem or make it work. Would senior editors, for example, be counted on to be as radical as say, Dan, the paster? You couldn't be both a radical and an insecure man. They had seen J Babu's fear of losing what he had if everyone began to have what he had....

Young Dan had surprised them by his ability to keep separate his identity from his place of work and to see his ties with it in purely economic terms. To each of Biran's questions on another night, except for the question of his salary, Dan had had the same answer.

"Who owns your paper?"

"I wouldn't know."

"Who reads your paper?"

"I wouldn't know".

"How many pasters in your paper?"

"I wouldn't know."

"What is the name of your paper?"

"I wouldn't know."

They had had several meetings since the first one. At every meeting, the boy had burst with irrepressible energy after the meeting had been over and then drawn around himself an opaque silence, a time when his face furrowed till his forehead was a mass of lines. When he would feel oppressed by his own silence, this too fair a boy with a mass of unruly hair, would annex the ongoing conversation to some or the other remembrances of his life and addressing J Babu with half-shy eyes, then Mir, then Biran, and just as suddenly set his head back with a jerk as though it had slipped out of a hinge, and grow silent again. They grew used to him and his interruptions and noted that the mention of The Party had a way of setting him off and make his eyes crawl around the room. When he spoke he was trouble, when he was silent, he was clamorous. His actions, full of unsaid demands, drew their attention; they were constantly turning their heads back and checking up on him as he sat squatting just about to suck in his lips to let out a whistle or flick the plaster chipping from the walls.

Once, he came head to head with Biran and Mir. He had signed his name at the end of a poster and said it must stay or he was out. He had made friends with a calligrapher in *The Meat's* artwork department, from whom he was learning to draw, a man he had since brought along, a man even more silent than he, and insisted about the credit.

Coaxed by J Babu to reconsider his position, he replied looking at Biran and Mir: "You speak. I write. Where's the harm? What you do and what I do make people stop and listen."

"No one is stopping and listening. Look around you," barked Mir, "when we started, we were eight, three months later, we are twelve more. There is plenty of work left in *The Meat* and it's your choice whether you want to stay or go. No time for anyone here who thinks he can sit in a corner and be an artist."

11

The Wedding Party

"What do we do about Danish?" Biran asked Mir on the way home after a meeting at *The Meat* one evening. A wedding procession drowned Mir's answer. The bridegroom, their neighbour's son, got off his cow to greet them. He coaxed them to join the feast at the bride's home around the corner. Pulled into the wedding party, Mir and Biran joined those on foot and stood in front of the girl's home at the side of a pipeline. A row of shacks, stacked next to each other and as stable as a pack of cards, faced them. Where were the walls, where were the roofs on which the wind could dance—even the wind seemed to have refused to stop on its path for some cruel play. Bags of potatoes, utensils, rags, served as divisions between floors; piled up on one above the other, they served as doors; if they moved a bag two spaces left or right so that they could stick out two hands without dismantling the roof, they had a window. The wind left them alone; too many human beings forced to live together didn't or couldn't. So no house leaned too heavily on the other. Camaraderie was given, from one to the other, between a man and a man, one woman and the next, from one child to the other, and constantly negotiated. It was a loan. It was not unconditional. A few jasmine buds grew waxy-white in these starved corners. The smoke from the factories floated over their heads spraying their upturned faces with a thin layer of soot but could not muffle their will to grow. The darkest clouds passed over each day and so would this. But the moon on tip-toe, killed them with her unbearable softness.

Month after month, production in the factories was peaking. Workers were being ground with the grain. New machines were moving into the factories that could just with the flick of a switch put every muscle of a man's body to work at a bone-wrenching speed. Fathers in The Frontier noting their incremental effects were beginning to hold back the young who filled the ranks in the factories and told them to stop turning up for work. Their sons were happy. They also did not want to miss the excitement that could be had by sitting around at home. The Dongs had ratcheted their propaganda for voting for their party during the Plebsicite and were driving in into The Frontier almost daily. Baba Lala and his son were holding streetcorner meetings and giving away hens—again. It was a double insult. Lala's goons, unknown to him, had slipped into their backyards and stolen their birds! They would have liked to cook his goose! Tempers ran high, there was talk of murder—when someone came running to say that the pipeline that ran all along the workers' shacks had cracked open.

"We have complained over and over about this! Someone is going to have to pay!"

At a distance where the wedding was taking place, the pipeline was pumping dirty water from the factories into the shacks by the gallons; the bride's little cousins sat on them till the guests finished their meals.

"What brother," said the bride's uncle, a man who had participated in the action at The Malacca, to Mir, "here we talk and talk and they just take and take. What after The Malacca?"

"After that you fall down and die," said his wife jabbing him on his bony back. Smiling self-consciously at Mir and Biran, she said: "This man just frets and growls. Since you two took him along, he refuses to look at me, this woman who has suffered him for thirty years. He just wants action...."

The room burst into peals of laughter and the festivities got off to a right start. Soon, the gathering moved outdoors. By now, the water coming in eddies had broken up the party. Someone shouted 'snake' and then everyone had to spot one. There was no longer room for politeness, panic pushed one neighbour to punch another. The children who came rushing in from outside had just about time to wash their bottoms having stuffed the pipeline as best as they could. They rushed towards their trousers which they had left inside and their little sisters squawked seeing them and then went splashing around the room to peep at them from behind the curtains. Then kitted out in clothes which their mothers had stayed up all night to darn, they stood in knee-deep water and powdered themselves all over with cheap rouge and stood in line for an old aunt to line their eyes with kohl and paint their faces all over in a furious berry pink. They urged her to hurry. They were at least 20 of them so they needed her to hurry.

"Up to some mischief no doubt!" she said peering into their faces but getting no reply she finished the last touch-up and surveyed the results. "There—now no one knows who you are! Binu looks like Jhinu..."

That done, they slowed down. The girls took one last look at one another and went to stand beside their mothers, who were still rummaging through the shack for the best possible gift to The Frontier's temple. It was dark inside, so no one gave them a second look. The boys went to the corner that was the kitchen. An old ram would be slaughtered and they needed cotton to stuff their ears.

The wedding rites were got over quickly. The fire had refused to burn. Water had soaked the pile of wood outside the bride's home and the people of The Row, where the shacks stood, who had looked forward to a night-long revelry, went inside their wet homes. Cold kerosene was poured inside the lamps and one by one the lanterns began to burn inside each hovel. The flame flickered, framed by the shadows that had taken over the walls. Someone in great hurry went down the road on a cycle. He pressed down on the horn and the shacks shook like old leaves.

A CRANE LANDED nimbly on a boulder that had been discarded by The Manora. It was the fourteenth ship of the year! Horo, the priest, had heard people splashing ashore last night as he lay in bed. Walking slowly towards the sea, he now took a stumble. His gnarled feet curled around the rocks—a split-second reflex stopped him from falling down.

"How many more men can The Frontier hold? There should be a law about it. In earlier times, we would have been consulted..."

But since that was too long a while ago, the memory of past prestige at a time when his was nose-diving, gave him no satisfaction. Nostalgia was an unsteady building; he did not want to waste his time connecting the dots. He looked at the ship half-sunk and upturned in the oilslicked sand, drab and undignified like a washerwoman drowned in her own tub. Once upon a time the sight of a ship in the horizon would have gladdened his generous heart—so many souls to save! But since the scandal of the book, his legs felt unsteady, his mind unable to guide his hand to push through a thicket of doubts. To put it plainly—he was suffering the pangs of professional men. If he lost the temple, he wasn't worth a straw; he would become a man with neighbours unprotected from common disourse; what Horo feared most was turning common. A noise a few feet ahead made him draw back. A band of rats climbing down the hull of the ship, were chittering madly and on landing, bouncing off, what seemed to be a rock. Curious, he inched closer, but his fading eyesight refused to cooperate. All that he saw was grey waves breaking evenly along the coastline.

His knees knocked against another boulder. This time, they hurt. Bending down, his hands traced the outlines of a box. He was unable to lift it. It was heavy and it was locked. He gave it a push—blocks of wood or metal clanged against each other. A box of tools left in a hurry by the sailors or the families that climbed ashore. They would return for it no doubt. But he should stop this lately acquired habit of pottering around the water at evening tide. A man had to be light on his feet these days, it was the only way he could add to his life in these hostile surroundings though for a ninety-year-old he had to say he thought he had not done too badly. Eighty years, and sixty of those years as a holy man, he had presiding almost on a par with the deity at The Frontier's sole temple. People tiptoed around him. Slowly they stopped asked him any questions—about god or anything else. "Just as well, do them some good to figure out something on their own sometimes."

The reputation of his temple, he told himself, had compelled him to protect it with a gate. The queue of the faithful would begin to grow again so in order to be available to them he had built his quarters above the shrine. Milk, melons and jackfruits came from The City's notables. He often went to sleep resting his head on a pile of bananas. From his dwindling flock in The Frontier, he did not demand much. After their work in the factories when they dropped in for a chat, they fixed the leaks in his toilet, plucked a weed or two from his garden, stirred the milk on the stove while he worked up a chant from the shrine.

"If I had prayed for my own well-being as much as I did for those curs, even the lord would not have found fault in it," he thought as he walked back to the shack he had propped up by the sea since the time The Book had disappeared from the temple. It had been the perfect excuse to shunt him to this wilderness. But not for long.

"One day it will be the colour of my teeth, next day, it will be the shape of my face—they were just looking for a reason." He wasn't going to put up with nonsense, he had put up with a lot since they all started talking of The Party. He looked forward to the meeting at the home of one of the richest men in The City the coming week. Yes, he would love to stay and pray in The City. What a relief it would be to find himself among people who avoided conflict.

"They don't push and scream, they are polite, even if their arm were to brush against mine, they blanch in terror, they say 'sorry.'" People in The City were always sorry about something or the other. Sorry was a city illness. He, Horo, knew how to cure it. He was what they had been waiting for.

As night grew over his head in this corner of The Frontier, he was less sure. He wondered if he had taken the wrong measure of his life. As a priest, had he not failed the very essence of holy duty? He had turned people away from god, he had built a temple to keep the sky anchored above his head.

"And now they are building their own."

His servant—a new boy The Party had allotted him after having got rid of the old one—would report the progress with undisguised glee mimicking how the hammer came down on the bricks and tuned them into dust, how they carted away the gate to smelt it into a stove.

"That boy Guli, our Uma Ai's nephew, what a boy! With one push, how he flattened two storeys of your house into one.... Tea, master, some tea for your throat?"

There was nothing wrong with his throat and the little rascal knew it. It was his heart they had bludgeoned with their rough ways. He felt weak and close to tears. So he said he would have the tea. The warmth of the cup would rejuvenate him, the salt of the winds would cool his ill humour. But the memory of privilege is a long one. Once it is gone, no self-respecting person stops crying about it. His father had been a priest for sixty years and his grandfather before him....

"Longevity—that's what they snatched from me."

He couldn't wait to reveal some of the things he had heard about some of them to the gentlemen of The City. "Guli. Whattaboy? What a devil is more like it! Just he wait...Baba Lala should know what his driver's precious son is up to.... " Mangu had returned to The City. But the boy had stayed back. Why?

He hadn't seen him playing near the shore over a month but he was sure he was up to no good. Each time a ship came by, he and his gang were as inevitable as night. Horo would cower behind his window as their hushed voices would grow sharp with excitement as they paced the shore. As the ship glided closer they would call out to each other like wolves and climb it with their saws, torch cutters, hammers and rope and drag the ship ashore. The night would ring with the sounds of its disembowelment. Their sharp cries and hoots as the masts came down with a pull of their rope and the slither of the long line of cable thud thudding down the deck to the grounds even as they tore it down, sent a chill down his spine. Slam! Rrrrrrrrr! Grrrrummm! The saw cutting through the veins of the ship as they met the resistance of wood and steel, started a dull pain at the back of his neck. His heart would thump. As the hours passed and the night cracked and splintered, speaking only in sound, he felt he was being torn apart with their little hands. It would make him forget his prayers, make him say them backwards. For nights on end, it would be like this and one day he would wake up with the same sense of defeat to see a clear sky and at one corner of the sandy strip, bits of broken shell.

"When life is not permanent, what's in a ship? All things that are put together can be separated."

But what a din they had made! With what sport they had broken it apart as if they were under oath to do it well! The dust of the dismembering wood and the inky fumes would keep his throat clogged for a week. He held back his sighs. The world had no consideration for an old man.

He hoped the date for The Plebiscite would be announced soon. It would be the cornice to build a new order. It would stop all the hanky panky. Everyone was on the make—even children! Who had given them the responsibility of breaking up the ship and dispensing with its parts? Where did they take the iron sheet and asbestos? To their homes no doubt, the little thieves that they were. He had seen them download big boxes from the ship and cart them on their back. When he had asked them what was inside they had given him the sauce and said they could give him a good price for The Book in case he had other older versions stashed away somewhere!

"You had to bribe people for respect these days," he muttered and his shoulders heaved. "There would no place even in hell for them."

Stars had blanked out the sky and proved wrong its infinity —every fold of the canopy had been filled, each space taken. The clouds hung around limply like defeated generals. A few escaped and went along their own way but the night unlike other nights did not seem governed by law, it did not inspire the trust that it knew it would be followed by morning. Looking skyward, Horo got no answers. All around him, the sea mumbled and groaned as if she was just about to release a troublesome child from her belly. The moon full of unspoken advice, paled, and went to hide behind the clouds. It was the time of monsters.

Horo's feet got him up and took him to the shore and he sat on the boulders for hours looking vacantly at the sea when a thought wrinkled his forehead. No! It couldn't be possible. The box still lay a few feet to his side. He decided he would bring a hammer and break it open the next morning to be free of doubts.

At night he was blind as a bat and any moment now his servant, would be here.

He thought he heard voices in the distance approaching his shack. He wiped his feet in the sand, then climbing up the incline went to sit on the steps before his door and crossed his legs. Fanning himself, he waited for his evening meal. As did Handsa-ai*.

THEY ALL loved Handsa-ai, they so loved her. And that is why they were happy to have her and Khandoba near them once more. But Handsa is what they had all come to see. But where was Handsa's idol? What was being put up was a blackened pot and a piece of worm-eaten wood on which someone had penciled a mouth and eyebrows—now that turned some people away.

"You here, Khaimee-bibi!" asked Uma, relieved to find a familiar face in the crowd that had gathered to look on as the deities were placed on two square stones facing each other on the mound under the sky.

"I was just passing by," said Khaimee, who sold dried fish in the market, pointing upwards to the basket on her head, but her eyes were blinking with a luminescent blackness.

"Not to worry—I won't tell," said Uma reassuringly, hugging her around her waist. "The children—all well? Sajjad back from the factory?"

"Huh, hmm," grunted Khaimee and slipped away. From where she stood, she could see a procession of lights bobbing, going around the blacksmiths' houses and moving towards the mound and she knew she could catch her children here. They had shot past her with their bizzarely painted faces in the evening during the wedding in The Row and she wanted to get to the bottom of it. The light bearers now stood around the mound—and they were not among them! Where *were* they? She pushed her way through the crowds and decided to join Uma who had clearly not given up on her and had been madly waving in her direction with every addition to the scene in front of them.

That night, everyone who was at home, was at the mound.

It was Handsa's consecration and from now on they would talk to her, fight with her, side with her and defend her against naysayers, whisperers, slanderers, moulds, moss, inclement weather—and even if the sky fell down. Handsa did not need them now, it was they who needed her.

"Hush now—the lamps are lit. But who goes there to light the lamp?"

"The sweeper's girl and the butcher's son."

"It is fitting. Our Handsa was married, but she was not a wife. She would not stay with Khandoba. So when they dragged her to the other end of The Lambda one night and when she came back, she spilled no tears. She climbed up a tree and stayed up there for years."

"Handsa-aiiiiiii!" "Aiiiiiiiiiii" The cry went up and they all milled around her, the daughter who had fought her own back from the wolves and starved herself up on a tree even as they had all gone about their own business around her—the rice-farmer in his rice-fields, the corn-grower in the corn-fields, in those days when every man had a farm.

"It was all gone soon afterwards. The cows died at pasture, then the goats by the pond, and that is how the land too came under the bulldozers' maws just the way she had said it would."

"Yes! Yes! This had been her curse and this is what came to be," said the women in one voice, now a group of forty, squatting on the ground around Uma, mother of Kanhu.

"But I had heard a different story, Uma," said someone interrupting her flow and all heads now swivelled in that direction. "I thought the factories turned the land barren. Or, Ai did?"

"Ai did," said Uma firmly fixing the sceptic with a look and drawing their attention to the saddle quern on whose flat surface rice and corn were grounded and the miller's stone which was used to pound it, being placed before Ai, their girl who had become a goddess. "One day, they came from the other side of The Lambda, and said they would burn our settlement down if she did not come down the tree," said Uma taking up the story, "but she was unmoved. Her cries of hunger kept the settlement awake all night, but she would not come down. Not even when they tied Khandoba to the tree. Years passed and as is the way with all of us, what we don't understand we turn into Gods or the devil. Handsa became Handsa-ai and there came a priest."

"Horo? Was it Horo?"

"Don't know. If a man does not behave like a man but like a parrot and repeats what he thinks the divine says, only in his ears, what use is there for him or his name? Horo, Maro, Daro—who cares? Yes, yes, Horo's father it was," she said to the gaggle around her. "Every morning, men and women came out of their houses to meet Khandoba, whose legs were tied to the tree but whose hands were free to write down his wife's predictions on the saddle quern. On some days, the people brought rice and fish, on other days, a cup of tea or milk, a dish of goat. Whoever had whatever brought that and sat around the odd couple—one at the foot of the tree, the other spitting down it. In the beginning, the saddle quern lay clean for days but as time passed, the slate began to fill—Handsa had begun to speak each day. That is how The Lambda knew that The City would grow out of The Frontier and The Gates would come up between them like a wall, and the trees would burn, and the land would go barren—all this was written with the blood that leaked drop by drop down the tree. Yes, they all came, my father and your father to have their fortunes read, but no one lifted a finger to help. So wipe your tears now."

"What did Horo's father do?" asked someone quietly but the teller of the tale seemed in no hurry to answer that question.

"Haven't I got dinner to make? Kanhu's father will be back anytime soon," said Uma getting up and walking away without even a look back in their direction. Around the mound, tempers had begun to rise about the eating of game in the premises that a few had brought from their homes to distribute, with the understanding that if this was an occasion there must be food, or, simply that there must be food at all costs. But for the moment, the fight was threatening to take another direction. The fight was for determining their relationship to god.

"There will be god but no more temples. No walls, no premises like the way it was."

"Fine! Then where will we hang the bell? Around our necks?"

HORO'S EVENING meal and their offer had grown cold in the same hour. But he had been wise enough to realise the gravity of the situation. The wind had carried the din at the mound and brought in its wake three unexpected visitors. He could not dismiss their words off-hand, he had to consider them. He told the boy to serve his visitors tea. His dinner, a small share that had come from the wedding feast, had been brought by the groom himself with some ceremony. The copper plate was covered and placed on a small table; a fish-head and a bowl of potatoes and peas peeped from under the cover. But by common consent, the men decided to walk to the shore.

"I had come for your blessings," said the new householder with too jovial a grin. Horo smiled, the skin around his mouth crinkled like old meat. With an effort, he kept the conversation fluid, asking after his parents and expressing sympathy for the hardship caused by the pipe leakage.

"And now the wedding is done," said the groom. That they all agreed was the situation. But the daily business of life, said one of the men, had to run on the same rails. He introduced himself, he said his name was Mir. The man sitting next to him dispensed with the nicety. He was Biran. His eyes wandering and yet terribly fixed, bore into Horo. Horo nodded—who hadn't heard of these two?

"But isn't The Party trying to re-order everything?" Horo couldn't resist asking. Sitting on a rock jutting out of the bay, he nevertheless looked for a grip to steady himself but the calm gaze of his interlocutors knotted the muscles in his stomach. The darkness was the perfect cover for his fear; if he had to go down, let it be said that in his final hours, he had been true, courageous and consistent. Sitting facing the sea, miles away from the heart of The Frontier, his craggy face must remain unlined in the face of danger.

So he said: "When you throw religion away you throw away a nation's childhood. If we cannot believe, we cannot love, we cannot trust."

The men before him laughed and then apologised and returned implacably for battle. "What is love? What is trust? If the man or woman next to us is discriminated against or is going hungry, and we are unmoved by it, God is going to be quite unimpressed even if we send upto him a hundred prayers on love and trust. He knows what is actually growing in our precious little hearts."

The servant brought them more tea and placed a candle in a cup. The wind picking up speed with the night, stamped it out. He asked the boy to move away and lit it himself, cupping his hand around it. This time, the flicker steadied into a flame.

"There it burns! But with what desperate passion to redeem itself," remarked Horo with a smile. Looking up, he saw the men had moved away and were standing at a distance away talking among themselves. Hearing his tread on the stones, they walked back to him.

"But my friends," said Horo picking up the conversation where they had left it, "if you were to ask the poorest man or a dying man in The Frontier how the world began, this I do know, he would imagine it in religious terms: God came first, Man came after. And even if you were to liberate him and his children and his children's children and make him equal to the richest man in The City, you would have his gratitude but he would thank god for you. After some years, he might even think of you as his god—you see people always need a higher power. Balance, protection, security are of great comfort to human beings. 'Anyone outside my door?' 'Is my house safe?' These are the last thoughts a man has before he goes to bed. No more tea? I could tell the boy. It's getting cold isn't it?"

The three men sat facing each other on the rocks again. The air staled between their faces. No one spoke, the silences were hard to measure in this rogue of a night. Expressions were hard to read and masks are worn longer.

The groom had left them a while ago. The servant, who had accompanied him part of the way with a lantern, had since returned. Mir asked him to get Horo's plate. Horo took a mouthful of the rice—they had insisted he eat—found it difficult to swallow.

"There does not have to be a quarrel," said Mir placing a hand on the other man's shoulder. Biran now spoke. "I believe we are looking at different things. So far religion has stayed inside the temple, the church and the mosque. We think it would be better, at least it is our view, that it should be followed by the faithful together at the town square." If God is made to side with the rich, the manipulator, the hoarder, he said he cannot be their God. "Then it is better that He be recalled or retired till He can be a better God. Listen! Can you hear the drum roll at the mound in The Frontier? You should go and see with your own eyes. Those who had never been able to set foot in the temple have taken over ..."

"What do I know sitting here, but the boy tells me there is trouble. That you, too, are having some difficulties...."

"Communism is a difficult slogan—it is difficult, at first, to rally people behind it. People think it is algebra, they have fears about it when actually the fears are about something else. So they tell themselves 'what if I am not able to understand it? What if I'm not able to be a good communist?' when the actual fears are 'do I have to share?' 'why do I have to share or share in this way?'.... But if *you* were to say that this fight is for God we think it would carry weight. People are used to having a priest, you would be needed ...."

The servant waiting at a distance gave him a glass of water. Horo sipped it slowly, he had to know what to say when he put the tumbler down. It was a bolt from the blue, an offer from very unexpected quarters. He needed time to think. The time had come for him to take sides but who was to say whether the rascals here were better or worse than the rascals there? He was too old to make a jump.

"There is a difficulty," he however said. But they were quick to agree that there would, of course, be some difficulties. The problem he said was in their concept of religion. "How can I let it be used?"

They dismissed it. "I don't think we have doubts about the most important thing. You say 'use', we see purpose. For us the most important question is, is religion to be used for the freedom of people or must it be the voice of power? Has God made the

Sabbath for Himself or for the people? Think about it. People who actually believe in God, you will realise, are Communists."

The sky had lightened when they stood up and they walked him back to his shack. They asked to be excused for keeping him up and said they would be on their way. Horo passed his hand over his face and rubbed his eyes. In a few hours the sun would be up.

"All well?"

"All well," he agreed. Yes, the monthly ration had been reaching him. Salt, sugar, soap—he had everything. He said he would think over what they had said.

12

Danny the Red

Mir and Biran reached the heart of The Frontier under a pale sun, each lost in his own thoughts. None of them said a word, each had delayed the moment to speak having waited for the other to speak first and the all-too familiar clusters of The Frontier had forced them into other conversations. Mir's proposal to the priest had certainly taken Biran by surprise, and standing in one corner of the middle of nowhere, he began to re-set the night's meeting in his mind in order to understand his dilemma. But his dilemmas, part of many small moments it was important to link, triggered the beginnings of other questions. His head felt as if it was about to burst. His feet trembled, but he could not lift it to take another step to go and stand beside Mir, already surrounded by the problems of other people who were saying they had, on his advice, "cut down mountains into hillocks." Biran wanted to turn his ear towards the conversation to understand the background of that fantastic claim but the walk had tired him. He was unable to remember how long he had been standing in the same spot. His legs had, meanwhile, grown roots to the ground. Any effort to climb out now could disturb the surroundings and impair all future movement. He decided not to take another step. The morning was rising like a powdery mist over the roofs of the factories but where they stood, the soil, dark and grey, lay coiled like the tides they had left behind. And so it had always been. The heart of The Frontier, he thought, had always been unmanageable. Why did they think they could gate the land from the sea with broken down pebbles?

"Biran! Where *are* you?"

Mir, he found, as they started walking back home, was still

drawn in by the problem of the pipe-burst. But they needed to discuss Horo. Their journey home, always extended, today gave them little time to discuss among themselves what weight each of them had put behind an alliance with the priest, leave alone prepare a common vision of the event when face to face with other perceptions in The Party. Well, they would know at the evening meeting Mir had arranged for before leaving for Horo's house the evening before. As they passed The Row, some women showed them the other places where the pipes had burst at night.

No man seemed in sight. They had to all leave for work. Who could afford to lose a day's wage especially with the number of job-seekers growing at the Factories' gates each morning? So the women sat away from the water hugging big unwieldy bundles of clothes and utensils and snapping at their children to quit playing with the mud, and drain the water from their homes, in little mugs.

Some of them had taken refuge at the mound last night on rubber sheets given by a merchant, whose three-men rubber workshop was located in the lane opposite The Row. Kanhu and Guli had persuaded him to part with a tarapaulin cover as well. The two boys had helped the women throw the cover across poles they had planted on four corners of the mound. Help had also come from the boys' house. Uma had sent over some rice and vegetables with her son and nephew to her neighbours. She had asked them to wait for her till she arrived. They hadn't. They had left word for her that they had work with Mir and Biran. When the two passed them by, they had left with them.

"Those two!" exclaimed Mhalsa-Ai to Uma, bursting to talk about her son's wedding. "Thank the Lord I say that I have done my duty as a mother... anyway so I said 'Sit here awhile, have a mouthful with us boys' but no! 'I have work' says your Kanhu and Guli, as if *we* have no work and to think these children were born that other day!"

Uma laughed aloud and sat with them. A few women had crowded around the two deities on the mound and were applying vermillion to the burnt pot and strewing rice grains around the block of wood. They saw Uma and called her to join them. But Mhalsa-Ai would not let her go and gave her a basket of peas to shell.

"What are they upto Uma with Mir and Biran?" she asked as she threw some peas into a pot cooking in front of her, the smoke covering her face. "I see them running around all day with that woman, Lavni, who runs the teashop by the railway line...."

"All of them work with Mir and Biran, Ai, and the time for the next edition of the workers' paper to be out is very close. They are all working on the paper—may be you could go through it sometimes, no?" Uma's voice had sounded sharp as a shot and then grown awfully quiet. She rubbed the side of her face against her shoulder; her ears, she was sure, had begun to swell. She wanted to leave but the more she made an effort to extricate herself from the conversation, the more she caved inside.

The water from the pipes were now snaking all around The Frontier and creating young islands and mounds. On the mound where Handsa-Ai and Khandoba sat, were now the temporary home of ten families. Uma found herself asking for another basket. She dug her hands into the peas.

"Well, we are illiterate people, but we too read newspapers Uma," said Ai hitting the burning coals with a stick. "But must say never found anything in 'The Will' to laugh and smile about as we see in its making, though I will be the first to bless the one among us who is brave enough to laugh and smile in these times... no, don't say 'no,' have a bowl Uma. The peas are piping hot."

But Uma had just had tea at home before coming to the mound but the women would have none of it. She had sent them rice, she must have something too. "Save it Ai," she finally said "and besides too much heat sits uncomfortably in my stomach while climbing up the stairs and there is also a lot of washing to do."

"You never washed every afternoon," remarked Ai, her head bent over the iron gridle on which she was now puffing up bread. "Since his promotion, Ai, I have a lot of work. Kanhu's father is very strict, he wants a fresh shirt to wear to office every day and I can't work as fast as you Ai," said Uma.

Uma's words had still not faltered but why was she adopting a wheedling tone? Why was Uma about to cry? Hadn't things begun to go well for the family? A month ago, Lotfi, who worked at Baba Lala's horn factory, had returned home one morning from his night shift saying he had been made permanent and his overseer had given him a bonus for sorting out some matter in the machine room. With the extra money, the family had tied up their bundles and hired a cart to take them to a three-storeyed building filled by permanent workers, a little further away from their shack near the railway tracks, up a flight of stairs.

It wasn't much but it was a room. A room with a small kitchen and a bit of balcony. Lotfi had flung open the door to it and they had stood, husband and wife, looking out to an open terrace in front of their balcony, built above a ground floor. On it curled a man with a child on charpoy and his other children under it. A woman slept on the other side of the terrace next to a tin drum, one hand over her eyes shielding them from a harsh morning. Uma and Lotfi had retreated indoors as the woman had suddenly opened her eyes and Uma had almost immediately started to set up the kitchen. She opened the bundles and stacked the cups and plates in one corner. In a few minutes, the milk, dripping into the pan, was on the boil. She took the pan off the stove and poured out two cups of tea. Now Uma no longer barked when Lotfi asked for an extra cup. She also did not badger him about the whys and hows of getting the promotion.

Lotfi had also started to come home early. Sometimes he came home with a man, sometimes two. Uma cooked and she looked out of the kitchen window and she would see the engines, run by the factory owners for industrial use, sitting enveloped in their own smoke on the railway tracks, puffing the same chanty day in and day out. Rested a half hour each day, when they moved, they moved with a tired screech and from the little carriers attached to their hind was heard the last rattle of junked machines on the way to the sea-side grave. Most of the days, the tracks curved towards the factories. Teams of glassy-eyed workers sat on bags of cement till the train stopped deep inside their production units to drop them off; both returned at the day's end in the same black exhaustion at the platform.

From her balcony, in which she had for some time stopped standing, or her kitchen window, through which Lotfi forbade her to peep, Uma could see little of this. But she had known the train for years; its daily chug and pant and whoosh of steam, was for her, a concrete and immediate pleasure. For The Frontier's children, the engine, was akin to many special memories—the first sight of the sea, the thrill of being chased up a tree, the greed for unopened boxes. Its coming, and its going from the plateform, added and subtracted from their lives.

From her new home, however, the scene was limited. The long asbestos roof of the train shed blocked Uma's view of the station. The smoke still rose into the sky like a big black rose but she couldn't do two things at the same time; the time for work and for watching engines go by couldn't be done in the same hour. In those moments, she thought of Lavni. If she could just spy Lavni from the window she often felt she would be at peace. Those were the days—when Lavni, who would keep moving her tea shop out of her shack onto the railway platform or near the carriage shed, would sometimes appear by her door with two glass cups of tea. And, to her chagrin, light up. Once or twice, Lavni had even forced her to take a puff, smiling with all her face, as she coughed.

"That two-bit woman and you pine after her as if she—" She had planned to put up curtains and invite Lavni and her husband, Hog Babu, for a meal in her new home. But Lavni would not come and Uma and Lotfi had had their first quarrel in their new house.

There was another person on whom the new house did not grow. Kanhu came by the house only to sleep. And now not even that. At first she had put it to the work he was doing for The Party but he had begun to stay over at Mir's. One morning she saw that he had shifted his school bag and books, so she had begun to wait on the balcony every evening to catch sight of her son on the way to the night school. Guli, her nephew, who had not gone back with her brother to The City—she still saw more of him. He would look up and sometimes wave at her as he passed down in the street. Sometimes he came up and she had started to thrust a hundred, two-hundred mukka note into his hands for their expenses. Uma no longer quarrelled with Lotfi but she could not get over her son's random absence. She could not understand it, she would not understand it. Climbing up the stairs to her room now on her way back from the mound, she decided to go over to Mir's home in the evening and kill two birds with one stone. If she went, Kanhu and Lavni could not but meet her. She, Uma, had every right to be there at the meeting in Mir's home tonight. She, too, belonged to The Party and Mir wouldn't turn her away. Without our men and women and our mistakes, she told herself with a quick shake of her head, hadn't he said there were wouldn't be new possibilities. The thought of Mir—they all thought of Mir as they watched the sun go up and roll down each day—now brightened her eyes and she wanted to be equal to his work for The Party that would bring about The Revolution.

But sometimes she did not understand what Mir meant. His words were a way to a meaning she could not reach. "If The Party will bring about the Revolution," she mumbled breaking up her thoughts and looking back at them, "why is the Revolution not about The Party?"

She would ask him. There was no scare in asking Mir questions. That was one way of keeping him in their midst.

The thought seemed to lift a weight off Uma and so when she heard the latch of her door shake and saw a hesitant shadow of a man outside it, she summoned up all the readiness of which she was able, and said yes, she was open every afternoon.

A DIVERSION IN the Frontier was never simply that. All the ways leading home could be taken to lead elsewhere. Mir and Biran had had to stop under every window from where they were called to stop for a chat. Kanhu and Guli, who had joined them at the mound, found it difficult to defer the usual discussion of everyday problems that one poor man has with another, especially if they are living on the same lane. But the paper had to be sent to the printer's by the next morning and there were still a load of articles to be proof read by all of them. In this issue, they were carrying another poem of Danish, the paster. Reaching Biran's room they took out the handwritten poem the boy had left with Biran's mother and moved the last few hours of work to Mir's home. Mir, they all noted, appeared restless. His body was pressed against the window rails for the cold comfort of dew. His hands gripped them as if they were the bones of a dead friend who had left them standing, for him, to remind him of some ancient vow. His smile, as he turned to face them, therefore, was painful to see.

"Mir, we don't have much time. What do we do with Danish?" they asked, who seemed surprised by the question. "We do nothing," he said. "Danish is a good boy. We didn't go to him, he came to us. See to Danish—don't ask me what to do," he said and sat down at the little table on which they were piling the proofs. "If he has the longing, he will begin to get it—I think. And his is a legitimate question isn't it Biran? No movement can ignore the individual, but that is a question for The Party, not the individual. I alone can't answer this. It's just that we cannot give undue importance to it at *this* time. Danny will learn, as we all have learnt, to see ourselves in connection to our politics. Seriously, if all this goes nowhere, I'm going to go sit under a tree."

Biran laughed out aloud—but he was thinking of Horo. As it turned out, he was the only one. At the meeting a few hours later, Mir spoke and all hands were raised in favour of what had already been decided at the sea-shore. Neighbour after neighbour saw the person on his right nod his head in agreement. "What a day to call a meeting", some, however, muttered as they shuffled out of the room onto the wet street. The trouble was no longer in the distance. Even those, whose shacks or dwellings were not circled by the pipes, found themselves wading in ankle-deep water. If someone did not stop the flow, soon they might as well walk into the sea. "Petit bourgeois this and petit bourgeois that! What is *not* petit bourgeois? The struggle not to be so, I guess. Now for god's sake Mir bhai, plug the pipes!"

After the last man and woman had left, Mir and Biran sat with Lavni, Kanhu and Guli for the last editorial meeting before the paper went to press. Danish came up again as Dipu another paster from *The Meat* dropped by on their way home. Biran and Kanhu exchanged a look as the hours sped past. The moon dropped sullenly over the roof. Each day, Mir seemed like a tree grown so tall that had no idea of the termites beginning their work in its trunks. At times, he remained impervious to the silent industry of the Dongs, who were plotting to finish them off since the word of their growing influence had reached Baba Lala.

Hog dropped by around ten in the night. He had come for Lavni. He said he had got off The Bus and had had come straight to Mir to give him the news of some developments at *The Meat*. They made space for him on the floor. After their action together at The Malacca and in the course of coming back later to talk about it, they had realised that here was a comrade even though his experience of being in a movement was a much shorter one and, largely, a personal engagement because of his marriage to Lavni, but he was here for his own reasons. Without his inputs, 'The Will' was not released. If need be, they delayed its release by a day or two till he was able to sit down for a final reading of the paper. The four-pager, distributed at the crossing, had started being in demand and read on the run the most at the tea stalls outside the factories and the tea and biscuit cabins outside government offices of The City. Since their work in *The Meat*, employees had also started reading it inside the office; first out of a sense of curiosity or to laugh at its ambitions, or to sniff out the first Christians. And then in ones and twos become a hive, unshakeable in their support. But in the beginning, their numbers were few.

The company packers had begun to slip it inside each copy of *The Meat* and on the last day of the month as Aristu's paper went around The City, 'The Will' travelled the same route in his trucks. As Mir and Biran began the push for a face-off, their paper, earlier a monthly, increased their production, appearing twice a week. Since Hog's involvement, their paper was better produced and edited. He brought in new ideas as well. As he now got off the floor—and they smiled among themselves as he tried to dust himself without drawing attention to himself—he leaned over the table and asked for a chair. He got one—he had earned himself one. It was on his initiative that 'The Will' had started a column on the daily life of a 'Worker', a term they used to include the teacher slaving away in The City schools with no influence on the curriculum; the contract labourer who was trying to organise his shift against the diktats of slave-driving superiors, often senior permanent labourers themselves, and the young girl pulled into marriage to cook for and produce a family and the journalist with no job security, increasing work hours and diminishing control over the work he wanted to pursue. To Mir, the goal of the paper was clear and he had communicated as much to Hog.

"Our paper is for propaganda, for bringing people to us, for telling people who we are here. Dogs must bark."

As Biran's work had increased, Mir had begun to entrust the work of the paper and the organisation inside *The Meat*, to him. Along with J Babu, in his or Biran's absence, they became the nucleus around which workers from different departments studied, learnt about each other's work and began to make their first decisions about themselves in relation to other people.

But right now what they all wanted to know was the news from *The Heat*. "You will like it," said the older man clasping Mir's hands and then drawing back. "You are cold, Mir!" he said rubbing Mir's hands, "Lavni...Guli... you haven't been taking care!"

Everyone suddenly got up all at once and with a scraping of chairs, crowded around Hog telling him to tell them at once what had transpired in the meeting at *The Meat*.

At one meeting, said Hog, Dan had started his usual ruckus, this time about being "fed up" about meeting on the sly when they were a good number now, and someone had murmured something about Dan being Dan the Hun and the two had nearly come to blows. "And then J Babu called some of us to say 'let's call the boy Danny the Poet' and with him in the middle we have been meeting him and that friend of his...."

"Has he begun to speak?"

"No! He comes regularly for the meetings but he's still giving us the silent treatment."

"So we've been meeting them, sharing cigarettes and listening to Danny's rhymes—and I think we do him an injustice by calling them so, the way the poems unfold you can see his arguments with himself—and since that day, for Danny it has been 'J Babu said this and J Babu said that.' He has also begun to stop by our desk in between work."

"Tell me what to do—I have hands," had said Danish one day. From the next meeting and for every meeting afterwards, he brought along his stencils and pens listening intently to the discussions, in which he still refused to take part. The last meeting had begun to excite Dan to such an extent, that he had been unable to enjoy the eating and drinking at the wedding of Mhalsa-ai's son. He had found nothing he could drink, nothing he could eat and there was no girl he wanted to dance with. In the end, he told himself, he could understand why no girl wanted to dance with him, but there was nothing to stop him from dancing with food and drink and so that's what he did. The next day was a Sunday.

He wasn't sure who—the sun or his mother—got to him first. Her thick fingers dug into his sides and the sun, streaming through the open window at the back of his head, did the rest. The meeting on Saturday night had held them up. They had missed The Bus and it had been nearly a six-hour walk from *The Meat* to his home in The Frontier. His head hurt, his back still felt sore—but they felt alright while they sat together or planned together. Each meeting had now begun to take longer—everyone spoke and so everyone argued; no prodding was necessary any more.

At the meeting, it was decided that it was time to again leave Aristu some gifts to make him hop on Monday morning. One of them kept watch while the rest of them had scrambled to Aristu's office to leave a new missive on his desk. These missives will create confusion and panic and lead to a fair bit of hell-raising and rumour-mongering..... Rubbish, said someone else, their series of letters were like a grape-shot, an accumulation of demands and defiance before a man who would know a threat from a challenge...shut up and pass the gum, someone hissed...the rest of them messed up the office, sawed open Aristu's leather chair, raised their legs and put the imprints of their muddied shoes on his white walls, tore up his selection of the day's stories and placed their own....Their first target had been Aristu's door, now his desk—and they were expecting a strong reaction next week.

Splitting up, they walked out of the front entrance of *The Meat*, met under a bridge on the way to The Gates and walked away in different directions. As they had walked home, Dan had lent half an ear to a fellow worker who was going in the same direction and was keeping up some inane chatter about his supervisor. Dan had interrupted him telling him he was trying to remember the few things he still had to ask J Babu. The thought, he realised, to his surprise, gave him keen pleasure this Sunday morning when he began to laugh his low cavernous laugh that his mother said did him no favour. You couldn't join him there, but it was all happening in some corner of his mind, the lobbing, the catching, the return of the balls to himself....

"That dog! What a dog!" He started to laugh. "That dog, that dog," he sat up in bed shaking his head, tears streaming down his face, thinking of J Babu's low-breed, he sometimes brought to office, who at every given opportunity showed his unwillingness to be led.

That he had met Soli, Hog, Dipu, he reminded himself, had also given him pleasure. But meeting J Babu, as the entire office called him, made him feel special. He could now look forward to the next meeting all week.... His mother sent his sister up to him to ask if he wanted tea. Tea! Tea! Tea! Every two minutes that he was home he was asked if he wanted tea as if they grew its leaves in their backyard. No, he didn't want tea, he shouted at her—now scram!

He pushed his back into the pillow and tried to collect his thoughts. As for The Party, what is The Party, who is The Party and should he put all his trust in The Party? Regaining his calm, he told himself that it was The Party that had brought him in touch with J Babu.... But when the revolution was done and won, it was not Biran but J Babu and who would be around to run things, would he not, and he sank back into his pillow trying to imagine the benefits of their association. For a while, he indulged himself by imagining himself at the head of a few heresies. By mid-afternoon he had exhausted himself and felt cross at his juvenilia simply because it was being demanded that he commit himself to a future that was uncertain and to relationships that right turn confrontational. A strong feeling of self-disgust took hold of him. He should set out of the house; he had stayed inside his room for too long, his mind had grown stale picking out threads from the same thought. It might be a good idea to set off for Mir's home and see what the others were doing.

"Shit," he said biting his lips, and kicking his sandals to another corner. He realised he had missed the meeting at Mir's home.

He left the bed and opened a window. The slats opened with a clutter—the sky had purpled but still lit with a low-hanging sun, it cast The Frontier in deep gold. The Gates of The City ringed the west like an iron waterfall. The factories in which those gates had been forged, were still at work. In a hundred foundries now, workers were adding their breath to the acid fumes, their legs were grazing or escaping nails and screws strewn on the floor. Then lugging and pouring gallons of liquid into a mould, they fooled their body to take just another step, blew their lungs with purpose—to prepare another iron cage. The smoke from the factories, never so far from a worker's home so that they would forget its poisonous coil, rose up once again through its twenty chimneys. By appointment, evening came when evening comes. There were men and women at work and there were men and women at home. It was six'o clock, the time, when with just a turn of a knob of the radio, they would be enveloped with the soar of Ghazala's voice as she sang the false promises and the illusions that a tired people need to mend their hearts on a Sunday evening. And this is why no one noticed when a small grey vehicle left the The City gate and began to move into The Frontier.

Dan took a look at the day's newspaper, made a few notes in his notebook and laid out the arguments with which to confront J Babu, who, besides the Statement page, also had a say in the lineup of news. A picture of that lilywoolly son of Baba Lala still filled some corner of their front pages–something should be done about that. Their meetings, he exhorted himself, were not meant to be their hour of private games. Till they could take charge of the paper, wherever each of them were, they should be moving towards building a workers' paper and extend that understanding not just by what they were saying but in practice. What was the use of their coming together in the meeting if they could not implement it in their work? He now felt ashamed thinking of how he had taken umbrage when Mir had heckled J Babu and made this very point in an earlier meeting. 'How dare he, he an outsider,' Danish had thought. Later, he corrected himself.

"Who knows, there was every chance that with J Babu behind the desk, it could be Aristu walking around again." On Monday, some of them were going to distribute some posters near the Dong's office, their first attempts at mobilisation outside the newspaper gates, and it was his responsibility to think of a new theme for a poster and write a few lines. Take the lead, Mir and Biran had said. It may not be your city, but take the city, they had said. Dan closed his notebook and took out his stencils. Placing them on a poster, he wrote—

> Once I went for a walk with my friends the snake, the rat, the cat
> And on the way the war broke out, so we decided to break our chat
> When I woke up one day, my mother sent me to a school
> The war is over so I told her, let's play the game of fools.
> But if the war is over, why do we have to crawl and sing?
> So I told my mother, bring me a few stones with a string.
> Once I went for a walk, and met the old king, the queen,
> On the way we passed a pool, and then they were never seen.
> Once I went for a walk with my friends the snake, the rat, the cat
> On the way we passed a pool, soon we had fish on the mat.
> But if the king and queen are dead, why do we have to give our fish?
> If we eat we'll die of guilt, so let's feed the rich, the rich.

Since his work with The Party, which had lately started calling itself The Partisans, words pushed themselves out on his tongue, his state of mind provided the rhyme. "From Danish the paster, do you know your son has become Danish, the poet?" he asked his mother one day as they sat in their kitchen eating. His mother would not look at him but then neither would he. It really wasn't that odd. Just that for years they had this habit of talking past each other, as if to acknowledge the other, would mean the acceptance of a bond from which they had not wiped out the condition of necessity, of habit. His mother never behaved like other mothers. She had fed him and clothed him when he was a child but had never protected him. When he began to do badly in school, she had told him to catch a snake and make it dance or break stones. "Fuck it, I'll break stones," he had said and disappeared for a month. After he got a job in *The Meat* he returned. His mother never asked him where he had been. He sat before her and she talked over his head telling him of the new roof they had just got made as if it was a son just returned from town. Even now, she talked to him as if the words were meant for someone else. It was she who mentioned Mili or whether she had mentioned it last night, he wasn't sure.

He wasn't sure what he had been up to last night. After returning from the meeting, he had joined his neighbours at the eating and drinking at the wedding. He remembered having talked such a lot that he had woken up repeating other people's sentences. He had also laughed and fallen off the chair a great deal. It had surprised the locality and he had felt Mili's eyes on him. Mili, a girl whose terrace was next to theirs and whose braids looked as if they were ropes of roses. She washed her hair on Sundays.... If he could hurry, he would lock away the sight and run his fingers through them in his sleep.

So he went up to his terrace and Mili was on her terrace. No one noticed the two gentlemen get out of a small grey vehicle and scan the windows of the rows of dark houses with their monocles. The engine had just come puffing from the factories, and lines of men and women returning to their tenements from the morning shift were craning their heads from the carriage to see if they could spy the child to whom they could shout out to start putting the tea on boil on the stove. But no one was standing on their balconies so there was nothing more to say but lug their tired bodies up the staircases. And this is why no one asked who they were and what business had brought them, such fine gentlemen from The City to a workers' colony on a Sunday evening so far from their houses, their Sunday rests and their Sunday dinners, in that hour. So the two men waved at Mili, who was just then leaning over with her wet hair and wet shoulders to hang out her clothes on the edge, and asked for the way to Danish's house. Danish was still watching the water drip over her arm as she lifted it to point at him when the men's heavy boots began their climb up the stairs, and his sister's cat shrank at the shiny piece of metal hanging from their hip belt and his mother, who always spoke over his head, came running upstairs behind them, calling his name and telling him to jump and Mili's clothesline snapped under her treacherous arm. And this is how they picked up Danny the Poet for the murder of Horo the priest, and even then Ghazala sang.

13

In April

Seeing that Danish was determined to go quietly, he didn't get hand-cuffs. I'll be back tomorrow, don't run after the car crying, he warned his sister, who was hanging on to his crook despite attempts by his minders to shake her off. To lift her spirits, he gnashed his teeth and pushed his eyeballs towards his forehead as he would do when she was a child to scare her into having her milk, before walking up to the car. The policeman gestured him aside with a wave of his stick. Be quiet, he said needlessly, the Bus is coming, and Danny decided he would make his day. This is my father-in-law, he joked to himself, stealing a sly glance at his bald captor who was cooling his face with his cap, and we are waiting for the family car to come around. A year ago he might have made a dash across the railway lines but he was this close to a dream, which was not really a dream but like the day of revenge—that of having The City forced to gaze on him, to have the lights turned on him, to have to listen to him speak, to be unable to hush him up, keep him down. So, he imagined The Bus to be an open carriage on which he would ride into the City, standing, to the astonishment of all its maidens and their good mothers, who would pull them off the balconies; he would shed his fears like a warrior and then pick them up like a spear; at every turn, the bus would run into a crowd, the whispers around him would grow, stones might fly, and he would no longer simply be Danish the two-penny paster with a tinpot house on an unnumbered street in The Frontier. He was Danny, the bandit poet of the coming insurrection and that they should know. And that they would, they all would, for when the sun came up in the morning, his life, would be re-routed through new ink, and he would be written about with the worst of intentions with the best of prose across the pages of *The Meat*. His life would in this way no longer be his and thank the lord for it.

With a smile on his lips, he entered the bus and made himself comfortable. The first line of a new poem was hovering over his brow. Seated next to the driver through the rear view mirror, he saw Hog pedalling furiously on his cycle towards The Bus. The Bus was making its last journey for the day. The seats were mostly empty except for a young boy who was trying very hard not to look at him and some artisans. Batches of artisans left for The City each day to work around the clock for re-modelling buildings, add fittings and slap new paint on to its facades. The age of cupolas and domes were over, they had declared with glee when they had first gone to work; within a week they were lugging on to the scaffolds and raising on crowbars crowned bulls and tuskers to put on building tops. Some of the artisans were making them and some were lifting them. "The Dongs are coming with the same bad taste," they said among themselves as they stared at the matted locks of the stone animals and the turbaned cherubs—legs seeking hands, hands seeking legs entwined in precocious play around lamps shaped like teats hanging from the ceiling of a deep portico. The animals that took shape under their hands told them what animals had always known—when old kings are dying the fastest to tear his throat gets the job—when someone working on the first-floor offices rushed upstairs to tell them that oil portraits that looked remarkably like The City's notables were being unpacked in the rooms down below. So all their speculation about The Plebiscite had been in vain. The selection of the next government had all but taken place even if The Plebiscite was still a few months away!

"Danny," the artisans urged as they surrounded him in the bus, "tell Mir, April is as good as October. It is a good time for tornados."

When you hear a thing like that it straightens a man's back, thought Danny, and stops him from growing weak with desire for stupid things. No one around him seemed to act as if he was going to the gallows, so it seemed likely he would get to pass on the artisans' message and also sort out a matter with Kanhu if he came along with Mir or Biran to visit him in jail—they would, wouldn't they? His thoughts returned to last night. He remembered he had been drinking on the rocks by the sea when Kanhu and the band of children had gone ahead to speak to Horo's servant. When they returned he had been lying on the sand, sleeping. They had lifted him up by his shoulders and that is how they had walked for hours, without saying a word, till they reached his home. He remembered complaining to Kanhu how Biran was turning into a bully and had all but scratched out the last poem out of his head saying they couldn't wait forever for his contribution. So, if he had been struggling with the poem for several hours before setting off for the coast and had fallen asleep while waiting for Kanhu, he wouldn't have been able to find time for a murder, now would he—which son of a bitch was passing off his act on to his head! He would sort out the matter with Kanhu and Mir when they came visiting—but could they?

There were five detectives behind Mir and Biran watching their every move. For the moment, it seemed part of a strategy not to pick them up, but the people the two met in The City, especially in the Black Quarters, so as to spread their network was given a harrowing time. Even they were being followed back home, their conversations eavesdropped, their women befriended by lady detectives over days till they made the unsuspecting offer to their new friends to drop by come home. Getting past the door, the detectives threw them on their backs, their demands of an arrest warrant were laughed at, their letters were opened and read, their beds were turned upside down, their cupboards ransacked for ammunition and incriminating documents. Once cornered, these man and woman neither denied nor confirmed that they knew Mir or Biran or knew people who knew them. If the plan was to present them as criminals, let them work hard to make their case. But as was becoming common with these operations, weeks of activity—of picking people and roughing them up— would be followed by days of a low-key vigil by the detectives. The vendor selling tea at the local market was surely one of them. During the day he hawked his wares and took position behind half-shut windows in a house across their street watching them. So there was a good deal of waiting, watching and listening on both ends. People spoke their minds only in closed groups. When they visited cafés, they spoke an unnecessary lot and aloud to mislead potential spies and disseminated bogus information to the opposite camp. Conspiracy hunting became a universal habit. The man sitting at the next table was suspect for reading the paper too long; the man who got up as soon as they sat down was problematic as well for the same reason. Everyone suspected everybody.

But there were reasons for the paranoia. In The City, supporters for The Partisans and supporters of the Dongs still went about masked. Other than long-standing and unabashed supporters of the two camps, it was still not clear who stood where in the ever-shifting plane of allegiance. Some were put off by Mir's insistence on the party being a combative association between different tendencies; some were aghast at his lack of personal ambition and his unwillingness to be boss; some were drawn to him for this very reason but demoralised that he could not be counted on to act on their behalf; some found there was too much emphasis on struggling and not much achieving; some understood achievement only in terms of state power and felt betrayed when they realised that was not the goal, some found 'knowledge' and 'experience', the gains of the struggle, too paltry an achievement; and some simply wanted the good old equidistance from The Partisans and the Dongs so that they could eat and hunt with both. The City's middle class, many of whom were simultaneously attracted and repelled by The Partisans, finally withheld their embrace for two reasons. First, The Partisans had made it clear there would be no compromise with the way things were—and they, the middle class, were part of things that are; and second, well, it was more or less because of the first reason.

"The Dongs are our neighbours," they said, "just because the Partisans want us to, should we now throw stones at them?"

So, well, there were two sets of supporters that The Partisans had if they wanted them—those who were with them and knew why, and those who were with them to support their own ideas of themselves as radicals and so wouldn't go too far down the road with them. The first group was proving difficult to break into; with the second, the police tried a different tack—they were alternately harassed and cultivated to pump out information about the first.

The Fairlander intelligence, which had by now started being staffed by many card-carrying Dongs, was however, of the opinion that they were forcing their hand too soon. The Partisans would in no way carry out their first hit in The City before October, and October was a long way off. Revolutionaries, they said with a grin, did not waste anniversaries so all they had to do was wait for them to plan their little action and then they would get their ducks in a row. The job of an intelligence officer in these times wasn't easy. You kept your ears to the ground and kept the pressure up. The raids, said Colonel Saunders, who had moved from active military to military intelligence, would have to continue. And they did, but in a haphazard fashion and sometimes caught the plainclothes cops themselves by surprise. The directives constantly changed behind their heads, and the wheels within wheels of intelligence hierarchies where some project of one of the bosses was being initiated so as to undermine the work of someone else, made junior officers live in constant fear of having their cover blown. The nights, the standard time for the dirty tricks of secret services all over the world, were suddenly voted out in favour of day. Raids, they were told, had to be conducted under natural light, so they got into the jeeps and zip-zapped through the city streets, blowing their horns, startling citizens on the way to the market, and brought their cars to a screeching halt before The Partisans's safe houses. After they were assured of a crowd, giving it time, of course, to gather, they knocked on the door with the Murkys bringing up the rear and took out their pistols from their hip pockets screwing up their faces like pugs. A member of the force searched out *The Meat* reporter from among the crowd. He was given the press release that had all the information complete with a police quote on the list of suspects and the number of laws broken even before the investigation was launched, never mind, sealed, so that they would not miss their page deadlines. "A long investigation," the cop, anyway joked with the reporter, "is a bit like a love affair is it not? We don't really want to know those pascals that well, do we?" What would citizens say, what indeed, if they spent all their time in watching these hoods, who dress their illegal activities with theory when they should be guarding the banks and government houses on Garisson Street?

Most of The City's re-designing, Dan had heard, was happening on Garisson Street. It was not an area he passed on the way to work in *The Meat* and he did not wander around the city anyway like some of them did, to stand under tall buildings, that were these days either coming up or down. The Bus, he learnt from the artisans, would pass the street, dropping them off, so he would be able to see these buildings first hand but that was not before spending many hours on the road; The Bus had still not moved. What were they waiting for, he wondered, when he saw Hog arguing furiously with his police escorts and then climb on to The Bus.

MIR AND LAVNI had left an hour ago to talk to a worker who had been skipping the public meetings so Hog had been the last to leave the room that night. As the Plebiscite approached, too many of them were insisting on doing their own thing when they should all be in this *together* and they all knew that it meant a bit of shutting up, a bit of having someone's finger up your nose or throat—but where was the harm in it if with a little bit of tug, a little bit of rub, they could change things for everybody? He leaned back in his chair, and stared at the white bricks of Mir's room that gave it the look of a newly built granary. An almirah full of old pamphlets, files thick with paper cuttings of earlier agitations, fraying banners torn off the hands of cops or factory supervisors in the heat of a confrontation, stood in one of its corners. On the bed was accommodated books, a few clean cups, some rolled up calendars, nothing in fact, that anyone coming into this room could not remove or push aside or claim for himself—with reason. He remembered Mir laughing his big laugh when one day a comrade, not too fond of reading, had barged in saying he wanted some of the newspapers and then some other comrade sitting in the room had called Mir a hoarder. "What will you do with the papers?" Mir had demanded to know. The comrade said his child had just broken their last plate so if he could... Mir had stopped him saying that it was a very good reason for wanting a newspaper and he should help himself to many more. Why should we collect these things he had said and set about to disorder his own archive. "Comrade you have shown us the way," he called out to his neighbour standing shame-facedly in a corner clutching his bundle. "We will stop this documentation right away. The experience of our struggles should be branded in our bones. If we forget what it has meant to resist together, then these will be merely paper and what will we do with that?" From that day Mir's room stopped being his room and became one of their many centres to meet, sit around after work, or sleep in. Even the contractor reached this room when he wanted people to do double shifts to fill in for those who hadn't turned up for work.

It had been an hour since Mir and Lavni had left, thought Hog looking at the walls, his eyes burning with the strain of keeping awake. There was something in the air tonight; sleep was fleeing from all the corners of the world. A sound from the roof distracted him momentarily; the brown owl that had grown old on Mir's roof was restless tonight. Her reflection fell onto the water trapped between the houses and startled the rats. The rats haven't failed us, they are still with us, thought Hog hearing them run along the entire length of the pipes that had since that night-burst, lain between the houses like dead larva flooding every bit of available space. So much water—when they did not need it. Hog got up, he suddenly felt that if he didn't set off now, he would never again be able to sleep.

As the night grew, the factory chimneys relentlessly smoked The Frontier. Workers entered their hovels and sank to sleep. The houses that had windows to open, shifted their beds so that the children could face them. The air in Mir's room had long since taken its leave, if he stayed in longer, he would be unable to breathe. He would finish packing and labelling the bundles of newspapers into cartons to be sent to addresses all over The City and The Frontier tomorrow. Tomorrow there would be more hands and they—Dipu, Danny—could all come back after work to finish it off. Aha, young Danny had again given them the slip. Why hadn't he come for the meeting that evening, he wondered. But perhaps he had had to finish the poster and must have fallen asleep after that. Working shifts did play havoc with a man's system, it kept you awake at odd hours. He had caught Dan many a time at *The Meat* catching a little nap on his feet, his head resting against a closed door in one of the corridors less frequented by members of the editorial staff.

"Still here, Hog?"

He hadn't seen Kanhu come in. Hog said he was just about to leave, silently bracing himself for the return journey but by the time Kanhu had finished with his account of the night before, all thoughts of sleep had vanished from Hog's mind. The boy was kicking the dust off his heels and smiling to himself. After a while, he went to sit on one of the pipes, and snapped his fingers at the owl still walking about giddily on the roof. When he finally looked at Hog, his eyes were sparkling like that of a beautiful beast out of a forest that has seen the road for the first time. And he said:

"Look, I don't know what we are all thinking but there is not going to be any grand march to The City's gates and expect that people will start flowing out from the houses towards us in support. The Revolution has begun in all corners and we have to recognise and support it even if it seems flickering. When we built *our* temple, it was the revolution, when Danny stops thinking of himself it will the revolution, what we did last night *is* the revolution, and one thing you can be sure, the people are on the move without waiting for Mir or Biran to blow their whistle. The Dongs are already in place so we must make the revolution vigorously and fiercely, and many times, with what we have, not in October, when we may be perfectly ready, but now."

"Be quiet, Kanhu, and come inside. Does Mir know?"

No, Mir did not know. And something that the boy had just said seemed to have passed on to him for he remembered feeling this excited many months ago when he had met Mir the first time. He took out the trunk where The Party kept its contributions, and looked around for the key. The key's cold metal, however, nudged his old fears that still troubled him each time he had to make small decisions. He was feeling mixed-up and angry but there was no external force he could blame for the turn of events. The problem had started, and they should have foreseen this, when Kanhu was allowed to take out another paper specific to children who worked in car-part ancillaries and began noting in their paper who was being brought in or expelled from The Party or who was being allowed to speak at meetings and who was not. Slowly, they had also wanted more representation at the core party meetings. When Biran had said no, and so Mir had said no, they had demanded the right to distribute their paper at their old posts, such as the railway crossing, as The Partisans had stopped to do so, being taken up with increasing the strength of the organisation and letting everyone know it was there. This was the time to consolidate and not for everyone to start demanding the right to strike out on their own!

"How many of you were involved?" He took out a few mukkas from the safe and handed them to Kanhu. "I think you had better run," he told Kanhu quickly turning his face away. How he wished Mir and Biran were around to knock some sense into the boy, who was looking like something fierce the wind and fire leave behind after a night of mayhem on their tin roofs. Hog felt inadequate to handle the situation but he knew he had to steady himself. If the cops were coming after Kanhu for the murder of Horo, they would also be after all those who worked for The Partisans, trying to make it seem that it was the random hit of a common gang without politics, positions or principles and had simply murdered a man. *The Meat* would, of course, behave like a bloodhound, and send its pack to write a rash of stories on the incident. He decided to stay back home tomorrow.

But Kanhu said he was not going to run, which could create a problem. Why should he run, he said. The Partisans should defend his right to take action. In Horo, Mir and Biran, saw an instrument, he said, for peace and win acceptance in The City in preparation for the Plebiscite. But did we need such an alliance, he argued. "We were in the shadows by the sea watching him... his servant, whose brother is a metal-worker, brought us the letter he had intercepted that Horo had earlier written to the Dongs requesting a meeting... we watched his eyes as he saw them off.... With time, here was a man who would again build a temple and become the law, so I killed him in the name of freedom. What did I do wrong?"

Hog drew the boy to his chest but said nothing. This was not the end of the story as they well knew and they had not a minute to waste. Since their paper was complete, they would delay its distribution by a day so that he could compose a pamphlet that would go along with the paper and serve as an editorial to put the action in context and why it was necessary. From time to time, Hog would still hesitate but this was not the time to wait for Mir or Biran. They had to assume they would agree with that he was going to write. He, Hog, had to write as if he was speaking for all, otherwise it would show in the writing.

"And so that's what we learnt by being in the party that only two people can take the right decisions," said Kanhu watching Hog hesitate, but right now Kanhu was only going to see things his way, thought Hog. By the time they were titling the pamphlet, the sound of feet running over the pipes from somewhere close by was heard. Hog pushing Kanhu back, rushed outside. Day was breaking over The Frontier and there were sounds of people stirring from the row of rooms. But there was no one outside. No new face actually, just one or two of Mir's neighbours who were sitting outside their door brushing their teeth or combing a child's hair for school.

"No, it's nothing," he returned to the room putting a hand on Kanhu's shoulders. "If they send the Murkys into these lanes, they know they would be butchered. When they come, and they will come, they will draw us out," he said and closed the door. A second later, it was flung open. Guli stood on the pipe, panting.

"Kanhu, they've got Danny."

14

Operation Rabbit

Around afternoon, when the sun was like an angry boil in the sky, The Bus reached the gates of The City with its cargo—a boy who had murdered a priest, a newspaper worker who seemed to be coming along as his friend, a young peon from a Fairlander office, a bunch of artisans heading for Garisson Street, and tailing them, a car of beady-eyed cops that were letting their guns go off by mistake at passing cows and goats, and then at The Bus's tyres, for a bit of on-the-job fun. The journey had taken longer than he hoped, but the driver knew he was not to blame. He had given an undertaking he would be in by two, so he had had to keep a note of the time but he had also to keep an eye on that lot in the car. Their capacity for violence was known, but for them it was fucking legal, and they clearly believed there was something straight and beautiful in behaving in an appalling manner and stopping The Bus every few hours to come around and ask 'How far? How far is it—from here?' as if they were getting late for a date, with no care about the sensibilities of that boy they were taking into custody only to string a dozen cases around his neck so as to string him up a pole. Let the child live a little longer, that would be his prayer to the Almighty. And this child would live; the entire city, said the artisans, had his poems pasted on the walls. Everyone knew him, and you don't let people you know just slip away or be taken. The Partisans had begun to hold their street meetings before those walls and pillars now crusted with posters, graffiti, poems—how many would The Dongs rip off? Didn't everybody know they were mainly ripping them off because they were scared their cadre would read and turn? But such ideas, that people like that are most scared of spreading, they don't realise are already around them so their act of erasure only reinforces a love for those ideas, if not right then, then thirty years later, and what are thirty years when you think of a Palestine and even if there is only one Palestine it is enough for those who are dreaming, and those who are not, to rob them of sleep. The police station was going to be his last stop for the day having worked all night... no sir, he was not going back for another run tonight. After he deposited the poor boy to the station, he was going to take along his son under the bridge near the newspaper offices where The Partisans had put up their posters and ask him read Danish's latest poem. He turned his head back to look. What a fine looking lad, he thought, noting his head bent over a scrap of paper. And that's the way things were at that moment when Hog came up from the back as The Bus crossed through The Gates and from the other side a car rammed into it as its driver lost control shielding his eyes from the sun.

IN THE MIDDLE of a room on Garrison Street, Cailean Dado, an officer of a little-known department of the Fairlander empire in The Lambda, was washing his face in a basin behind a wooden partition when someone knocked and told him about the crash at The Gate. "Hmph," he said in response as his mind was still on his assignment. He took out the fresh shirt he had left folded on a side-stool before he had set off and looked at his reflection in the mirror. A dirty blonde moustache curved downwards to meet the tuft on his chin. It showed the face of a man pushing fifty, with a square forehead and sunburnt, leathery cheeks. A checked scarf girdled his wide neck. A faded beret, that ill-fitted his head, kept sliding off to sit over his ears from which one or two clumps of hair curled outwards like a kitchen hook. All of this, he felt, gave him range. He could be Doug the Sailor, Nathaniel, The Traveller of the Orient, or Tidy Baxter, the opium merchant returned from China—men of experience but not of fashion. Nothing, in short, should trace him back to this office on Garrison Street. He would try every trick that would give him access to the Rabbit and, if all that he had heard was true, Tidy was the trap to catch him. He had said as much to The Boss and the name had stuck. The old bulldog had given him one of his rare smiles and made his day. And so it was that seven months before The Plebsicite, they had launched Operation Rabbit, all bets off.

Cailean moved away from the mirror and stood under the fan hanging twenty feet down from the ceiling. For a mid-level officer, he had too large a room. The room belonged to someone else, a senior official who had thanked the lord and just flown out of The Lambda. As the deputy of his deputy, who himself hadn't made up his mind whether he wanted in or out and was thus working out his confusions from home with the help of his mistress, it was quietly suggested that Cailean move into his room. In the beginning, Cailean was pleased. He had imagined a shift of power with this inheritance and in the ensuing weeks was seized with the spirit that is noticeable in young missionaries setting up the first church in strange lands. A chest of drawers carried by two solemn mules and downloaded by Cailean himself—hat-racks, umbrella, stands of finest teak and bookshelves with ceramic knobs went up the stairs on the backs of the bearer boys for days and, to no one's surprise, marched out again with the turn of the month. Caelian's colleagues on the first floor tittered; the peons, the courier boys and staff attendants while making way for the procession to pass, bit back their smiles and said he was another of *them* who was coming unstuck.

The madness ended within a month. The wood, sweating under The Lambda's blistering heat, had begun to peel and his furniture began to look like auction rejects got cheap. The rascal who had promised him first-rate stuff at half-price knew not whom he had crossed. He would have his shop sealed! He really could—with just a letter. Calming himself down, he had finally taken a measure of the room and with so few visitors saw—what his servants had seen long before. It was just a room at the end of the corridor and as elegant as a cow-shed . Perhaps, he didn't need so many chairs. Or a hat-stand. "What matters is what I do in it," he now said and having come to this realisation all by himself, ordered his boy to look sharp and get him a packet of pens from the market.

Caelian went back to his report-writing by long-hand.

Despite repeated petitions, his boss, cross at having to re-join work and find he had been moved out of his room, did not grant his request for an assistant. This was just as well. Caelian wasn't sure if he knew about his assignment so the contents of his reports remained between him and the general. The character of his work though was changing—its clandestine nature made him feel that he had been put on something big and his role was part of a calculation to right the wrongs done to him. Who knows, perhaps he might be rewarded, as people do old retainers, at the fag-end of a career. Myriad possibilities floated through his head and sweetened his thoughts. But only for a while. It *was* somewhat odd and lonely to be out of the general thrust of work that his department was doing. By now, everyone knew that the Fairlanders were on notice and was working out the logistics of a Plebiscite while *his* work was to....Well, well, he had been told to hang in there and that's what he was doing.

Caelian's work hours were long. What he did in his off-duty hours was to confirm and re-confirm that all he was putting down on those sheets of paper were true. It was an exercise in futility—in The Lambda, things were changing hourly. For some time now, he had a suspicion that no one had a clue what was happening anywhere. His spies reported one thing, while the decorated officers in their offices, asked him to execute something else. It didn't seen right. Was someone playing a dirty game?

The plaintive moan of the large swing fan soothed his frazzled nerves; the yellow bulb popping out of a saucer-shaped light-holder stewed his head. As both effects cancelled out the other, Caelian thought he would agitate the stupor of his soul with a few simple movements of his body. He bent over and tried to touch his toe but he was in no shape; when he bent side-ways, he pulled a muscle. This was doing him no good, he was getting all worked up about the assignment for nothing. As a disguise, he had erred on the side of caution by setting his story closer to the truth. Tidy Baxter, the fixer—there was no reason why he couldn't play the part. It may have been years since he had left chasing the dragon, but there was not a single day when he had not thought about unlocking the drawer in which he kept his tray and his opium pipe. Sometimes, he woke up in the middle of the night on the side of the bed he used to lie down to prepare the pipe, and experience the acute craving that comes with the return of a decade-old loss when from some rut of memory in which we have buried the chew of all our old loves, we meet an old lover.

The curtains at the window to his east frip-fripped—a sudden gust of wind had bounced off the verandah and touched the muslin on the sly—and the blast of warm air that had surprisingly felt cold on his cheek, dried out his mouth. He was desperate for a drink but there was no bearer or boy in sight. Since the announcement of Plebsicite, the lads fancied themselves no end. He was having to shout twice for anything to get done these days. He came out to the corridor to look for the chap he had hired last month, a cheeky young thing who dared to give him the sulks if he interrupted his chats with the boy of the next officer's room or was made to fetch more than two cups of tea from the pantry. He had ensured that his first week was gruelling so that he knew the difference between work and play. But where was he?

"Golum! Golum!" his voice glumly echoed around the room. Huddling under the stairs no doubt with the others scratching his bottom or adding some mindless strand to some petty conspiracy in the belief that they could lay a scratch on the mighty oak of the empire. Well, for their sakes, he hoped they would be happy with what they were getting in its place. He cleared his throat and walked up to the basin to rinse the dust off his mouth. He had carried back with him the grime of the dim-lit alleys next to The Malacca. He found himself standing out on the verandah for air when the giant clock hanging from an ornate hook under the balcony of Colonel Saunders' office struck four. There were rumours of a national-level promotion, never mind the shape of the nation for the fellow, mused Caelian as the hawk-nosed colonel stood up from behind his desk and made his way to the balcony. Caelian dipped his head to nod and moved indoors. He was expecting a visitor but he was late.

For the past few months, since the department had set him up on the job, the clock had turned into an intimate creature.

Every movement of the clock-hand, however, slight, seemed to him like a talk-back from some corner of an earlier life. When the clock struck after every full hour, the sound would buzz in his ears like a bottle-bee. For his work in The Lambda, he had put three oceans, moody volcanoes, the world's largest swamps, dead kings' tombs, the wolf-ridden taiga and horse-hoven plateaus between him and his family. He wasn't sure they believed him any longer when he wrote back saying his superiors were tight-fisted about leave. Each movement of the clock-hand over its white dial inflamed his hidden anguish for spring—on the side of a rocky slope in the Northland, pale brown leaves flecked with snow were now falling all over his farm. He would not stay beyond April—in summer he would be home. Caelian looked at his wrist-watch. It showed that it was a minute past four. No one but him knew that it had arrived a twenty-million second later than yesterday.

Sometimes, Caelian got the sense that he was not the only one working in this case even though he would have been happy and relieved to be able to discuss its progress with a team.

"This is your baby, Colin," said the general when he had been handed the assignment in another office block, months ago. The summons had put him on edge all morning, but he had calmed himself down. He had bolted the door of his office and lain down on the sofa for a quick smoke when a boy from his superior's office, had knocked on his door. He straightened his collar, gave his head a quick comb down and set off for the meeting—it was probably about his leave. It must be about his leave. He had grown old, it was true, but they wouldn't pull the rug under a fella, would they, when his retirement was just a few years away? He still had a few tricks up his sleeve, he consoled himself as he palpitated outside the closed door before the fresh-faced attaché gave him permission to enter. He could still be very useful. But he was also very naked and feared that the longer he stayed in The Lambda, he was giving proof of his nakedness. Before the general, he had however, been self-possessed and detached, even when he forgot his name.

"Colin, we are depending on you old boy, to get us the Rabbit." It was decided at that meeting to refer to the project in code even while filing reports so that no trace would remain of this enterprise planned from the core of the Empire during the countdown to the Plebsicite.'The Rabbit' would be the code for the man, key to their plans for The Lambda and he, Caelian, would sign it as Bickers. It would not implicate him, he was told, even though the nom de guerre was from his part of the world. That was just happenstance—"Human beings are born everywhere, names can come from anywhere," said the boss looking at him meditatively across the table. But wouldn't he need other people working on the case with him when the stakes were so high, he had asked.

"You are the case leader and its cadre, Colin," the general had said. "You will report to me every week—I will let you know the day, one day in advance. That'd be more than the advance notice I would get from my boss in my day...."

"This is an award, an honour," Caelian had managed to say as the attaché came to stand beside his chair to take him outside. But the general hadn't finished.

"The problem with us, Colin, is that we have grown too lax. When we sit behind our desk every morning we think we are bulls and we snort and roar and expect everyone to do our work because they fear us. We have got so used to all the fetching and carrying that we have forgotten how to use our own limbs."

Fine thing for a man to hear when he had spent forty years in service. He didn't talk like that to anyone else, did he, thought Caelian as he walked back across the courtyard refusing to look at the clock, its hand still perversely raised, he hoped, over the same mark on the dial for the last one hour. Let the day be a long one! Why must he be the only one to suffer?

He wanted to ring the bell for tea but changed his mind. A sheaf of papers that he had not clipped to the file, fell off the desk. A scribble on the side caught his eye. It was not the general's writing. The tail of these ps and ds ended in a short squiggle. Clearly, more than one pair of eyes was looking at his reports. He had noticed two sets of pen inking comments on their sides or underlining some observation of his and then tacking a question mark at the end of the sentence. Sometimes, the boss, to whom he had started briefing every week, contradicted his observations, which meant they were relying on other versions. He wondered, then dismissed his misgivings. No, he could not claim to have been discriminated by his bosses just because he was from the Northland. His career had been slow, but steady. He had not— not intentionally at least—given anybody any trouble except for the initial years when he had been very angry and quick to take offence. The training programmes had sorted him out and smoothed his rough edges. He did not want to be the unhappy recorder of his missed opportunities, which is why with a clear sense of what he was about to do, he had enlisted for a position in the Lambda when a vacancy was posted in their offices in the Fairland.

As a career choice, it was not the most brilliant one. A Lambda posting, when it was clear the empire was folding up, would enrich him in what way? As an officer in the intelligence department, it would mean entanglements in the grundle of the empire, covering up intrigues that were half-heartedly begun and were hence sticking out like shittle and being part of plans that would end one way or the other in the favour of the new nation. The mines, the roads, the sea—were all gone or going.

"You've got it all wrong Cael. There is no more any motherland or fatherland to protect even though it is a useful call for getting fools like us all het up about going to war. What they need now are people to go out there who have a head for business," said his mates as they met at pub for a farewell drink a month before he set sail for the Lambda. "They need guys with whom their guys can cut deals and not someone who has faith in the Empire—wake up Caelian."

"You are doing all the right things for turning into a wimp," his wife had said to him quietly the day he told her about being accepted for a position in The Lambda, before starting one of their daily squabbles. Now when he went back, his old woman wouldn't recognise him, he told himself with a smile. He had learnt to be quick and they had taught others to be so as well. The sense of time would be their gift to The Lambda, he thought, as he now shot a quick look around and rested a thick foot over the other on a stool by the basin. His head had again begun to feel heavy and his body seemed strapped to a block of ice. Lately he had been catching a chill ever so often that he had taken out his old spirit lamp and started to light it in this corner of the room at all hours of the day. His old cravings rose inside him and he wanted to hold, just hold, his pipe in his hands. There was too much work, too much pressure and no one to share it with. Worst of all, he was never able to be himself and so he had lifted two chairs and joined them behind the partition to go horizontal and feel a little comfortable.

"I want to be able to sit for a drink with a fellow and say 'Fuck the Queen' 'Fuck the Fairlanders' and not get hauled up... or get ticked off for being inconsistent.... Fuck 'staying power', that's what I want to say...."

He decided he would get a bed. There was enough space behind the partition to squeeze in a small bunk. He shut his main door and switched off the lights. The room seemed to float in a purple haze. He went to lie back on the chair but couldn't keep still. A strange anxiety gnawed at his soul. He needed fresh air—that was what was needed but he didn't want to catch anybody's eye right now. He got up to stand beside his window and slowly parted the curtains—no, no one was standing in a neighbouring balcony. The view was clear.

From his boxy verandah, just enough space for a person to stand really, secretaries in the adjoining offices were extracting new sounds from typewriters. The offices around this square courtyard would be the first official bloc of the new indigenous government of The Lambda—if they wanted. If they wanted it, thought Caelian, looking at its walls, they would inherit more than structure. Well, they would also get the worms. Those winged creatures silently bred and multiplied under the beds, desks and chairs in all seasons. Anyway he would be out of here by April and once home, would try to get back his old job at the grain inspector's office. When he left The Lambda, that was the last he wanted to hear about it.

From his office on the first floor, he saw office boys surge towards the bicycle lot outside the gate, cackling and howling as if the sky was falling over their heads. For months now, they were being driven to go with the flow. Letters had to be ferried, and responses brought back so that the massive bureaucratic enterprise of Plebsicite and the simultaneous and hourly dismantling of the Fairlander empire would go hand in hand. He saw one of his boys, whom he had sent into The Frontier on an errand last evening, cross the courtyard and exchange a few words with a group that was about to get up on their cycles. Minutes passed—the bunch grew.

"Chat, chat, chat...." he muttered. No one had watered the ferns in his balcony for days and you send them on an errand where they spend the entire day and on coming back they hold a bloody convention!

"Well?" he barked at the boy who reached his room a good half hour later. "Which dead dear stopped you in your path? Which grandmother came in your dreams?"

Without any change of expression, the boy took out a sheaf of paper and said:

"Oh master, from across The Gates they are saying freedom
From your door Golum is saying freedom, I am saying freedom,
From the dreams of my father I am saying freedom
From the womb of my mother, my sister is saying freedom
From the blackness, the blacksmith is saying freedom,
from the clock of the shift, the factory is saying freedom
Oh master, the land you are killing is saying freedom,
the wounds you are bleeding is saying freedom
our broken jugs are saying freedom, our mouths are saying freedom
our guns are saying freedom, the man who has hidden his face is saying freedom,
Oh master, but freedom cannot be all that we want."

And with that, he folded the paper on which Danny had scratched his last poem back into his pocket, and walked back the way he had come. Some of the boys who followed him out of the building, said they had seen him join a crowd that was milling around The Bus as it went past their street, its hood bashed in, a tyre gone, its trunk riddled with bullets, but still rolling its hulk inch by inch on its three remaining wheels with the help of a few hands that had come out of the crowd, ready to give it a push.

15

The Flag on the Roof

A few hours later, the sky dumped the night like a load of coal over The Lambda and a foul wind began to howl over its head. The City gave off a single shiver and went indoors—to those that stayed out, they had not much to say. This night had started out like a night they had known many months ago. They had heard the whispers, seen the signs and they had survived so long by paying respect to both that they could not be ignored. Old bad habits can be beaten out of people only if they are willing. Word had got around to all of those sitting inside the houses now that the young rioteers who had accompanied The Bus till the gate of the police station were gathering around The Malacca to wait by the tea shops. Among them was a friend of the poet who the youngsters had pulled off the bus at the very last minute and who was now being requested to speak. Benches were straightened, the thin peppery tea dripped into the cups, but the talk was low, muted. This time, Hog did not hesitate. He spoke of Danny his friend, Danny who was a worker in *The Meat*, Danny who had many faults and how he had finally decided to be one of them.

"Don't make Danny out to be a hero. We are all little people," said Hog. "We all want importance. But what we are fighting for, if that doesn't get importance, what will we do with our own importance?"

This made the group around him discover their toes because that is precisely what a whole lot of them were thinking. A hero sometimes becomes an alibi for people not to do anything—great deeds are best done by others—other than cheer or gasp outside the ring where somebody else is howling while his groin is being kicked. The Dongs had been their heroes some years ago, said Hog, and they had seen how they had already stepped into many of the Lambda's offices, with a total disregard of people's will and had made the Plebiscite, still a few months ahead, into a farce. The Dongs had chosen themselves—where was the people's choice? But what would the people do if The Partisans failed them too? What am I saying, thought, Hog taking a pause, and he thought he saw Kanhu, and Kanhu smiling in the crowd, but he found that he was unable to stop now. Have faith in The Party, he said, but more with the desire to organise and not to form an organisation. "Claim the streets, arm yourselves and organise yourselves into groups that speak to each other and work together and go with the most radical tendency there is at the moment, and one that uncompromisingly keeps the workers' cause foremost." And this made many, many people go a little wild with joy—a man speaking the unspeakable in the middle of The City was a great leap in any direction—and men and women of the scavengers' union, the bus-drivers' union, the security guards' union, the press-workers' union, the teachers' union, the maids' union rushed to lift him on their shoulders. If they did not seize the moment, he said, The Lambda would have no bottom, no space for commoners, no corner that a man could come upon by himself to realise that he had taken a wrong turn and then turn around to make something else of himself. There would be no more sea, no more sky, day would arrive only by lamp light as the Fairlanders had tried to make happen near The Gates and they would all have to live around those spotless white houses of the City, as if they were in hiding, fit to skulk around the streets like a mangy dog only when night had fallen.

The night wore on. The teashops expanded like tents. The crowd around Hog grew and each person made space for another person to get a place, chairs were being brought from inside the homes in the Black Quarters and there was much talk of meeting up later to discuss what was to be done, and that there must be discipline of having some programme to decide where to take this next. Just coming out on the streets was not going to change things. The decisions made on the street, they knew, would be difficult to defend when inside the home but that was the real test: to be kind and interested in one's own is easily understood, but to stand with people one does not know means being open to various risks—to one's person, to one's home. That is difficult for most people to do.

Those who stay in the ditch, probably love the ditch, so let them stay there. A stray has to be accommodated at the bottom of the stairs. The wind of the street cannot be brought in to stay inside a vase. A desperate knock at any untimely hour does not mean that the door has to open.... If any of these house rules are broken, all laws, they fear, can be swept away. So each person took from the meeting whatever he or she *could* take.

FROM THE WIDE staircase of The Malacca, that had been once carpeted with splinters of glass and bullets and licked with blood, Mangu, the driver, was scanning the tea-shops for a boy not older than fourteen or fifteen. His concentration, however, was being disrupted by the melee right in front of his eyes, not even a feet away. A bunch of The City's toffs had run into some new recruits of the Fairlander army mid-staircase, and were delighted at finding themselves among like-minded people, such as those who liked roasted quails and were unfussy about plates and knives if they were being served in the middle of a forest, started to discuss suitable places for a camp. Each group tried to best the other's picnic venue. By the time they had reached the top of the stairs, The City's princelings, who had spread the net wide and laid out the offer of a feast that would have fed an entire barrack, seemed to have got the honour to host the party. More talk later, each group decided to go their own way as the street lights spluttered into life illuminating parts of the pavement and throwing back some of the light on the stairway. Mangu found he had nowhere to hide.

He had recognised one of the young men of the group that had just gone by and saw that he had let his friends go ahead when there was no reason for him to do so. It was Guru, one of the friends of his master's son and the way he had stopped and remained standing at the head of the stairs told Mangu that he had been noticed. Was it wrong of him to step out of the hotel when his master was inside holding a meeting? Heart thumping, the old man climbed up the stairs, then looking up, said he had come out for air.

"What news of Guli? Still not back from The Frontier! Working in a factory there perhaps.... That's no job for one of our boys I keep telling Polo" said Guli. Bring him over, bring him over, let him handle Polo's new car. What power that car has, makes a man feel really good behind the steering. Let's go in now, what have you been really up to?"

But what was Mangu up to? Nothing really. He had simply been waiting for news of Guli. He had heard that he might be on The Bus with the prisoner. But his son had not got off The Bus nor had he been among the crowd thronging the teashops. Even though he had been standing at the foot of the staircase for the past two hours, not one man or woman coming out of the shops had so much as looked in his direction. That man called Hog, who was holding forth on Danny, would he not know Guli? Could he not have said two words about Guli? He decided to follow master Guru inside the hotel and for a few minutes, or so it seemed to him, forgot all about his son....

Mangu was wonderstruck! If even before Independence, the master's party could create such magic inside a single building what could they not do for The Lambda if given the chance for five years! The thousands of poor are safe with them, they would be able to eat with them around, may the lord bless the master, may His light shine on him, may his son Polo prosper, may his house prosper...but for now, he wished he had more than a pair of eyes to take in the panorama that some mysterious power had been unfolding like a fan before his eyes. The voice of master Guru receded and then reached his ears from a distance. They were now in the atrium and his eyes unaccustomed to such richness tried not to give offence by staring at the walls, the placing of tiles on tiles, stones on stones..... The dots and tints of silver and gold moving all around the atrium would dazzle anyone's eyes; they addled Mangu's brain. He wandered around the room and bumped into a few gentlemen who had got him into the habit of nodding back at them when they were visiting his master's house. Here, he found the same etiquette need not apply. Here, they hurried away towards a circular open-air space cut out from the room where dinner arrangements for about fifty had been made. Little glass tables and chairs bandaged in white shot silk sat waiting for their distinguished guests; the identity of the fifty was the subject of bitter speculation all down the hall. Mangu peeped here and he peeped there and could not remain still. He came upon a fellow chauffeur like himself in a peaked cap who was looking up at a gallery of portraits in one of the adjoining corridors leading out of the room and bit his tongue on coming close—it was Colonel Saunders, the dashing leader of the dreaded Murkys who had fought with the rebels from The Frontier, why at this very hotel, some months ago! The floor was solidly carpeted, his old shoe did not give him away. It left him free for a few seconds to debate his next course of action that servants of important people learn to do in the course of their service, if they want to remain in service. How big or small should his next gesture be? Mangu doffed his cap, better to keep things small, but the Colonel seemed particularly taken up with a portrait of a mustachioed officer brandishing a lance seated on a steed and was ignoring the coughs, sniffs or any kind of competing exertions by his admirers standing at some distance from himself. The group fidgeted but did not move away; placed in the very equal and undeniable position of rejects, they gave up their initial hostility and started talking among themselves hoping that at some point the great man would turn around and accept the attention they were so willing to shower on him. Suddenly the Colonel said, 'Ah!', and stretching his arm towards his left moved in that direction, making his little cortege look west as well.

Baba Lala was emerging from a room at the end of the corridor with Kuberos, the hotelier, and seeing him, he waved at Saunders and walked up to lay a paternal hand on the officer's scarlet coat. "You're still in your uniform! I was just telling Kuber that when we have our own army we will let the men have a bit of fun. Enjoying the evening I hope, Saunders—you here with your men?"

The Colonel was enjoying the evening. The weather looked miraculously changed over his head and he was like a man who after a long winter was now facing the sun. Having taken off his cap, he was rubbing it like a mitten and seemed ready to grow smiles in the most inhospitable crevices of his face. His body could clearly be bent on special occasions. He leaned over to listen, he bent to the floor to remove the creases of the carpet before Baba Lala stepped on it, he laughed. Long years of practice in military parades now saw him effect a perfect half-turn and, balancing his spare frame on his ankle, swivelled his waist to face an eager bunch, an assortment of second lieutenants, corporals, a petty trader selling grain at the military store, an artist stalking him for months to make him sit for a portrait—all transformed in the last few seconds into 'his men'. He barked out an order of 'salute'. Mangu's heart nearly burst with pride at the sight of the old Lambda paying their respect to the master of the new one, and nodded philosophically to think that the wind turned equally for kings and clowns, dogs and serfs and everyone has their days of glory and shame, and they enjoy it not for one day more or less than what is in their share. Kuberos's tale was just about to confirm it.

"Captain Saunders is scared of mongrels," said Kuberos with a little giggle that seemed as loud as the pop of twenty bottle corks in the narrow corridor. "Did he tell you—no? Then I will tell you a little story...."

"*Colonel* Saunders," hissed a loyal junior eager to be the first one off the mark to note the insult by the owner of The Malacca. Kuberos was not going to be put down by such minor details. No man was going to run his motor on his, Kuberos's strip, without thanking him for building the road and as Saunders had done so, he would be paid back with this 'little story', which actually began in a year when the first fictions, the first seeds of unfairness, began to sprout all over The Lambda.

One spring morning before the sun got harsh, a young Saunders had got off his grandfather's car and jogged a lap around a tree where a pony, his shoulders sloping but his eyes alert, was waiting for him. Both horse and man were taking part in an equestrian exam to be eligible for a place in the army. That year it was instituted, by law, that men of breeding were to be given a head start in jobs of state as it was wisely said that responsibility comes with privilege, people who stay in mud houses do not defend forts. In short, young Saunders was not entering the force as a lieutenant but as a colonel. Rules of course were rules and the young man "had to at least get up on the horse", sheepishly said the balding brigadier, a distant relative on Saunders' mother's side. As the man conducting the exam and as a relative, he was, he said, demanding this bare minimum. For a good five hours, the horse and his rider tried to get along but each had their own idea of doing things so an alternative had to be made. After a kick on the animal's sides to set him off, the brigadier took out a square sheet of paper with a sigh. As exam officer, Brigadier Rarebit testified to the absence of a suitable horse for the occasion. He recommended that the horse be made available for the next round of examinations. He next proceeded to ask the candidate on hand the following question: "If chased by mongrels, would you grab a horse and be able to cross a fence?" Colonel Saunders, the examiner noted, replied: "Yes."

The effect of this narration was exactly what Kuberos wanted, every cadet present there was shovelling through his solemnest memories so as not to laugh. In the end, Saunders was rescued by a pebble. Various unrelated remarks were meanwhile passed in the brief interim, someone said the phones rang too loud in this hotel...donations for the Dongs' widows' cell had exceeded expectations...aquariums, someone had heard, was going to be a tidy business...when a pebble broke through a glass window and whizzed past Saunders' ear. One of his lackeys caught it with a neat jump while crashing into a side table but produced it to universal relief. Saunders gave the offending piece of stone the attention of a mango dropped from a tree.

"Small for a missile," he finally said. "But sharp." True, it was a curious bit of rock, as if a knife had been whetted all evening around its edges, it was still that warm.

Kuberos, moved towards a window, his face ashen. "It is beginning again," he said peering into the night. Except for the dim fires around the tea shops where a few boys were clearing the tables, there was nothing that should catch his eye. The wind had stopped howling and a light drizzle ran gently up and down the street threatening no one. The approach to his hotel was clear except for The Bus that had come in hours ago from The Frontier. It was now standing near the police station opposite The Malacca. It should have been back in the depot by now, he was going to ask one of his fellows to haul up the driver, but something made him change his mind. The party was on, the bar was full, the meeting was on and the good businessman that he was, Kuberos did not want to upset his customers. What if the driver kicked up a storm and was known to his staff, a most volatile bunch always on the look-out for trouble? He could not risk another riot on his premises so soon, perhaps someone trying to put him out of business but he dismissed this thought as well. From the atrium, the low gurgle of Koo, his latest acquisition, crested and troughed to the sombre play of the pianist, and the night spun around the tap of her heels. Koo will never have what Jaba had, he was thinking, when he began to pass out.

When he regained consciousness, he was told the matter was under control, words that heightened his sense of panic and brought about another spell of dizziness. Under control – under whose control he wanted to know. But Baba Lala silenced him with a look and made him a stiff drink and for the second time this summer Kuberos felt Lala had imprisoned him in his own property in front of, well, everybody. His eyes moved around his private quarters in the hotel tower when a young corporal rushed in with a Roman air to say the situation near The Gates was serious. Sounds of marching had been heard coming from all directions towards The City.

Saunders effected another of his half-turns and in a voice dripping with resolve told his men to secure the entrance of The Malacca, where the rebels were no doubt heading. This time, he was going to put those bastards through the grinder, this time, he could not afford to fail. His orders from his superiors were clear and unambiguous. Saunders my good fellow, sound effective and, well, be effective. He gave a last salute to Baba Lala and left the room in steam.

A few beads of perspiration dripped from Baba Lala's

forehead to the floor—where was Polo, he thought exasperatedly and then remembered. He allowed himself a sigh and got up from beside Kuberos's side to look out from the window. The sky was lightening but it was still many hours to the morning. His eye rested on *The Meat* easily the grandest building in the neighbourhood, then stiffened. He thought he saw a shadow move at one of its windows in its top storey but his eyes were probably playing tricks. Aristu, he knew, had placed his men in each of the floors since those Reds started breaking into his office and now one of his staff, he had heard, had been brought to book. Ah yes, it was the Horo affair but there was something about the murder that he wasn't able to figure out. 'Must remember to ask Aristu more about it,' he muttered, a mutter loud enough for Kuber, that fat fool, to be disturbed and raise his head and bleat in terror—all that went through his head while he was awake or asleep was his hotel, and that some unseen force was waiting to jump on it. He wouldn't be surprised if he suspected him too of something or the other, these days whenever they met he was so full of false bonhomie that to cover that up he had taken to telling stupid stories at the drop of a hat and if not that, then to complain about the costs of knives and spoons. But they had known each other for long, their fathers had made their fortunes together, they would hunt together, and well, had died together, but that was another story. Lala shook his head at the man on the bed forbidding him to stir and turned his face back to the open window. The black squall that had roared over The Lambda in the evening seemed to have blown over, a few gusts of strong wind simply shook the shutters of the neighbourhood's windows for a brief while and rolled the moon all over the horizon. In the east, daylight had begun to blink when a sight stopped him in his tracks. How had it escaped his attention? The unmistakable red and blue flag of The Fairland fluttered from a familiar roof in the distance. When he turned to talk to Kuberos, who had by now propped himself up against a pillow, he, however, said nothing that would betray his state of mind. What he said instead was:

"That man, that man in the portrait our boy Saunders was

looking at in the corridor, turns out, it was his grandfather.... Take slow sips. Or shall I call for more?"

Kuberos was in no mood to show any interest in Saunders' family tree. The presence of a doctor standing woodenly with his case at the foot of his bed just about made him hold his peace. "Good of you, I must say," continued Lala, "to keep a place for a portrait of Saunders' old man in your hotel. This I will instruct all our men to do. No taking down of old emblems and portraits, our history was the experience of both our communities. We asked for what is ours and they are giving it back. The Lambda needs a sense of continuity to keep it running, their time is up but why make enemies and rub Fairlander noses when it can be business as usual if you stay friends?"

Baba Lala's words were beginning to restore an ill man to his health. But Kuberos did not want another lecture on how to run his business, which he knew would be followed by a request for funds for this or that national initiative. "How is Polo's meeting going? I gave him our best—the Crimson Room," he whispered feebly from the bed and asked a servant on stand-by to turn on the radio and shut the door. He looked around for Mangu, whom he remembered having seen close by before he had passed out. He could massage his feet unless Baba Lala had other work for him. "No, don't call him," said Baba Lala brusquely. "Let him enjoy himself a little while longer downstairs..." and continued to look out of the window as Kuberos tried to overcome the rebuke in pointless chuckles.

MANGU DID not know how long he had been slumped against the wall. Men and women in myriad hues stood about smiling as if they were inside a painted garden, or sat around the huge embroidered sofas, their eyes glittering like a lynx, hands folded tightly one over the other on their laps. Thick chains of gold clasped to the women's napes squeezed out secrets that unstable trees tell the air before a storm. Their hands never far away from their necks, managed to rub them with a fragile air, closing the gaps in conversation—Mangu had never seen women so beautiful. But something irrepressible and inexpressible radiated from their eyes on being looked at so from a distance that

Mangu, now drunk immediately lowered his gaze. His lashes parted on their own to search out the silk and billow of those clothes that were framed by deathly pale limbs curling like larvae by their side. Every now and then the women cupped their hands over their mouths to stifle back a laugh to attract or reject the company nearby, or curved up their shoulders to look over them as if not to miss the birth of something wondrous behind their backs. What songs could the orchestra play to fete such loveliness? Mangu, the driver of Polo, the rising star of the Dongs, surprised by nothing and therefore everything, was unable to close his jaw. He didn't know what more the night had in store.

The Malacca had innumerable passageways and rooms that open into other rooms and passageways that give the impression that some of them had been built to tell on the people staying or walking past them. Everything could be the matter for a report. Not too far away from where Mangu was standing was a door. It was the door of the Crimson Room and one of its walls could be moved—only a few people know which one—to reveal a ladder that could be climbed right up to the tower. This was a long rectangular room cut by eight doors of equal height. To those who had not entered it, this may seem an irrelevant observation but to those seated inside they would understand this well. The room had only one piece of furniture—a long mahogany table around which twenty chairs of unequal carpentry were placed, and to be asked to sit on one and not the other was the same as being asked for tea without being served sugar. The slight, thankfully, would first be felt in private, by the rear—some chairs had cushions, some had not, some were covered with the best of wood, some were a bed of nails—and the experience could be used by the individuals concerned as lessons in self-reflection. To get a good chair at the next meeting had to be the goal. The chair at the head of the table no doubt accommodated the most significant rump.

By ten, everyone had been seated and had taken the first sip of the goblets being handed around by the hotel's attendants. After a few minutes everyone kept looking at the door when Polo nudged himself to speak.

"The plan or programme for freedom," said Polo in his opening remarks, "is the real thing. It is more important than freedom itself. The question is: are we ready or not?"

"The people are ready, we can learn from them," said a theatre director from the other end of the table.

"What rot, that's like the dog letting its tail decide for the head," cut in a fellow attendee, and with that they went after the first fellow for half of an hour till Polo clapped and bellowed, a difficult thing to do with a falsetto, and got freedom back on the table for discussion. Everyone struck their foreheads but ideas don't drop like coins no matter what people say.

"The moment you have an idea," said S Forth, the doctor, "you let everyone know and even if it's the last time you can call it your own, you feel happy that it is taken up and happier still when it is implemented. At this point the only thanks you are ever going to get is the thought that you have freed others from thinking...."

S Forth was cautiously covered with congratulations; a chit made its way into his hands on which it was suggested that he keep the tone respectful otherwise he might have to change his seat. They put his suggestion in a notebook anyway, which someone had the decency to bring.

Molox, the livestock merchant, was among those who had so far said nothing, and this made people suspicious of him. As he had neither said anything in support or criticised what had been said so far, he was feeling the pressure and well he should. When he spoke, he said he wanted to share a dream that he had had last night. This immediately put off people because at the end of it there was sure to be a puzzle—when somebody said they had a dream it usually meant a lot of work for other people.

Said Molox: "I dreamt I was going on a journey but knew I wanted to return home. I got up on a boat and each time I passed a tree or a standing shrub or a piece of stone I did not know, I marked them.. The journey took long and I passed through strange and wonderful towns and by the time I had done an arc I was pleased with myself. When I woke up my most vivid memory was of the first tree on which I had put a cross. So did I even move? I think not."

The room was equally divided on the issue so everyone looked towards the head of the table for a resolution but as Polo looked as if he was about to dive under the table, a Dong faithful stood up to holler for some finger food. He got nuts.

"If peanuts are all we are getting tonight, who will be a monkey?" said Jot, the lawyer, resentful that he had been called to a hotel to sleep when he could have done it better at home. He was not the only one. Except for the distraction of a communal lynching, that any person who attempted to raise his hand after Molox was bound to get, the atmosphere in the room was funereal. When Baba Lala joined the meeting, he found Polo sitting in one corner under a fan that ground to a halt, defiantly looking left and right and people trying to slip away through one of the doors in ones and twos. Seeing him made many of them retrace their footsteps. He took a chair next to his son, waited for the house to be full and then spoke.

"I will be brief. I often tell my son Polo not to make me his idol. Don't grow with the expectation that your father knows everything, I said. But this makes my son very unhappy. He asks wasn't grandfather your idol? I said no, *he* wasn't. It was sometimes Hall and sometimes nobody at all. But everyone must have an idol, says Polo. How do I explain that I learnt this from *my* father.... He never said I know everything or ask God. So I say this to you, Polo doesn't know everything, but the meaning of everything is there in the dictionary. Look for it. And now let us hear you speak. I have spoken enough. But there is one another thing tonight I would like to speak of—whatever we do, we should never try to get ahead of ourselves and for this I will take your time to tell you something that happened recently. Just the other day, we went to a meeting where we invited some officers of the Fairlanders and some of our poets. Polo was there—ask him about it later. Poet after poet got up and recited their piece and filled our ears with 'God save our King, God save our king's city of Pandan from the evil eye.' Then someone got up—and I don't remember his name. He said: "King oh king be victorious/after the war meet me/I will have brought you a guava from my tree/give me then my independence, don't say never/and I will be tied to you with a golden thread for ever and ever...'or some such thing. I asked some Dong members to hush him up. People took him aside and said: 'You mad fellow, who are you to ask for independence?' And the fellow says: 'Why, haven't the Fairlanders themselves said they will give it to us? It was then that I took him aside and said: Let *them* say, *you* don't say that. Polo is my son and it may take some years for him to be his father. But you will have to wait for him."

A few people filing out of the room had a red eye but Lala's work was not done. He was waiting to call it a night after a report from Saunders on the situation at The Gate. He beckoned Polo leaving the room but he seemed preoccupied. Polo was, in fact, thinking of something else. He was late for another meeting. But his thoughts remained frozen in the moment his father had stepped in to take over the evening. He picked up Guru from the atrium and headed off towards the barracks where someone was waiting for him with a tray and pipes. A small grey sedan followed him at a distance. The man driving it had his target in sight but his mind, too, was elsewhere. The march could be halted. But the flag fluttering on the roof of *The Meat* was something to think about.

16

The Falcon is Coming

In *The Meat*, the march was already the subject of much talk. I'm not writing about it, said some reporters, till I can see some sort of smoke coming out from The Frontier, or only if The Partisans were right outside our building said others, laying out the rules of engagement. The truth was that Aristu had resorted to the old tactic of bribing people at work, instead of pleasing one, bribing pleased two, a bribe after all means burying differences and being encouraged to like what you, left to yourself, wouldn't like, isn't that right? But to look from the other side, as is the fashion, you could think about it in another way. What Aristu was asking them to do was something very little, for, as reporters, they wouldn't do a *big* compromise—it's not as if they were being asked to lie—when even a little one would go a long way. For those who were born disagreeable, there was the door.

"And I suggest they take a good long look at what's behind it as they leave," said Aristu drawing on a cigarette at one of his meetings with some of his senior recalcitrant reporters and flicking ash all over the floor.

Just then his secretary popped his bald head in to say: "They are here Sir." And a line of men and women walked in hands at their side. Aristu took a last drag of his cigarette and placed it on the day's paper on his desk. The paper curled, the room smoked. As an aged editor passed out in one corner, Aristu signalled his secretary to switch off the fan, close the door behind him and go, leaving him to survey the scene he had just organised and was now waiting for to unfold. An hour passed, when still no one spoke, Aristu got off his chair and looking at the direction of his older group of employees and asked one of them to open the window. The light and fan came on next. Pouring himself a glass of cold water, he waved the two groups into one single file with a jerk of a finger and sank back into his chair.

"There! Now I think we will all work together. It's not so difficult just look at Neut. How well that boy is doing!"

Neut was a new recruit. He was a quick learner, he soaked up what he was told. He never said No when he should say Yes, he never said No, period. He wrote of what he knew and of what he could see out of his window. As he never travelled far for his stories, he was a boy who never missed his deadlines. When he went to the newsroom and scanned the headlines of other newspapers and saw that they too had reported nothing on The Partisans, he scratched out a few lines he had written on a lean day based on what a vendor outside *The Meat* had told him, and accepted the gratitude of his seniors for rubbing out the copy before it caught Aristu's eye.

"But should we not try to study The Partisans just to see what they want?" he asked one day and got his reply.

"Sure. That's how doctors discovered a cure for tuberculosis."

Neut shrugged and went back to his seat. The good thing about Neut was that if he could write about parakeets, he could write about water ballet; put him in an orphanage and he could spin a story that would make the oldest orphan cry; throw him into a slum, he could come out with ten good ideas how to remove them with the approval of its residents.

Soon enough his voice began to be heard loud and clear in the newsroom he had joined only a few days ago. And so defined and definite were his opinions that his fellow workers began to hold back their thoughts and their opinions for fear of giving offence to their young Octavius. His ideas left a trail, and *The Meat*, a fertile ground always for the birth of myths, added a new one to its name. His admirers grew outside the newsroom, everyone knew who Neut was, and people would constantly place themselves in his path in the office corridor for a chance at private conversation. And because he spoke well missing neither pause nor punctuation, they elected themselves as his envoy and took it upon themselves to repeat him without any deviation, with accuracy. Neut was what young blood looked like and Aristu was looking out for him. "That was a good story you did last night," he said walking into the bureau one day. "I want you to do many such more. But you can't just file one story a day!"

"If I do three a day, sir, they won't be very good."

"Dear boy, have I said they have got to be?" With a Delphic smile Aristu stopped his protestations to say, "Hey, someone have him introduced to Darius. Both of them, I have a feeling, will do great things together."

A SMALL AGENCY, The Thump, flourished at the foot of *The Meat* these days. The source of its boom was a matter of speculation so we will only state what we know for sure. Its proprietor was the stocky Mr Darius, a former publisher and writer of devotional books on the known and unknown deeds of the gods. Owing to his girth, Darius moved slowly but his moves were timely. The man who has participated in many races was the real achiever, he liked to say. "Arriving in town was the main thing, any goon with a gun can take the town," he would say with a straight face to his three-hack team, who were aware of his back story and would mumble as soon as Darius's back turned: "It's his old pain, we'll never hear the end of it..."

Noticing a change of climate in The Frontier, Darius had followed a small exodus out of The Frontier after the death of Horo around whom a coterie of cloth, grain and book merchants like himself had flourished year on year without divine intervention. He left one night with a sack of essentials and one trusted servant and took a room just above the street on a pavement opposite *The Meat.* To contain the news of his flight, he did not take The Bus but walked for a full day to enter The City. Then he slept. On waking up, he expressed surprise that the sun had gone down and sat down before a steaming plate that his servant, with the practice of years, handed over to him heaped with rice, topped with lentils, two pieces of fried potatoes and a fish head. Not a single grain of rice or lentils spotted the floor. He did have the knack of clearing up things cleanly. When he was done, he climbed down the stairs to dust and line his books in his small space on the road and fanned himself as he observed the lay of the land. One day, he saw a man get off his car and walk into *The Meat* and Darius recognised him in an instant. The face was the same, the walk was the same, the legs that used to walk around barefoot were now taking their strides in expensive leather. In The City, Aristu, his old acquaintance had done well. But Darius, who had always stood on ceremony in one court or the other, knew that to get past the high door, he must have his own game. So for months, he put heart and soul into the book business but the clientele just would not grow; The City was fridge-cold to celestial exploits. By nature he was lazy or he may have given up too soon, but the pomp and spread of his former neighbour's clout visible just across the road and which he could only measure by the vintage of the cars of *The Meat's* visitors, daily humiliated him. He was an ant at the foot of a tree. He was a pumpkin born out of season.

"This daily business of sitting and waiting for customers is not for me. You can bring cows to a well but how do you force them to drink? Godless! Blockheads! Bloody bores! This is a city of illiterates. I am clearly wasting my time," he grumbled to Axe, his servant, who stared stonily at him and then started picking his teeth. When Darius gave him a poke to turn his wrist towards him to fan him faster, he bared his gums.

It increasingly became clear to Darius that he was not going to get very far in The City without patronage and he decided he would present himself before Aristu and say so. Having made up his mind, he downed the shutters of his shop one day, crossed the street, and appeared on the editorial floor and followed Hog who, he recalled he had bumped into a few times before in The Frontier, to the canteen. Even though he may not remember it. Darius seated himself in front of the proofreader and took out a bag full of books. It was a thin enough list and unlikely to support his next claim.

"I publish the unpublishable—all right I know how that sounded, so let me say it better—I don't go by canons, I publish the brave, what no one is talking about. I hear you are writing something, I could look at it, don't be shy."

Some castles are taken through a long siege, some are entered by a side door. Darius was well aware of Hog's political affiliations, the fellow, after all, used to live a few streets away from his old house at The Frontier (though he had heard he had moved to The City). Hog, he knew, could not chase him away without calling attention to himself. Seeing the man sitting in front of him stiffen and look warily over his shoulder, Darius realised his gamble had paid off. He immediately changed tack. Would not Hog, an old hand at *The Meat*, get him an introduction to another old neighbour, to Aristu Argot himself? "I do know him of old," he hastened to clarify, " but you don't announce to an emperor do you that you are here, to call on him one has to wait—but I don't want to."

Each time Hog hesitated or tried to drive the discussion elsewhere, Darius raised his chin resting on his chest and brought up the book. Face to face with a will that would brook no indifference or his opposition to the project, Hog tried his best to keep his voice low. His tormentor carried on regardless, his voice soaring over the general thrum of tea-time conversation, to reach other tables. A few workers turned to look back at the two, some raising a hand to ask him if all was okay.

Hog smiled back in response and braced himself by ordering another round of tea. This went on for a while until Hog placed his hand on his, and asked: "But how do you know I'm writing a diary?" There was really no point in putting this off any longer.

"Journalists keep scribbling something or the other don't they? So a diary is it?" And the man jawed the subject for a good half an hour like a leech that has seen a new opportunity to feed. By the time they left the canteen, Hog was sure that no one in the room had been spared the details of his exertions with the pen. But he was in a slight fix, there could be implications of being helpful or unhelpful in this case. So he put in a word with Aristu's secretary and left Darius with him. As he turned to leave, a voice rang out loud in the corridor:

"Write, write, put down all you see, don't miss a single day. It could all be very important...."

Darius began to be seen in and out of Aristu's room in no

time. It is said that he became Aristu's link man to other smaller papers and fed them, with Aristu's blessing, the main news of the day in order to maintain the continuity of opinion about the main events of his time. Reporters got used to the rotund man lurking around the boss's office and slowly began to meet him at his own post, downstairs. Darius, a former writer and publisher of devotional books, was now the head of a news agency. He hired three boys—the only test he had them submitted to at their interview was their willingness to answer to the same name—and had them clean out the basement Aristu had given him. Within a few days they were put to supervising the digging of the floor and knocking out some walls of the basement. Sounds of pickaxes knocking against hard concrete was heard by *The Meat*'s employees who stayed in office late at night.

"I wonder what they are up to," confided Soli in Hog one day.

"They don't do this in the day, the diggers come in after the entire building has emptied out."

"Should we go and check?"

"We can't. Darius's dog is always around or one of those Blone boys are—do you know he calls all those boys by the same name? That man, Darius, he either hates Aristu or idolises him but he is in some hurry to become him."

Soli and Hog had a good laugh about it but the conversation had stuck in both their minds. Soli decided to investigate. To avoid being noticed, the next day he took along a bunch of newsroom interns and showed them around the building, talking loudly and animatedly about the history of the building, its first editor and their current one. Their approach was noted. Axe, Darius's servant, suddenly seemed to pop out from somewhere behind the walls and stood glowering at them but as they were standing on *Meat* property, he opened his mouth in an angry snarl, but did not say a word. He nevertheless asked them what they wanted. Soli was prepared for this moment.

"We are all very excited about the setting up of this agency, nothing like getting the city news first," he said in his best professional manner, taking out a cigarette and offering one to the guard. "Could we..."

The short answer was No. No, he was not going to give them a guided tour. He had not been authorised to do it, he did not see the necessity for it, and what was there to see? It was an office like any other and moreover it was under construction and they would only get in the way. He was about to disappear down the basement but something made him stop to administer a sweetener.

"Besides, the young ones with you will trip over the stones and rubble, they will hurt themselves—Not like you sir, who can go anywhere, ask anything."

Soli did not give up. He kept up the rounds with a new bunch every day. When he could not catch hold of an intern, he coaxed one newsroom colleague or the other to stand near the wall where he had seen Axe appear and smoke a cigarette or two. Sometimes he took out a notepad and pen and scribbled some nonsense on it and profusely apologised for bumping into Axe, whom he pretended he had not noticed being immersed in deep thought. And he kept up the daily circus, the loud praise and the warm curiosity of Aristu and Darius's joint enterprise within the earshot of the latter's employees, waiting for the ice to crack. The Blone boys were less formidable. Whether it was the basement syndrome, the life instinct that goads some species to be sociable after being buried deep in the ground, or the prospect of meeting People from Upstairs, he found them more open to a chat.

"They even nod or smile when Axe is not around but none of them will say what their real name is. It's just bad luck to have got this far and then no further," he told Hog.

And one day, something happened that broke the jam. Axe had not reported for duty and the youngest Blone was in charge of the work to fit the door leading down from the ground floor to the basement in front of The Thump. The lights down the stairs had still not been fixed and in his hurry to speed up the work, he absentmindedly stepped on a pile of bricks lying around and went flying down the stairs and had a concussion. Soli, who had just entered the office and was about to take the stairs upstairs, took him to a doctor and brought him back to

The Thump. In the evening, just before leaving for an assignment, Soli climbed down the stairs to the basement to check on him and found him holding his head. He got him a cup of tea from the vendor outside and advised him to go home early just to avoid breathing in the dust rising out of the debris. The boy suddenly took his hand in his and came out on the road with him. He was still standing as Soli drove away on his bike.

"He said his name is Jallar," murmured Soli to Hog while giving him a report to sub. Their work with The Partisans was fairly obvious by now in *The Meat* but they still took care not to out the connection among others. "Jallar stays in an area outside the Black Quarters. He is newly come from The Frontier, but that means nothing so we will just have to wait and see who he is."

Jallar and Soli met quite a few times after that and Soli didn't even have to press him to go out. Being in the same building of course made it more convenient to meet, but knowing the watch that Darius put on his employees, his slipping away from his seat was an act of reckless courage for the quiet, shy boy that he was. Sometimes it seemed to Soli that he smoked his cigarette outside *The Meat* to wait for him knowing the time he was likely to come into office just so that he could nod and get a nod back, or if Soli wasn't in a hurry, share a smoke with him as he wheeled his bike to the office car park. Within a few days Hog was ribbing Soli about it. Yes, that boy did seem to look upto him. Whenever the two met outside the office for a bite, the lad would find some way of not letting Soli pay for the meal.

"Then I'm sorry we'll just have to stop meeting Jallar," he told the boy as they walked back to work from a cabin after wolfing down some sandwiches. But the boy smiled luminously back at him as if he had a hand in making them—it was a hopeless situation. But the frequent meetings were beginning to yield some information even if they were not of the kind Soli had in mind, and so he decided it would be unwise to let the connection grow cold when he had put in so much effort to make it work. It was really just that.

"His father was a senior clerk in the telegraph office at The Frontier. His boss, who did not get along with his own children, had taken the boy under his wing and sent him to college. Every Sunday when they..."

"Next you'll be telling me about the jar where his mother would keep her biscuits.... Soli, where's the investigation? You're handing this boy with kid gloves," said Hog, his voice breaking with worry. 'Plebiscite is just a few months away and the Dongs with Aristu is planning something big—I just know it. Dig deeper and for Chrissakes, hurry."

The Thump began their operations two or three evenings after that. A signboard was stuck to the little glass door and Axe, looking day by day like a thug, stood guard outside it. All manner of people came in and out of that door that led to the news agency housed in the basement of *The Meat*. Soli and Jallar were by now meeting twice every week after work but the boy wasn't very forthcoming about talking about his office and its visitors, stopping Soli's volley of queries with a light reproof:

"They are *The Thump's* clients as we must build our own source of information. *The Meat* mustn't get its hooks on them otherwise why will you buy the news from us?"

After that, things cooled down between the two for a while. They still greeted each other when they bumped into each other at the entrance, but no further invite was issued from either side. Once, Soli found himself visiting the tea cabin in between The Malacca and *The Meat*, that the two would earlier stop by after work. The waiter, this time gave him a puzzled look when he ordered a beer for himself and a plate of mince cutlets and then understood why. Two cabins down from where he sat, he heard Jallar's voice—and was surprised by its loud, confident pitch. He was debating whether he should go up to him when the waiter pushed aside the curtain and brought in his order.

"Beer and cutlets with a dab of mustard on the side, no sauce—the way you like it Sir," he said and then hung around with a question on his face. "Your friend's in the next cabin, it doesn't look nice"—he said or perhaps he hadn't really said that but Soli's mind, that had been restless all day, was adding words desired or prompted from within his subconscious. A young couple in the cabin before him were fighting over some point that could be major for their relationship and their ruckus was anyway giving him a headache.

Soli rang for his bill. He wanted to leave the joint without catching Jallar's eye but his presence had already been advertised it seemed. Through a tear in the curtain, he saw the waiter signal towards his cabin to Jallar who had come out to settle his account.

"You were slipping away without saying hello—why?" asked the boy as he came in to stand before his table. Soli was taken aback at his appearance and could not stop himself from passing a cheap remark. "Garters and tie! Is that how we will now see you in office, dressed up like a Fairlander?"

A shadow crossed Jallar's face. "Fancy dress—sometimes I do a bit of that. Aren't I pretty? "

Soli was thankful for the dim lights, he reached out for his spectacle case and slipped the glasses on. Looking up, he gestured the boy to sit down and lit his cigarette.

"That man you were with, I have a feeling I have seen him before. Doesn't he serve under Colonel Saunders?"

"He's someone I know," said Jallar without answering the question. "His father paid for my tuition—I've told you that before."

"So you did," said Soli, his voice steady by now. "So what have you been up to? Since your office started I haven't seen your face, it must keep you very busy."

Jallar did not answer. He was seated in visible tension, his shoulders pulled back, his palms gripping the arm rest as if he was waiting for that one word that would release him from his surroundings and let him escape it without damage. But as he was not making any effort to talk except for that burst of emotion that he had shown when he had barged into the cabin, it was difficult to gauge his thoughts. His eyes would not hold Soli's gaze. His face seemed drained of colour, he looked as if he was on the verge of a breakdown.

"My God Jallar—what is it? Are you in some kind of trouble?"

"And he said 'No—you are,'" said Soli to Hog telling him about the encounter the next day. "His voice had dropped to a whisper, it was dark, but I thought he was trying to tell me something. We were in one of the cabin-cafes you know that's always filling up, people constantly climbing up and down its stairs, chairs being dragged from one corner or the other to add to some table that an hour ago was going all empty and now everybody wanting to sit around that one, bearers being called out by their names—that you can hardly make yourself heard. But I heard him quite clearly. And Jallar told me, he had met a Murky, though his friend, who was sympathetic to The Partisans and who had told him to warn me: "Great ideas. Heart's in the right place. But don't step it up, don't do more." Intimidation—what else? But we've been warned."

"I see. And then?"

"And then he takes me completely by surprise. He starts screaming that I have been following him around! That he never wants to see me again—and he was responding to what? All this while, I hadn't even said a word!"

"I wouldn't take it very seriously. His friend, the Murk was still around right outside the cabin, waiting for him to leave isn't it ? All this must have been for his benefit. But your friend Jallar is a very interesting man, keep him close to us."

The following days proved Hog right. Jallar again began to seek Soli out and clung to him this time as if in fear of being shaken off. It was as if that evening had never happened. To divide the burden, Hog had suggested that he could come along on one of their evening outings, but Soli would immediately grow evasive about his plans. Writing to Lavni, still at The Frontier, Hog wrote that it was difficult to fathom who was under whose spell. Soli had also begun to depend on the boy for leads to city stories. When Hog tried suggesting that he keep the two kinds of work separate, he had given Hog an earful about doing his best and that he was tired of being constantly watched and having to bring Hog up to date about all his activities.

"I can't constantly watch what's coming out of somebody's mouth and then weigh on its consequences for Mir—where is Mir? Does anyone know? Has anyone thought of asking him? And if I go ten steps out of *The Meat* without telling the party, it's a conspiracy! Look, all that I've been up to is working on an early tip-off from downstairs on some stories that will keep my arse in the job. The City is a few square kilometres of land and there are 50 reporters sniffing around for a story in the same stretch...."

"Summer has done what summer does, Soli was not the only one feeling the strain," Hog told J Babu one day as he walked him to The Bus. "We're all going a little mad. A few months ago all that we talked about was the cell inside *The Meat*, then we banged on about The Party, then we forgot about The Party, later we named ourselves The Partisans, now it's about the Plebsicite because we realise that the Dongs have beaten us at it—and so all that we have been doing is thinking it will all add up, something will come out of it—that some will learn discipline, but we know some won't, some will ask where we are headed, some won't, but we will all learn to swim in some manner. But will we? For Mir, revolution used to mean not just a new set of people at the helm, not a change of managers but the birth, as it were, of a new society, of society thinking of itself in a way. A Society, Society, Society, not Country—For Mir that was the word and that was the dream and yet now even he doesn't put a stop to all the talk about The Flag and a Country. All that Lavni writes about in her letters these days is The Flag and how they are touring The Frontier with it."

A bit of news to gladden their hearts, however, got confirmed through unexpected quarters. Lately, Darius's servant seemed to have had a change of heart. Whenever he saw a reporter from *The Meat* on his way out, he stopped him or her with a sideways dip of his head and asked with a show of great solicitude, would they step in for some coffee and cake, —as if the treats were being paid out of his pocket—and as there was no harm in coffee and cake, most reporters would. The office, they found, was a chamber of wires—wires hung from the ceiling, they were coiled all over the walls, the team hung at least three around their ears. On seeing the reporters from *The Meat*, the staff would unplug the equipment and get up from behind their typewriters and make a move as if to rush to greet them and take them to the cafeteria. Standing in, as it were for their master, who was never in sight.

"The City's become hot again, they know The Falcon is coming," said Jallar one day to Soli under his breath and then broke into a loud laugh as if in continuation of a previous conversation. He had heard someone stop to stand behind his back.

"What's so funny, young Blone?"

It was Axe.

"Dogs are coupling with cats, I've just got a call from a stringer on the ground who said he has seen ten instances of this in The City. I bet you never had such a thing happen in your Frontier. Well, we have just pushed this story to both *The Meat* and *The Limpet*—what do you think I do all day listening to the goddam wires our beloved master has strung around my neck?"

Axe grunted. His eyes shone, his voice grew gruff with pride. "Limpet, Mimpet, you name it, our news goes everywhere. The day is coming when we are not going to have an office in this hole." The thought cheered him considerably and laying an avuncular arm on the reporter, he looked at his empty glass, and said with a wink: "Enjoy your coffee and cake and then write about the cats and dogs in the paper tomorrow."

But not everyone depends on a newspaper for news so opinions are made and unmade all the time. Despite Aristu's efforts to build a bias against The Partisans and make it seem that their politics was a local Frontier activity, many people in their offices and on their terraces, in the street and under the bridge, were, in fact, scanning The Frontier's sky for direction: when it moved, they would move. Meanwhile, they regaled themselves with stories about The Partisans, which in these fraught times were difficult to verify.

A favourite point of discussion was on their number. Some said they were five hundred, others swore their strength was at least fifty times that count and a nervous excitement ran down their skin to think what could happen if those many people should turn up in the middle of the city. Just thinking about it made their safe steady noses quiver, they could smell their coming, but they had nothing to worry, they blew their noses regularly and kept them clean. Besides, tomorrow was tomorrow and the marchers wouldn't make it here tomorrow so they munched their cobs of corn, shuffled their pack of cards, placed a mukka or two on their Kings and Queens and laughed into their Jacks while each of their discussions gave birth to others, just as the evening grows out of the morning without asking why.

"I met Mir once," said a man who believed The Partisans were five hundred. "At that time, The Partisans were not more than thirty or forty people—basically those laid out by the factories, you know, due to plain laziness or aggression. Then Mir went inside their homes and brought them out to stand outside their old places of work. Some even had hashish, but they came. Men and women. Because they came, their children came too. The kids who could not come because they were in school, by evening they were all there outside the factory gate. I realised then that forty people was not a small number. The factories had their goons ready by the gate swinging their truncheons but people who have not had food but have hashish in their stomachs, if you hit them, how will you hurt them? And that man, Mir, he was the catalyst. When that ragtag group had taken their beatings and given a few back they returned home with not a small measure of achievement. They sat around comparing their bruises, the bruises made them brag a bit, it's a good idea always to talk out the pain, and Mir, who was there all through, the first truncheon had come down on his back, yes, by the time he had got them all back home, this group became his group, and he had identified among them who could be leaders and then moved on."

Not all the stories were complimentary or even half-way complimentary. Some people talk because they feel it is their duty to expose other people, the day's meal sticks in their throat without it, at night they burn in bottomless pits of frustration, talk is their tablet.

"I met Mir once," said another. "Once a worker really got his knife into him and was jabbing it good and proper. He was saying that if you are free to tell us what you want, we are also free to think of you what we will. Wait there is more. He said, 'Mir, while you talk it is your duty to communicate to those in front of you, so that you are understood in the right manner.' And that's the great leader for you and the story of his loyal followers.... Look, let's not spoil our card-game, we are fine, we are safe, no one is marching anywhere, no one is leading and no one is following.... His horde, a few of those that remain, are basically telling him that we can go with you, but why should we, what are we getting.... How did Mir take it? If I had known you'd ask, I would have stood around to see."

Other people had other stories, and depending on their motivation, they told it well or didn't. Everyone has a story they like to tell but sometimes you really have to tell that one story over and over again for people to believe you. Now faith is something else. It is that unfinished painting, left incomplete, but always before us hanging from the wall. But is faith enough? These are cynical times and it demands constant proof not just of the consistency of consistent people but guarantees for all time. Thou must not fail! Thou must never fail! The Partisans had activated their cells in *The Meat* months ago and Danny, remember, had been part of them. How many from this group were now with him? How had the common faith in a new society fared in these months of turmoil since the cell had been set up in their paper and when one of them stood accused of murder? Because every murmur sits at the tip of a mountain of belief, let's go back into their story and ask The Partisans to give a sense of what has been happening all this while inside *The Meat*. If their commitment still holds good, well, we will march with them when they are here, otherwise scram. We are a bit tired of people dropping the words resistance and revolution to see how well they will do this season.

Some of The Partisans meanwhile decided they must be seen to do more. In all this while, with new people coming and going, the core in the library had remained intact but as the group had grown, The Partisans present in every editorial and non-editorial department of *The Meat* began to feel that the time had come not to be tucked away in some secret corridor or garret in waiting for coded knocks as if they were a bunch of adolescents trying to play snoop and solve some weekend mystery. The time had come and that time had really come now, they said, to hold their meetings in a public place inside *The Meat*, say the newsroom or the staff canteen, that would put them under the glare, give them the best visibility in order to be able to say as openly as possible that they were here, that they were not in hiding, and in a sizeable number right in the middle of the city. But you, of course, don't declare things like that outright and not in an individual manner, it's not a matter of your personal credentials and so no matter how many of the other members of the staff went around asking, no one knew what *The Meat*'s Partisans were going to do next. Because no one was telling them anything and why should they—we don't consult our neighbours, do we, about what we should put on our table for dinner—they spread the rumour that these Partisans were doing nothing. This outward pressure, of perception, began to create stress across all sections of the party cut off from The Frontier as they were, quite immediately after the death of Horo the priest due to the heavy surveillance mounted on the road leading to The Gate.

One group of party workers was of the opinion that they should start agitiating the cells, small though they may be, in other newspaper offices and actually look beyond newspaper offices over the issue of Danny and his incarceration, and then go beyond it, so as to delegitimise the Dongs and their institutions that they were setting up föllowing the manual of the Fairlanders, talking all the while about freedom and representation and liberating and representing nothing. If bad ideas were what the Dongs were after, they had only to ask them, they had a couple that would be sure to give them a bad name, and anyway the time was right, this group of Partisans said, for a show of strength and perhaps take over The Lambda. The City, they felt, was restive, the Black Quarters was ready, The Frontier was sure to be so, they had friends in The Malacca and they should go around The City and start identifying at least ten good people, among guards, masons, maids, teachers, lawyers, gardeners, blacksmiths, and if they were not ready then the cooks, scribes, clerks, acrobats, salesmen and the peons, people in different professions, well, just about anybody who was convinced and willing to make it a problem for the old regime to be renewed under a new name. When other people joined, it was understandable that they would bring their own songs or slogans even if they are not their songs and slogans and they would see if it was a problem or not to sing or shout them all at the same time. For this group then, the revolution clearly was nigh and it would, in a stroke, set right everything, the years of disrespect by their fathers, the lack of solidarity among workers, the attitude of bosses, the disparity in wages, breathe new life into their dessicated relationships, and keep it that way if not forever, then at least for a long, long time.

Sounds good. But.

The other group advised caution and said they should wait till they had word from Mir or Biran. You don't go to your leaders as if you are going to a restaurant and start demanding things and the problem, dear reader, was that by this time this group was so sodden with respect for Mir and Biran that they were incapable of asking them to hurry it or move it or anything. Once petition becomes the key to negotiation, all that you are able to get out of the mouth are appeals. So the decisions that could have been taken if not in the next one hour then at least the next day by those in *The Meat*, started getting delayed and the energy that comes when many people together push against a wall started getting sapped, while giving those standing close to wall, the impression that a lot was still happening. And certainly a lot of bad pamphlets, but a lot of good pamphlets were being written as well, poetry was being read or thought of and put down on paper or on poster, posters were being nailed on walls around The City and if the nails came off, they found that somebody or the other who may have liked the poetry or the poster had glued it back. When they ran out of ideas, they dipped their cycle tyres in paint and ran it around the borders of a poster to give it some kind of a design, for example, to depict chains; if they ran out of things to say for propaganda material and you can be sure they did not want to repeat themselves, they put down their own anxieties. Not everyone spoke well but paper was inexpensive and expressive and in this way these posters helped The Party appear and articulate its message. It also established a new medium of communication between The Party and The City. All fine, but what else? Aristu, for one, was turning out to be a curious problem. In the absence of any concrete threat, he had been the peak to conquer, the first wall to smash and for many months had saved the Partisans from staring, arms akimbo, at their own sores.

One morning, they arrived for work and saw a truck standing in front of their office. To their astonishment, they saw Aristu's lackeys grimly loading into it his black busts wrapped in transparent cellophane and setting them on the truck floor with the courtesy accorded to a bunch of bananas. When questioned, the man handling the operation had nothing to say or wouldn't say. By mid-afternoon, gossip had become event and Aristu, said his detractors, was as good as gone. But in the absence of a confirmation, the speculations began to swing between two extremes, from the possibility of another takeover to the necessity of a summer cleaning. Old buildings do need that much more care. The likelihood of the last was, however, quashed as no other furniture had moved. His office attendants shooed away all queries but they were less rude than usual. By the end of the day, those hated busts that presided like ghouls over every free space in *The Meat*, were gone. None could work that day, deadlines were missed and passed over in silence. Around six in the evening when senior editors lined up outside their cubicles and made their way to Aristu's room for the evening meeting , they found Aristu gelled, waiting and smiling, two of his front teeth filled with gold, tapping his pen from behind his table. The meeting was over in ten minutes flat. The editors, barring none, realised they had never been more in agreement with their proprietor and after these hours of uncertainty, Aristu was almost a beautiful sight. This incident bolstered the myth of Aristu: he no longer needed to strew his office with his logo. By removing his bust, he had, in fact, closed the distance between them and life in *The Meat.* From then on, the staff stayed in their seats like neat little trays of eggs inside a refrigerator.

The Partisans were caught unawares by this development. It was as if Aristu had wound the clock back and left them where they had started, that is, even before they had imagined themselves as a collective. They were not harassed or intimidated, they were simply left alone. Aristu, who seemed to know who they were and how many of them they were, began to nod at them at work but with one exception. J Babu was quietly removed from the editorial page and made editor at large, a shorthand for saying he was on his own and had to find work for himself in the newspaper. Some of the people, who had joined The Partisans out of some prurient desire to hold their hand over a flame to see what it felt like at least once in their life, began to leave. If you get no scars around which you can build own adventure story why stay?

Which is just as well.

But the call for action from within The Partisans did not let up. One day, a poster appeared about some of the senior comrades on the door of the canteen and the walls of the toilets. Binti, a young sub-editor who had been one of the first members of The Partisans in *The Meat*, had sat with her partner, Jiro, a worker in the artists' department to pen the text of a poster:

Boss, give it a toss
You told us to love
Now you are telling us to hide.

Not just these two, the first group had begun to say in their private conversations: 'It's as if we are still debating the problems of the Treaty of Versailles during the time of the Normandy landing.' It was no coincidence that around the time, one blistering afternoon, some cycles in the office car park were smashed and party literature laced with spit were found in some letter boxes. The culprits were known to all but they couldn't be thrown out, only Mir could decide that anyway, and it was difficult in the circumstances to decide whom to praise and whom to criticise but what it started was an introspection in what was being lost and what was being gained by both these stands and in this way a strike began inside the party against the party. J Babu, the acting chief of *The Meat*'s Partisans, treated this as a minor incident, for after all, there is work that has to be done on a daily basis within the party for it to grow and when something has been born, it has to be fed and bathed and massaged so that its legs are strong. It should not collapse under every freak wind.

"This is a party, not a twig," said J Babu to Hog, who was not in favour of disciplinary action against the rebels. "It will not do to appear weak. It's rank stupidity without any preparation or coordination to pour out into the streets. After you come out in the street what then? Stand? And what if The City goes about its own business and no one else joins us? It takes time to prepare miltants – our work among people in other institutions is not ripe for action. Will we get these people out on the street too just for a beating? What's this great hurry to be seen doing something? We have to wait for Mir. Let Jiro cool his heels for the moment."

If you minused Jiro, a new entrant, whom they had suspended from active duty—they had not taken action against Binti only because, well, it was still unclear why—there were ten more people waiting to join them to do Jiro's work and the party had work for all of them. But J Babu had been rattled by the protests, even though a week later he was singing a slightly different tune. "If people want a museum to show that man has been to the moon, what do you do? What can I do if people want to celebrate?" he said to Hog and the two men, one grey and the other growing old, passed the ball between themselves in a corridor near the press. This was still among one of the safest places to talk in the office, and was favoured by The Partisans to decide their time and place of meetings under the clap and clang of the printing machines, they, who knew what this new talk of transparency really added up to. Aristu's current receptiveness had in many ways meant a closing down and was harming them in other unforeseen ways. A few workers seeing them, reached out for a ladder and climbed down the machine tower and began to question them closely on the goings-on in the editorial under the 'new Aristu' that everyone was speaking of these days, and to fill them in about the mood in The City since Danny had been brought from The Frontier. 'What now?', was what everyone was asking.

"What they are not saying is, where is Mir and Lavni?" said

J Babu to Hog, and felt like kicking himself. Hog looked at him without expression, he had answered this question so many times that he no longer flinched when asked another time.

"Some questions have two sets of answers, J Babu, and I can't seem to get even one of them out," said Hog and the two men laughed to hide that each was apologising to the other. This brutal summer they would have few opportunities for mirth.

The days were growing heated from hour to hour when J Babu made another disastrous decision. The Partisans of *The Meat*, everyone would see, were a tight bunch but it was definitely not a closed group, so he thought there should be no harm in opening its doors a little wider so that the party could begin to function as an open organisation and everyone could know where to find them. Aristu, ironically, had made accessing them easier. There was no need any more for any sympathiser to hang around in the library pretending to read a book in fear of being watched when all that he or she was doing was to see which one of the Partisans would emerge from behind that closet and then catch him for a quick discussion on overground strategy and fine-tune who was taking what responsibility, sort out the drawbacks of an earlier or a present action or simply talk of the great revolts of history and then shape theirs drawing from those lessons. But without the pressure of discovery, the skills of subterfuge fell into disuse, and that room in the library with all its attendant functions of study and debate, tactics and coordination, work and practice, and all that happens from defending a movement under attack, began to be put aside in the favour of a space and a spirit that seemed to fit a club.

When Mir finally arrived with Biran at the end of the month, they found the party split into two, cadres who had decided by themselves that they would only do cultural work, and cadres for whom it was all political or nothing. It was just this sort of division that Mir had always wanted to steer clear of. Why shouldn't everyone do everything? The question of his hideout in The City was also worrying him. He decided to stay with Jiro. When asked why, he said after so much talk in the day, he needed to rest and the smell of paint that was sure to be in the home of an artist would help him sleep.

Jiro was beside himself with excitement on knowing that Mir was to be put up at his home. At *The Meat*, he talked of little else to his confidants and spent all his time thinking how he could start a conversation with Mir so that he could end his suspension. He could illustrate, he could paint, he knew how to typeset, and he had worked a year on the party paper and he wouldn't mind being put back on it, but he would insist that he be used only to do the artwork and not be pulled into making posters, he was through with making posters, but if Mir said so... But Mir said nothing. Each night he came up the stairs once the rest of the house had gone to sleep, to enter Jiro's room on the terrace, had a wash, said no to food, and lay down on the bed, one hand under the pillow to read a book. When this went on for a month and he had not been able to exchange a single word with Mir, let alone, bring about the topic of his suspension, Jiro decided not to wait any longer, and ask him straight out that night. When Jiro returned to his room that night, he found Mir sitting up on his bed waiting for him.

"What comrade, you took so long to come, will you not offer a fellow comrade some tea?"

Jiro hurriedly washed his hands, threw his shirt on a chair in delight and went into his kitchen to prepare two cups with great care. The room was as hot as an oven. He wished he could open the windows, but he had the strictest instructions from The Party not to keep them open till the time Mir stayed with him. He nevertheless pushed the window out a bit to let in some air. Not a bird must know he was in The City; a movement in the next terrace made him draw back the kitchen curtain. He filled the kettle with water but his stove chose just that minute to run out of gas. It took him a good while to get the second one running. He balanced the two cups on a plate and went into his room to find Mir asleep, and started laughing. The next morning, they talked. Mir asked him about his family so he told him about his family. His father was an electrician in one of Baba Lala's factories in The Frontier. Their home was beside a canal. Mir, he discovered, had grown up close by and that he had passed the place often on his way to school, till the time he had been in school. Jiro also told him of his flight to The City and the incident involving Baba Lala's overseer that had got him into trouble.

"He was always harassing us for extras. Someday he was out of blades for his razor, someday he wanted a young lamb, and other days.... No sooner did a girl and boy like each other, he had to have her. We put up a play during one of the factory's official functions when Lala was in the audience with a few episodes based loosely on the overseer's escapades and fixed him."

"Good. And then?"

"And then he fixed us. One of the girls took fright and got up on stage to say it was not about her! But he had his revenge. He got father moved to a heavy engineering unit in the factory, he held onto his job but lost his eyesight. I could not finish school."

"Neither did I," said Mir with a laugh, "but look how far you came."

This was the opening Jiro was looking for but when the moment came he could not bring himself to talk about the suspension. He saw sitting before him a man not too older than him and a face turned towards him that was interested in his life, the good that was in him and yet telling him that he was looking out for him, that his work was of worth and not just telling him but giving it respect, that he felt that he had to be the best that he could be. For this man, he thought, I am ready to give my life, what he wants me to do, I will do, what he is doing, it will lead to good, and tomorrow, which only the wise have seen, will be better for all of us.

"I haven't seen tomorrow my friend," said Mir, "but I can say with some degree of confidence that a few things will happen, and for that the spirit must be buoyant. Revolution in thought is as important as revolution itself. "

When they met again that night, Jiro had another question for Mir. "Do you think I will last? Will I remain with the party or not?"

"Before you came to us think about how you felt and how you feel now. If there is a difference, you will have answered your question. Now tell me what else is happening in The City?

What is this story with the rats and The Dongs saying that we have brought them into The City? J Babu and I talked and he said you are the best person to take them on. Keep the message light in the paster but take their pants down. Danny is in jail otherwise he would have contributed. We would have had his poems and your art. Now let's see what you can do."

Jiro sat working at his table with his box of paints that night.The next few weeks, he held time in shackles and squeezed out night from day, the day from night. The splits in the party, which were arrested with the arrival of Mir and threatened to break open into a new crisis every now and then only to be resolved at his intervention, did not touch him. In the morning, he earned his keep. At night, he sketched. No camp could claim any more that they 'had'. Jiro—the boy with whom Mir stayed. When asked which group was closer to Mir, he knew what to say. To those who were spreading the rumour about Mir's diffidence to action, and the rascals perhaps got that in their dreams, he laughed openly in their faces. Mir, he said, was neither excited nor frustrated about the possibility of the revolution but he had seen him agonising about a few things—that it should not be degraded and that it must come from the most genuine, the most joyous, the most humane desires of a hopeful people. And as Jiro explained Mir, unknown to himself, he grew in confidence. As for the poster—there it stood on the terrace, the sun drying the paint, the writing gloriously bold as in love's first love-note. What would Mir say? But he didn't return that night.

17

The Walk

Many things happen at night that are best not spoken of in the polite hours of day. Paris stole Helen. Macbeth killed Duncan. His lady killed sleep and went sniffing her hands thereafter. When we pick up things like these we go running after light forgetting that the day first rises by the sewers; its light still touched by night is first sighted on its waters slipping as it does through the sewer grates. All these divisions—night and day, lunch and dinner, six o'clock or nine o'clock—actually arrive without intention, if we were not to stir from the bed or were to die today, they would still swing by on a pendulum, be present, and then get by without us. There is, however, only one time, the time that we are all waiting for, that daily howls for us down the shaft of an abandoned mine telling us we have a future if only we are ready to hazard hanging from the tails of bats. Hope and courage can be drawn on at any time. For that, the day doesn't arrive early enough and you can't give birth to them at night.

Two young men are walking on the street. Seen from the heights of buildings or from the widths of streets, they can be measured against nothing at all, they leave no shadow and may leave no trace when they bend off to some other street, and even if you like their faces you can't ask them where they are headed. When people hide what they are thinking, they are unlikely to tell you where they are going.

Jallar is walking with Soli, rather Soli is walking and Jallar is walking around him, coaxing him to go somewhere. Jallar's request is at times taking the shape of a jab but Soli is hanging on to his reluctance.

"It's getting late. You go. I have a father."

"And I don't?

"Look here, I don't want to go anywhere and feel lost or sit with my mouth locked."

"I'm precisely asking you to drop the lock. And besides we are not going there to make friends. We'll just smoke a bit and look around. You don't understand it's important in my profession."

"I understand less and less of what you are doing. Is The Thump a news agency or a listening post?"

"What's the harm if it's a bit of both? Did it harm you to be the first to tell the party that the Falcon, the Great Mir, was coming? I don't remember you complaining about that."

A nerve twitched at the back of Soli's head and he turned to look at Jallar but he was no more at his side. He had crossed the street. The signal turned to red, a stream of cars and near-empty buses from the other side rushed in to fill the space, some slowed down to let a beggar pass. The beggar's metal bowl tied to a tail of cloth hanging from his waist, grazed the ground and then fell out and a blast of car horns barked into the square like dogs. Soli saw Jallar pull up the man and his bowl to the pavement. For a few seconds it seemed, the man and his benefactor were unwilling to let the other go, but that time was brief. What Jallar had to offer, he had.

The signal changed and Soli crossed over. Jallar's eyes still shone with the feeling of condescension with which he had matched the beggar's gratitude, but to show that kindness was an everyday act for him, he searched for a subject that would let him talk of generalities while keeping the recent incident at its centre. The man in the rags meanwhile was sitting on one corner of the sidewalk and giving him slow grins.

"These guys are champs, Soli. Don't be fooled by their slow gait and the impression that they will collapse under the indifference of the world. They have a sixth sense about when the lights will change and that is when they begin to cross the street so that they can fall at somebody's feet. How he stares towards us—I think I'm going to give him some money so that he can look elsewhere."

And saying this he was gone in a flash and was throwing

the man some coins before Soli could stop him. The traffic was unusually heavy on this road that night, all the offices on this road would have shut hours ago, and he wondered if they had crossed over to some other street which he had not noticed while talking.

"If you are feeling unwell, we can call it a night," said Jallar who was now staring straight at him, his thin face lined with stress. It was this unspoken pressure of spending time together Soli found most troubling and it brought him time and time again to keep standing by his side while feeling no connection with him at all. With Hog or J Babu there were long connections of work and of politics, that despite periods of intense personal frustration that comes from holding different view-points on their common work, brought them back to the same place day after day to fight, to argue, to accommodate, to negotiate. With Jallar what did he have? And yet the little horror had grown dear to him like a brother. Somehow Soli wanted to believe this boy mattered and not just as a source of information for The Partisans.

"No, let's go. I suddenly want to. Note the spring in my steps."

"Don't humour me, I can smell your disapproval. But to lighten the air let me tell you a story about these chaps. But first I need to wet my throat."

So they walked ahead but the eateries were all closed. Sounds of snoring rose in waves from behind closed doors. They climbed the stairs of a bar they frequented—it was their only hope. A boy appeared from behind the door with a half-open eye to the sound of the banging and asked them if they wanted their legs broken. But he had not accounted for Jallan who had miraculously fished out a horn from his pocket was blowing it with some detachment as if it was not he but the instrument that was directing an invisible orchestra; with his other hand he was opening his zip. Surely he was not going to pee! The dull pain picked up at the back of Soli's head so he rested his head against the wall as he watched the waiter blanch and then get down to negotiate. The matter seemed resolved in a while. As the boy went in and came out with a bottle and a packet of chips, Jallar threw a triumphant look down at him so Soli started to climb up the stairs. He had got the boy to let them come in after all! He wouldn't mind resting his legs, the long walk in the humid night—perhaps he shouldn't have left his bike at the parking lot—was acting on an old leg injury. They could stop a while, while he pressed his leg in the restaurant; he would scold Jallar for his high-handedness in getting the restaurant re-opened later. But Jallar stopped him.

"You wait. I'm coming down."

"What happened? I thought the matter was sealed. You—you didn't scare him? He scared you?"

"Go on laugh. But I've wrangled a bottle, haven't I? And we get to sit on the stairs."

"That's one hell of a deal. Can I get a glass while you get started on the story otherwise I'm going to doze off."

But Jallar had other things on his mind. He said he was saving it for the party. The place they were going to was swell, he said. He busied himself in opening the bottle and munching the chips. Soli had asked for a peg and he got one too. Just after three pegs, Jallar was as high as a kite and clapping his palm over the mouth of the bottle, he changed his mind again and got ready with his beggars' tale.

"What if after the party we have no time?"

That, agreed Soli, could be the case.

"It was the day we were leaving The Frontier. It was windy, specks of dust clotted our eyes. As we got up on The Bus, it began to rain. We sat where we could, we didn't get seats together. I wrapped a blanket around myself and must have dozed off. I woke up after a while to the sensation of sharp little nips to my toes. Before I could look down, my neighbour, a scruffy old man, whom ordinarily I might not have paid attention to but for the fact that he was carrying an inordinately large sack with strange bulges, raised himself like a mountain, and erected a podium of sorts in the centre of the bus by piling up somebody or the other's suitcases. I remember that as we were settling down, my leg must have landed on his luggage and a pitiful mewling was heard. When I expressed curiosity about its contents, that rascal looked at me straight in the eye and said "Cabbages." Cabbages indeed! Well, I was not the only one. Around the time I was being attacked from the toes, other passengers were not spared, so when the man stood on his podium, he had everyone's attention. "Sons of pigs!" "Children of dogs!" he growled at us, as at least ten little piglets and pups began to emerge from under the seats of the bus and began to line-up next to him. As you may guess, the driver and the conductor were in cahoots with him. There was even some petting going on there—"Come boy heel," they were saying to his four-legged squadron and tickling their ears. The man was in his elements. His bag was next to him. He put one hand inside and half the bus leaned over to see which other creature would emerge from its depths. What came up with his hand was a bottle. Make that plural. Bottles—scores of them—all filled with some dark liquid, some even congealed, they were that old. The guy had it all worked out. He knew he had a captive audience and so he delivered his final pitch with a pup and a piglet hanging from either crook of his arm: "Sons of pigs, children of dogs, if these were to Bite, here's the Medicine and by God, this is the Bottle!"

"How many did he manage to sell?"

"I had some loose change in my pocket—I bought one too..." said Jallar and in the dim staircase illuminated by a single naked bulb, his teeth, the only feature of his face now visible to Soli, they gleamed. "I was glad to help," he continued. "No harm in helping people. Not everybody you know has the time to think about what's going wrong with their lives and fix it themselves. You Partisans don't understand this. People don't want to fight. They want to be helped."

"That may be true of people you know," answered Soli unable to resist an attempt to get a rise out of Jallar. "To be tired, Jallar, is not the same as giving up. And we all grow tired at some point or the other don't we?"

"Why are you doing all this? Why do you want to foment trouble?" said Jallar and Soli startled at the edge the boy's voice could sometimes take, wondered what feelings of anger and humiliation must a man be chewing all day sitting inside that garrett for him to turn against a friend.

"What will you get by denying The Dongs when everybody wants them?"

"Who is everybody? Just because they look like us and the Fairlanders don't, doesn't mean that The Lambda under them will be any different with them in charge."

"So any other party other than The Partisans is a problem. And if The Partisans come all the problems will be over, Soli?"

"I'd really be curious in how you understand the, as you call it, Our Coming. No passive quick-fix is going to happen from our end. There is not one man or woman among us who knows the best way to do the dream. But, say, I'll begin by asking a question, and you could ask yours. In the process, you could shout and we could fight, but in the end we'll sight the road, figure out how we should behave on it, what we should carry with us and when we should begin to walk down it. So to answer your question, let us be sure this road will not be rolled down from the heavens, it may take us time to find it, adopt it, and that all this will be a struggle, but in the heat of the struggle, who knows we may be close to some answers."

"How is it to be done?"

"The first thing we are saying as a means of going down that road is, let us reorganise work, the way we work and the distribution of work. Work will ensure equal opportunities to be in power, which means equal opportunities to be involved in the dynamics and processes of social power, which means a democratic deciding of hours of work, of study, of leisure, the fixing of wages, fixing of work-specific bodies who will represent us, watching over the work of representatives, letting them do their work, then recalling them if needed, so that others can take their place. All this will not happen passively and then pause. It will happen over and over again with debate, with arguments, year after year. I must say many young people are excited to be involved with us to do this."

"But can you guys dance well?" asked Jallar getting up rubbing his back. For him, clearly, the conversation was over. "I am very scared of people who say they can't dance. They usually don't like people who can. Come now we're getting late for the party, give me a hand otherwise I just might fall."

Soli steadied him by the elbow and the two came down the stairs and stood on the street, beside the closed shutters of a shop. Its owner, lying on a mattress on the pavement, sold them a few cigarettes at 10 mukka more than what he was selling in the evening.

Jallar returned grinning: "What did I say about these chaps?" He drew out a cigarette and asked Soli for his lighter. But Soli had left it on his desk in the office so the two made another trip to the shopkeeper for a matchbox. It was only with the fourth matchstick, that Jallar was able to light the cigarette. There was a simple explanation: he was high, his hands were unsteady, but he continued to spew acid.

"The bastards sit on their matchboxes I'm telling you so that they are spoilt and you are forced to buy another one....but hey, to return to where we were, we were standing before a very cheerless future you are painting. Will it not be better that, just as an example, I or anyone for that matter, can now aspire to make policies that will govern the Lambda after we are free?"

"Through elections you won't. If a poor man's vote has the same value as a rich man or a middle-class man, in the balance of power the poor man will always be at a lower position than both of you. With money, the rich can lobby with the government of the day to give them privileges because with their money they can bail out or support the government. Their wealth will always be used against both your interests – unless, of course, you collaborate in the spread of his wealth because you would like some of it as well. The rich man's wealth cannot be accumulated if everybody has the same as him. It depends on you having less than him."

"All worked out I see! Well, when I need all this broken further into how more miserable my life is, or can be, I'll know where to turn. And who better than a friend to teach me how to take it philosophically?"

Out on the street, the time seemed not to want to reveal the hour. If this was night, it was standing on its head, losing all its warm, wet expectations one by one in a labile drip. Would it rain? The sky was an impenetrable slate, a colour, that young children sometimes draw into their eyes to keep their souls out of the grasp of determined adults. A turning away, a 'I won't say', as opposed to a 'I don't know'—Jallar sometimes behaved like that with him. And as he was jumpy tonight, so to any question of his, he was not going to get any answer, even if it was as straight as asking where they were headed. He should have looked up at the clock when they passed the post office but at that time, his eye had been caught by the crown of the building where perched on a scaffold now empty of workers, an owl was just beginning to stretch its wings and take off. Soli shook his wrist but the hand of his watch would not move, he must have banged it while sitting on the stairs. It had stopped at a quarter past three. Now, the sky looked an hour older, its greys matting themselves round and round the still blue moon, catching the rising vapours of the first day-dreams of a working day. On the glass facades of the houses, he thought he caught the reflection of the bird circling, stopping itself in half-flight as if it was making up its mind and he involuntarily ducked to escape the shadow of its wing.

A thin rain had begun to fall on The City. Soli looked around for Jallar so that they could stop and take shelter in the porch of some building but the boy was almost on a run—and he was leaking along the way. It was the untimely liqor and he had drunk a great deal of it, murmured Soli.

"When I talk, he'll let me go on and on. When he drinks, he'll control the bottle, he won't drink with me."

But the road was turning and Jallar was running and the rain was now falling on the skin like pebbles. From ten paces ahead, Jallar was shouting and waving at Soli to hurry but as the rain began to fill his mouth, no words came out. Soli found himself panting, unable to keep up. He was skidding on the rain-licked street. Once or twice, he slowed down to turn back. The road was empty but he thought he heard the low wheeze of a tyre about to go flat. In a few minutes, they would be running into Garrison Street whose outlines were now emerging like an artist's impression through the darkness. Rows of buildings stood like biscuits behind an unbroken border of gates. Some half-hearted hand had imposed this design on each of the buildings and then forgotten to flatten its tops; its domes were the perch of ageing eagles. The Jail and the Officers' Hall, purgatory and power, sat like conjoined twins on an elevation in the interior of the compound. Only the turrets of the mint shone as they have for thousands of years. Which of the last secret meetings were now being held there to decide the quantities of nickel and magnesium to be melted for the good-conduct medals to be distributed on the eve of Plebiscite among the dwindling loyal pack? And here he was now passing them by and had almost caught up with Jallar, and just about to stretch his hand to tap his shoulder, when Jallar turned back and stopped him with a look.

He put his palm up and gestured at him to rest a while against a lamp-post. Swiftly crossing the road, Soli saw him approach one of the sentries guarding the side gates of the vast compounds of the government offices, then point in his direction. So the venue for the party was one of the Fairlander offices was it—no wonder Jallar had been evasive—and as it looked, he didn't even have an invite. It was a pathetic situation and he didn't know whether he should be beating up Jallar for this or laughing with him. To be waiting around the Fairlander offices for entry to a party! If J Babu or Hog got wind of this, his excuse, that he didn't know, wouldn't wash. It was now too late to go back but given his early morning assignment, Soli had a few things going on in his mind. He would hang around just long enough to see the guest-list, it would be good to know who the Fairlanders could still count as friends. He could also grab a phone inside any one of the offices close to the party venue to pass on his assignment to a colleague who owed him a favour. Jallar and the guard, meanwhile he saw, were still huddled at the side of the gate.

From the other side of the road, even from that distance, he could make out that tempers were fraying and sooner than later one of them was going to strike the first blow. But he seemed to have judged the situation wrong. Soli saw Jallar fish out a card from his pocket and hand it over to the official—an ID from The Thump was hardly going to impress a vigilance officer of a high-security government zone. Surely Jallar should know better than that! But it was, surprisingly enough, leading to some discussion so much so that a car-horn had to break them up. An officer of the Fairlanders leaned out of his vehicle and wagged a finger at the sentry. The iron gate screeched open and the headlights of the car shone a little unnecessarily on the newly laid bituminous road. Night was finally passing and the day was imminent with all its graces. A gardener was snipping off the spent flowers in the garden by the gate. A posse of young Murkys in white sun shirts and their trademark glasses were running the field. The city's best bakers come to supply bread to all the officers' pantries, suddenly found themselves in their path, and were trying their best to dodge them. Standing under the streetlight, Soli watched the car leave the compound and disappear into a residential enclave outside the gate. The Bus, meanwhile, rising on the crest of the road was coming down in his direction.

Out of habit, he checked his watch. It had begun to tick but the time was still wrong. It showed four past five, it was probably an hour more.

Driver Gorora, an old acquaintance, stopped The Bus right before him. A few workers returning home to The Frontier raised their hand from inside it in a sullen wave. Soli sidestepped their questioning glance by asking them about Mir and Biran. They replied with a question of their own.

"What am I doing on Garrison Street? I am going in," Soli replied quickly to cover his embarrassment but the expression on their faces told him he had just confirmed their worst suspicions.

"Another rotten apple! I'm through with all this, I'm not taking this any more, Gorora you tell him," said one worker and buried his face inside a paper, refusing to look at him any further. Soli knew this face. Red as the bricks he had probably just basted, this was Pogosh, an uncle of Kanhu, and as hotheaded. He, alongwith around fifty workers, were returning from building a new fountain on Baba Lala's grounds whose waters bubbling down a height of twenty feet had to empty itself without spilling a single drop in a gigantic bowl at its base. It was enough to put them in a bad mood and who could blame them?

Gorora took out a paper from the overhead box and gave it to Soli to read. With a surprise he saw that it was not *The Will*. *The Will*—the party's old paper that Mir, Biran and Hog had matched their wits to decide what to put on its pages, the paper for which Danny was serving time inside, the paper through which workers from The City and The Frontier had first spoken to each other—where was it now? In all their talk of the way forward, they had had learnt to wade in crises after crises, but they had buried something they had made and was now building another paper with the old bricks. Soli couldn't remember the last time Hog had brought it up in all their discussions at *The Meat*. In all the faces that were now looking at him or were looking away from down The Bus, Soli saw faces that was like the face of the sailor who has been on many seas and has just seen the wave which will sink him.

"The Will stopped coming on time and one day it stopped. We had grown used to one paper and now we will grow used to this one," said another worker darting a quick look at Pogosh who was sitting on the same line as him.

"Fine paper it is, I say!" growled Pogosh looking all around. "Fine name too, I told Kanhu when he came to show me the paper. 'I'm calling it *The Hadi*,' he says to me, Hadi–'The one who will show the way'. 'Fine boy', I said to him, 'you call it that'. We workers have been crowding under a tunnel waiting for ages for somebody to throw a light down at us and say 'Come up, this is the day when we are all going to take it back.' And then somebody does come, but he asks: 'Can you stay put a little while longer, we'll call you when we've fixed everything?' So I told my boy, you tell us where you want us and we'll be there with our hands and feet, that's all we got. I am sick and I'm growing old waiting for something to happen. Aren't you? I, for one, would like to know where all this talk of the revolution is headed—some days Mir says it means this, then Biran opens his eyes like a sage and says, 'no, no, when Mir says this, he means that.' The meaning of all great ideas like bread and water should remain the same always—right or wrong?"

There were protestations from The Partisans' loyal followers, some furious words did fly. You couldn't filibuster everybody and certainly not a fellow worker though you could try just as you cannot turn the direction of an ear of wheat if it wants to sway in the wind. A mason, who had been part of The Partisans' first attack on The Malacca, shouted from the back of the bus, and lit into Pogosh. "You stop your grandstanding right now, you hear? Listen all of you, it was all planned from what I know," he said pulling out an old copy of The Will he was carrying in his pocket and throwing it on an empty seat. "Kanhu took on the duty to distribute The Will and then stopped doing it one day because how else was his rag to survive—who would want it, who would read it? Then he gets into a room, locks its door and comes out saying this was a meeting. Well, that meeting was attended by five. The average age of the people attending it was ten. This is not courage, this is trying to have your own group, and I have the strongest objection to a revolution led by children whose hands are dirty!"

Soli shut his ears to the tattle. He knew Mir and Biran and he also knew Kanhu. What he was surprised by was *The Hadi*'s reach—even Gorora, who had grown to be a party sympathizer but was not really a Partisan—was picking up *The Hadi*. He looked through the column of contents and turned to its first page. The newsprint he suddenly realized was of a better quality than their old paper and its printline said it had been rolled out from a different press than used by *The Will*. Their earlier press had been financed by a scrap merchant whose brother was a member of the party. This one, however, had a City address. He would fix a meeting with the proprietor—there was no harm in having the full information about the kind of people associating themselves with The Partisans or any of its wings. He saw that *The Hadi* had also kept the old sections of *The Will* but had introduced a few new sections like Letters to the Party in which the rank and file could write openly about any party decision and call for a debate and knowing Kanhu, he had a fair idea what the thrust of those first debates were going to be. Looking up, he saw Gorora sitting in between Pogosh and the mason, trying to effect some sort of rapprochement between the two. It was difficult to follow the conversation while standing on the road but from what Soli could gather, the driver had managed to make them see the benefits of returning to their seats so that they could resume the journey. The guards at The Gates would obstruct the path if they arrived beyond the hour fixed for the passage of The Bus into The Frontier and who among them didn't want to get home? Returning to his seat, Gorora busied himself in cleaning his space, slapping up a dust storm with his whacks to the wheel. He was upto something or perhaps he was just trying to make himself comfortable for the long run ahead. His first hunch proved right. He motioned Soli to move nearer to the window and slipped out the new paper to him as he started the engine.

"The Fairlanders want to meet The Partisans," said Gorora dipping his voice. "Mir is sending Lavni. I see trouble ahead."

18

A Day in March

As The Bus disappeared down the road, Soli found himself holding onto a copy of *The Hadi*. He saw Jallar grab a paper from the outstretched hand of a paper-boy riding by on his cycle and wave it at him. The sun was up, a crow flew down a tree and skipped near his feet, but it felt as if they were still part of Jallar's plans of the night. But Soli was unable to move. He needed to sit down, the pain in his legs was shooting but he had one more thing to do before he crossed to the other side of the road. Sitting down on the kerb of the road, he was stuffing the paper inside his shirt when Jallar came running, his thin brown hair all over his eyes.

"What was that in your hand?"

"A paper I had forgotten to read—but you were very long..."

"Just chatting up the guard now hurry, hurry, before we lose our advantage. I played a trick on him and now he will let us in."

"What did you say?"

"Simply narrowed my eyes like this and said: 'What is your name? Mirish he says. 'Yes, Mirish isn't it?' I say as if I had known it all along. 'Mirish, I've a complaint against you.' The man is taken aback but I can smell the fear on him, he thinks I'm someone important but he can't quite place me. 'How is it possible I've just joined today,' he actually splutters and finally faints—had to take him to the first-aid centre closest to the gate he was guarding. Why else did you think I was taking so long to come out? Swear to God, Soli—that's how it was! Anyway, we're going to be having a lot of fun now—I've called up both our offices to say we died last night and are taking the day off, don't you scowl."

And with one hand pulling at Soli's elbow, he was in a split second back to being the old Jallar in whom god had poured the play of twenty children and the secrets of twenty more.

The gates to the Fairlander compound opened easily this time. This time, the guard struck a salute and clippety-clopped his feet but they could feel his eye on their back. In front of them was a cobblestoned path. Ending in a long meeting of trees at a T, its twin arms might lead them down other paths, but even from the distance it looked as if this road had run its course, some roads are built like that from the start, from the time the first layer of gravel is laid to its last bed of asphalt, its mind is made that it should lead nowhere. A man or a woman can, of course, get off at any point and say this is not for me, or I made a mistake, I will now go elsewhere or go home. There's still another choice , that of walking on this road, not to be getting off, not to be afraid of its outcome no matter what, staying the course as the saying goes, and so they did.

Sand-coloured buildings of various heights and purposes began to appear beyond the tree-line. But for a seat of government, it was beginning its work inordinately late, there was no one about in the part of the compound where they were. No office boy or attendant passed their way to ferry messages on the run in between the various offices. No citizen crossed their path on the way to any of the government departments to push some petition through the nearest gate. No gardener, it seemed, had trimmed the grass in this area in years. He hadn't seen Jallar ask anyone for directions, he just hoped they were going the right way. The party was, of course, a fib that much was very clear to him now but you never knew with the boy. Perhaps he had an early morning appointment with the Fairlanders and perhaps he hadn't wanted to go in alone—who could blame him, but wouldn't it have been simpler to tell him that? Would he have refused if it had been put to him quite like that? He tried to call out to Jallar and rib him but Jallar, his face red from the exertion, was striding resolutely ahead, the soles of his feet barely touching the ground.

In a little while, they were at the head of the T point. Jallar turned left to take a path that seemed to have been raked out by force. They trampled over the heads of shrubs clinging on to its sides. Stones, big and small, made the walking difficult, the small pointed ones entered their shoes and lay there like a sixth toe. Soli asked Jallar to slow down as he sat on the side of the dirt track to tighten the buckle of his shoe, and then froze. Between one of the little hillocks of scooped up soil piled all along the road, a mongoose was biting off the head of a bird that had probably landed on a pile nearby looking for a worm that had itself crawled out of a hole—it had so nearly been a fine morning under the March sun. The grass, green and rustling, though overgrown, was back. In the sky, the dark clouds of last night suppressed by an ascending sun. Even look at the two of them! Here they were, playing truant from work, bumming on a broken-down road among bushes and brambles with no other aim but to join a party, and a party for what, a party that some topdogs were holding for other topdogs, the last pulsations of a string of celebrations that the empire was planning for a week, to stage its final goodbyes. Well, well, as that's what they had come here for, they should move on. But Jallar was transfixed by the roadside murder. The bird was living out the final moments of its life in jerks, its eyes closed as if it was telling itself that this was a dream—there had been no killing, it was not bleeding, it was flying, for the last time, dear god, let me spread my wings.

"Look Soli. Who would have thought about a sparrow fighting back? But it's fighting. Wait! Do look! Sometimes life can be snatched from death with just a change of argument...."

Walking on at a brisker pace, they reached a clearing. There were signs that sometime ago, here, there had been a wood. It looked as if they still had some use for it. Devoid of a single standing tree, all around were ochres and browns of opened up bark, the smell of leaves burnt in haste. There were signs of men and women at work, their tools left behind, of work being done in spite, or of men and women being made to hurry. Here and there were trees that had been brutally cut down or cut open or had been left to fall on the arms of another tree, breaking its spine. The heads of sprouts growing at the base of a giant oak had been pulled off, the little Jiji flowers that grow on the floors of woods didn't stand a chance. Someone had tried bending the branch of a tree and then had changed his mind only so as to slash it with a hand saw. But this tree would live, even if broken. A few axes lay on the stumps; wood cut in rectangles lay around, the frame of doors. Perhaps.

"We are now close to the jail," said Jallar who had come to stand next to him. "You can see this area from its left wall. Soli, look."

The grey façade of the building had been visible all this while but he sometimes failed to see what was right in front of him. His attention having been drawn to it, Soli now found he could not tear his eyes away. Built like the funnel of a ship, the unblinking lights behind each of the grilles of the cell windows, all of a sudden held him in a pincer and his throat choked as if filled with the smoke of all the fires that had started at sea. He opened his mouth to take in air, but was unable to breathe.

"It's giving me the creeps," he finally said when his breathing returned to normal. "You know Jallar, I am attending this party for two minutes and then I'm out—are you sure we need to go, we are very late aren't we? See, there's this sense I'm getting, don't ask me from where, but there's some funny business here. Did you see the wood cut in tiny rectangles in the clearing? They were too small to be the frame for a door, too small for a window, a man can barely squeeze his head through it."

"We are not late. This party will go on for a week. They are letting the staff relax a bit before they disperse all over The Lambda to conduct the Plebiscite and also, I guess, they wanted all the important people on all sides to meet on a common platform without letting anyone forget, and certainly why should they not remember it, that it was the Fairlanders that had set it up. Baba Lala is coming from what I hear. But if you want to go, go," said Jallar, stubbing out a few caterpillars that were crawling out from a mass of dead leaves on the ground, his face ashen.

"I was asking what these wood cuts are for, who visits the wood—you didn't answer that. I don't see anyone around. Who has cut the wood down?"

"What are you getting so agitated about? A jail has all sorts of people inside—could be interesting for you to meet. Some of them will be performing at the party; you could ask them what they use this place for. Can't be fun inside. It's not big. The air is stale, the light in their cells come from a bulb that's on all day. Sometimes the Murkys, who guard them, might let them play or exercise in a different area, bring a woman, without disturbing others in the cell. They might have been sent here to cut wood. But where are the trees? In a wood even as empty as this one, there's always a tree to cut, weeds to remove so that some tree or the other, which you want to grow, which is of use to you, can grow. Does your leg still hurt? We are nearly there. The hall is just a few steps away."

"I can barely stand up. Alright, you want to go, so I'll go, though I'm warning you—you'll have to attend to me at the party," said Soli, still casting around for a reason to leave. But it was as if he was addressing his words to the wind. Jallar had decided not to pay any heed. They were by now both talking without any pretence of communication, something had gone wrong, something had gone wrong from the start, thought Soli. In a jail, there are all sorts of problems, Jallar had started to say, but he hadn't asked him about that. He let it pass. But perhaps the problem was his, the pain in his leg was now driving him crazy and he was almost looking forward to the party so that he could rest his leg. His eyes were also feeling blurry, he was finding it difficult to focus and there was a pain in his jaw. But Jallar wasn't still ready to let go.

"Sometimes the fight is about work. Oh they want to work in jail alright. Working is better than staring at the wall, eh? This one here has very thick walls I'm told."

Given a choice, he rather liked staring at the wall, said Soli. It was an odd sort of point to quibble in the middle of nowhere even though nowhere is usually the place between widely separated walls, and a good place as any to make a point, and true, the surroundings did keep the words flowing as if without it, something terrifying would take its place and then they would have to look at it, name it, and then accept it, better to turn their attention to the twin buildings, now clearly visible. They were rising over the clearing side by side like brother knights guarding their lonely corner against all sorts of uncertain conditions such as the two-legged creatures just coming towards them.

The officers' hall was not distinguished by any unique feature, its entrance was fronted by a wooden door as was the jail's. Both were half-open, Soli drew Jallar's attention to it. He shrugged. There was no point of contact between the two, there couldn't be, he said. A narrow removable passageway, much like a gangplank, however, did connect the two buildings roughly in the middle but it may have been put in there later. The corridor was, anyway, not permanent. It was to be lowered or pulled up at the officers' will and would be useful for surprise checks, one never knows what these people do all day in their cells, said Jallar. For even when they are doing nothing, they were doing or planning something harmful to their way of life and that could not be allowed till the time they controlled the gangplank, the road to The Frontier, The Bus, The Plebsicite, heck, with so much to do, when were they going to live their life? Soli looked at Jallar in surprise, he didn't realise that he was turning into an advocate for the Fairlanders, many things would change if he had, things he could or would say to him, for instance. Looking up, they saw a man standing there—who could that be? A worker come to clean the facades? An officer hoping his ear would pick up the fledgling conspiracies being hatched from inside the adjoining wall? Who knows. Who knows, if these curious structures would still stand in a new regime, said Jallar. He proposed they go around it and see what was on the other side. They did. Other than heaps of rubbish and a mole that slunk away into the bushes at their approach, it was an unremarkable diversion. So they decided to go back the way they came.

"Don't stray too close to the wall, those characters don't miss a thing. They'll see someone under their windows and before you know it there is piss on your head streaming all the way down to your stomach. Anyway, as I was saying, staring at the wall is no fun, Soli, ask anyone who is locked inside a jail. From what I hear, the groan of a saw in the wood we just crossed has even pushed people inside to lose their bearings, commit suicide inside this jail. When you sit and stare hour after hour, and if you are inside year after year, and all that you do is sit looking at the wall, that's no leisure, it is work and it is hell."

"That goes for anything a man is forced to do. Even if you are forced to sing for seven hours, you are in jail and you are at work. If your house has a time for getting up, a time to eat, a time to shit, a time to read, a time to make love, an appointed time for each and everything—bring it down for then it's a jail. But look how we are still carrying on, Jallar. Are we never going in?" he asked looking up. The man was still up there in the middle as if he had been pasted to the plank. Something in the way he stood reminded Soli of someone—could it be Danny? But the vision disintegrated against the flickering light, the sun still perverse, would not show its face. On earth, everything was made ambiguous, and the fears and obsessions of his life began to form connections and demand that they be acknowledged as one. Steady, Soli, steady, he told himself, now was not the time to go under but he was losing it, his thoughts speaking in half-sentences and failing to attain their full meaning. From the corner of an eye, he saw Biran hanging Lavni from a nearby tree; Jaba agreeing to sing; and the man on the plank raising his hand at him—now the last was possible, he muttered, overcome by a violent shudder, the others must surely be phantoms of his mind. "You have had too much to drink", said Jallar laughing. No, he had not seen any man standing on the skywalk, let alone see him wave.

"We should go in," he tried for the last time, weak with pain.

"What's the hurry? Will you just listen to that music coming from the officers' hall? It does make me wish I could play something!"

They had now come to stand at the foot of the stairs leading to both the buildings. A Murky stood guard at both doors, which earlier ajar, now had their mouths open. Soli and Jallar began to climb up from the other end near the jail, to wait their turn. "It will be less crowded, you won't get pushed", said Jallar. "There, you can lean on me", he told Soli, "don't be embarrassed, it's dark, no one will glance at us." And no one did. Something wet trickled down Soli's chin, but the circus in front of him gave him no time to think of himself. The Lambda's nobility, family in tow, were joined like termites outside the officers' door. What are they waiting for, why won't they let us in, rang an uncouth shout from somewhere and everyone at the top of the line heaved a sigh of relief that there was still some difference between *us* and *them*, now with the same tailors and clubs notwithstanding. A wave of sulphur billowing out from the neighbouring entrance made those at the bottom of the line the first to get the full blast of the fumes and the queue was in disarray. The Murky at the door was unmoved, the door would stay open, he said.

"They are fumigating old mattresses in all the cells, I presume", whispered Jallar in Soli's ear, and he was not the only one. There was a lot of whispering all around, about the remoteness of the venue, its similarity to a barn, about the tunes that were being banged out on the piano, and the proximity to dangerous people whose passions might be aroused seeing them dance. And on this very thought a feeling of genuine solidarity began to bind the entire line—but not for long. Matters were coming to a head, the situation was tailor-made for a fight. It broke out soon enough. The sound of raised voices and a few bodies jostling against the other was heard from somewhere close to the door of the jail. Someone had pushed a judge and his lady inside who were now being made to prove that they were who they said they were. The convict who had an hour ago been transported from the barracks had taken advantage of the melee, to disappear into the officers' hall.

This is utter nonsense, said a man in whose voice the blues had been cooked with the bile in perfect proportion. No one calmed him down, every minute or so he would voice a new complaint. "Who'd build a building like this next to a building like this? It's like a creature with two mouths!" he cried. For the first time, he had actually voiced the general sentiment. The crowd, refused to stand outside a minute more, they were all going inside this very minute, otherwise the women might as well get raped in front of everyone, who knew how many criminals were at large. The Murks grew restless, they were unsure of the direction of this charge, rape was still not part of their job, but they would not budge and meanwhile, the smoke continued to surge over their heads.

"But first things first, find the convict," someone said. The tone of authority in this voice made everyone look in his direction and a man, who they had all noticed come out of the hall a while ago, and had been standing aloof from the line, now emerged. No one knew who he was but everyone made way. He stood silently in their middle as they milled around him, nodded at a few he knew, doffed his hat at those at whose homes he had dined, and finally looked over their heads as if searching for someone.

The rain had stopped a while ago. The evening was here. The birds were retiring, here and there the floodlights of the cantonment were crackling into life, the odd fox that someone had seen at a distance a short while ago, was running away towards the clearing, didn't it know that the last tree had been dead an hour ago, there were no bushes, there was no place to hide. It was time. Caelian Dado swept their faces with a glance and in the quietest voice that felt like a pat on their taut nerves, he said: "There's your man. We have found him."

And then suddenly, there was heard a shout.

I'm bleeding, said Soli with some surprise looking down at his shirt, all wet, blood when it comes out is so puzzling, he tried to air the cloth, trying to understand, pressing his fingers to his chest—all wet! And it felt so uncomfortable before so many strangers, and his ears were raw with trying to hear what had happened, what were these people saying, he thought he heard the word poison, who had been poisoned, what should he believe? Why was no one helping him? "I'm bleeding, Jallar," he said looking around, but the effort made his head wobble. Jallar, in the meantime had gone over to talk to a man who had been standing apart from the crowd. There was some mistake, Soli thought as he found himself slip to the ground, his arm, now freezing up, perhaps with the impact of the fall. Someone was tearing the shirt off, easy, easy, he wanted to say, as Jallar had been saying so long, what was the hurry, he didn't mind missing a dance. A few words entered his ears as the two men came closer and stood looking down at him. The rest of all those strange eyes had been made to move away, he didn't know them, he didn't care, but Jallar was here now, and he would, any minute now get help. He wanted to sit up and make sense of a few things before he lost consciousness. So much blood—he just couldn't get over it— lying all round him like a ribbon. Two rough hands were hauling him up by the shoulder, there must be some mistake, but Jallar was talking and he moved his head to that side, if only his head would stay still and not fall on his shoulder, it could be important—for Mir. And in a slow flash that comes to a man when he knows he is dying, he understood what the game had been all along. What would they say or do, when they got to know, Mir my brother, Hog my brother, will these eyes ever see you? The mind might not know what to throw or keep of these moments, but he would listen, but it just wasn't making any sense to try. Rabbits! Why was Jallar and that man talking about rabbits?

19

My Friend, the Murky

Kirit, the hawker and Woegore, the Murky were meeting after a year in Judge Charmis' villa. Looking at the judge sitting on his garden chair, the same thought crossed their minds. They had lugged a year's worth of legal documents, given up a good day's work and had been frisked by two sets of guards to meet a dog taking the breeze. It was a good ten minutes before the Judge, his nostrils upturned to receive the sun, so much as looked in their direction.

"Woegore," he said, snapping his fingers at Kirit. From 'Kirit', he would hardly take two questions during the brief period of their stay.

Kirit could not believe his luck but he decided to take it in his stride. There was no point in being thin-skinned about being called by some other name if it came with better luck. The Dong office bearer had told him this was his lucky day but he hadn't believed it at that time. Now he did. The provisional kindnesses of the rich and the powerful went a long way if you could discern the one or two things you could do for them to show that you appreciated the good turn. It was a good arrangement, provided they really did want just one or two things from you and then left you alone.

"Just give this chit," said the Dong, handing Kirit a piece of folded paper, and then had lost interest in him almost immediately. Kirit would have liked to show him the deep gash left by the stitches after the damage to his right lung but the man simply didn't have the time. He stood for a few seconds holding the chit when a shove from the back pushed him out of the line. He came up against the baleful stare of a woman who had been waiting in the queue right behind him to meet the office bearer. He wondered if she would be interested in the siege of The Malacca, and his role in it—well, he would make up something or the other—the noise the hotel's curtains made as they caught fire, the kitchen full of marinated meat waiting to sit on the grill, the hail of bullets as they struck the glass, the cutlery lying on the ground like crushed ice! Oh, there were some stories he could tell if he got some respect but her two children with their hollowed-out faces had begun to gnaw at her hands with their sharp little teeth.

He hurried out onto the street and asked the way to the judge's office. After a few wrong turns, he found himself standing outside a high iron gate flanked by dragontrees. He pulled the knocker. The gate opened by an inch, he stated his business, the sentries seemed satisfied, and the door opened an inch more. Word had perhaps reached the Judge from the Dong office and the reception at the gate was beginning to make him feel that his luck was finally about to turn. Kirit, you fool, you are too ready to think well of the world, he told himself after the hard hand of an officer landed on his face and his bag was snatched from his hands. His small bag of coins was extracted from a bottom pocket and dumped on the ground.

"What is this you scamp?" was shouted into his face. Kirit said what it was.

"Coins he says!" said the officer goggling at his partner who dutifully goggled back. "Do you know that nickel is the base metal for a gun!"

Kirit swore he had not known and even if he had, he would not have put it to quite that use.

"So this is just money to you? To buy bread, rice and eggs—is that what you are saying?"

"Just bread and rice sir, perhaps a pinch of salt. Egg once a month maybe, the last Sunday to be precise. "

"Egg once a month maybe, he says," said the officer calling out to his fellow officer once again, "the man thinks he's dictating me a prescription—but I tell you he is making me feel very unsafe!"

Outside the gate once again, Kirit slowly put back the contents of his bag and began to wonder how he could make the judge intervene in his case without being permitted to meet him. He saw someone vaguely familiar coming in the direction of the gate, then slow down. The man made a half-turn as if he had changed his mind, then looked again in his direction and then picked up his feet to move towards him. As he came closer, Kirit shrank back. It was the Murk! Without his uniform, his attacker seemed more frightening, more arbitrary, a machine without ifs and buts, but Kirit calmed himself down. There were visible changes in the man. His once smooth-shaven face was now hidden in beard. A twitch on the left side of his neck jerked it from time to time. An unnecessary jacket hid his bulging stomach—his entire bearing seemed like that of a man who had been thrown out of his house and had no idea if he could or should piss on the street. But why should he come to such a pass? Judge Charmis, at the time of the trial, had been the Murky's lawyer, so now as judge would surely keep batting in his favour.

You fool Kirit, he cursed himself, stop imagining things, and wondering about bats and balls, just watch what this fellow is doing, see that he doesn't cock up a gun again and this time take out your kidneys.

If asked, Woegore would have told him that was the last thing on his mind. Kirit could keep his kidneys. He was more concerned about his own possessions. It seemed he had to find something, or he had lost something—it wasn't clear but he was groping inside his haversack and his frustration was rising by the minute. Whatever it was, he didn't find it. Kirit saw him throw his bag on the side and begin to lurch down the lane kicking high the fallen twigs, squashing some ribbons of paper bunched up into a ball lying on the side of the road of no use to anyone. Then he began to bellow. After he had let out a string of abuses against the judge, he turned his attention on the judge's neighbours and then the world at large that slept on even as half of that world whimpered in pain. Escorted back to the judge's house by watchmen who were getting off on the scene, Woegore had avoided Kirit's gaze, his cloudy grey eyes peeping out from behind a dirty beret like a cat who knows a wallop is coming down on his head. At the gate, like Kirit before him, he was told to beat it and try his luck, at the gate with the garden entrance.

Kirit ended up leading the two. He couldn't trust a man who had buttoned his shirt all wrong to do that. The man was blind as a bat! He didn't believe it when the case went up for trial and the Murk was let off on this ground, thinking this is how the Lambda treats drifters like him but he had to admit he may have got it wrong. If he played it right, this final meeting with the judge could lift him off the street—the Dongs had certainly given him hopes of that. If he could manage to persuade the judge to get a bit of cash out of this chap, the first thing he would do is go up a certain flight of stairs, get a woman and be treated like a gentleman at the door. "God is late, let's eat Kate."

The man next to him turned towards him in surprise. "I haven't heard that one, mate! What does that mean?"

"If nothing works, apply Formula 34."

"I haven't heard that one either!"

"Nothing my dear fellow, just trying to keep things a little jolly. Umm, what are you expecting to hear from your man Charmis? I just need a bit to tide me over for a few months in case work dries up. Don't want much, all I am looking for is some fairness. After all, you did shoot the lung off my chest you know."

The talk died down between the two after that and from the iron gate to the garden entrance was another half-hour walk, and Kirit and Woegore travelled that distance in silence. The guard at the garden entrance was kinder, in these sort of houses they probably had a guard who would let you in and one who would keep you out, and even though he had helped himself to some of Kirit's coins, it was such a fine day that Kirit refused to feel he had been robbed. For here they were now making their way to the bower where the judge was within sight, taking in the sun.

With the empire winding down, Woegore told Kirit, the whole way of doing business had changed. A military action meant mapping beforehand the damage to be wreaked, who you could kill, who you should bruise, whose arm to take, whose tongue to cut, whose child to touch, whose wife to threaten, whose husband to scare, which family to injure, which to decimate—there were equations that had to be left untouched based on what people were trying to build on a common past. Present equations, too, had to be protected so that everyone, and now don't ask who is everyone, could begin to trade with everybody.

"The Murkys are becoming an embarassment. They now want to hide us away by putting us on duty in jails. But I didn't join to get up in the morning to stare down and then clean toilets."

So what did he get up in the morning for, but of course, Kirit didn't ask him that. "Can't you tell them that straight, I mean talk to your superior so that he could talk to his?"

"Oh, they are dead," he said with a laugh and immediately went very quiet. But for the jerks to the neck and his hands fisting up in his pockets, you would think the man was having a seizure. They were now crossing the lawn just before the bower but Woegore wanted to take a detour. Kirit was not unhappy at the suggestion. After a while, they sat down under a tree where Woegore told him about himself.

"I didn't like school but I couldn't find a reason to leave. One day, a friend of mine got me some news. He had read in *The Meat* the Fairlanders were setting up the Murkys, and they weren't throwing aside people who were blind like me, so I told myself, if you don't grab it and make this work for you, you'll never be able to leave the school compound and you'll hear your father gripe till the end of your life that the best job in the world is to become a teacher and that I had missed it. *He* wasn't blind, didn't he see my grades or what—See, I was already a strong, big sort of guy, but I had taught myself to be strong in a good way—if someone hit me, I hit harder, but I hit clean," said Woegore, the thought clearly brought some good memories and kept him cheerful for a while. "In the beginning, being a Murk was really nice you know. It was nice to have things to protect. I was told the land was mine, the coast was mine and The City was the Lambda's fort and I had to protect the people in it. But then the road gets built, and those Partisans start sallying down it pretending they are god's chosen knights with all their talk of giving people this and that as if it's theirs to give. In the beginning, we are told we have to kill them. Then we were told we are not scared of them, so we won't kill them. And now I don't know what they are saying. The Dongs are no better—I just feel humiliated listening to their talk of taking people along you know, as if we are talking of going on a picnic and not the protection of the nation."

Kirit agreed with him saying he would feel a lot of better if someone could stand up, speak clearly and mow down all the uncertainties. We need people with a proven record of being in charge, said Woegore, not boys with exciting dreams, everything is possible, everyone is equal, question everything, what kind of talk is that? My father, even though he is stupid, is my father, or isn't he, the sun doesn't hop around on the grass, it stays up on the sky, doesn't it, you really can't go around disturbing the way things are, by sticking questions into everything.

"The world does get better, I agree, with someone to look out for the people," said Kirit letting himself be swept along by Woegore's story. There was some truth in what the man was saying. The coast, the land, the sun, the sea, the City, all surely had to be protected even though for the life of him, he could not come up with a single source of danger posed to any or all of them. He would ask Woegore, he would know, with his experience of being a soldier he would know the experience of being in a fight. The enemy was masked, that much was certain.

He got a rap on the head from Woegore. "What are you whispering for?"

Kirit flashed him a sheepish smile. "No, nothing, it can wait... err, weren't you saying something?"

"Just was getting around to saying that, all said and done, I wish I had learnt to do something with my hands, you know, like something useful. What is there for me to do now? They are now saying I'm not really a soldier—but I'm telling you I don't just kill."

But there was one other thing Kirit was not able to understand. Neither by his life or by his death was he a fig's worth to anyone so why were they making an exception of this man for shooting at him? Woegore had been under Colonel Saunders' command when he had shot at him during the Partisans' first attack on The City, so what purpose was to be served by demoralising a Murky that would have an impact on other standing staff? Even if the plan was to use this as a reason to disband the Murkys, which Woegore suspected was the case, would suspending one of them make the rest more amenable to becoming janitors? The two stopped under a tree to put down their bags. Woegore held a notebook in his hand and took out his glasses from his pocket.

"Eight thousand and ten mukkas—that's the money they are withholding from me since my suspension. Close your mouth, " he said enjoying Kirit's confoundment. "Yes sirree, I've been getting my eyesight back. Now don't you go and tell the old fox when we meet him though, you never know what else he might steal from me. I'm living on my last mukkas and if he doesn't revoke the suspension soon enough, I'm going to offer myself as a bodyguard to Aristu Argot. I've heard..."

"The owner of *The Meat*—why him? Who wants to kill him?"

"I don't—look let's talk later, otherwise the guards will be after us and say we've been preventing their roses from growing by looking at them or some such thing," said Woegore suddenly getting up in a great deal of hurry. The day, indeed, had rolled and the judge, they saw, was now closeted with the morning paper.

"Don't you want to get on with him while the day is nice and fresh and make the case go your way?" said Woegore with a slight smile to Kirit.

"He was your lawyer, will he not still be your man?"

"Of late, he has been avoiding me, so this could be your lucky day. I'll tell you what, you meet him first, and then wait for me under that tree. "

"BE QUICK, man," the judge told Kirit as the hawker stepped forward and stumbled over the main points of his case, nearly forgetting to hand the judge the chit from the Dongs.

"What were you doing there in front of The Malacca when you were hit? None of the usual lies will do," he snapped. You fool Kirit, he told himself, don't you again breathe a word about selling nuts, you have seen what telling the truth did at the sentries'. Say instead that you were crawling along the sidewalk looking for crumbs, it might make him pity you, or better still say nothing, let him suspect the worst and then on that dark state, let him shine a light of grace, you have to constantly let people know that you are at their mercy for them to do good by you. So Kirit said not a word, he hung his head low, simulated a few sighs and waited to be called to raise his head.

What the Judge said, however, threw him. He said he was issuing orders for the re-opening of the case and would now privilege arguments from his side. It would not contribute to the security of a new nation to keep a blind and an infirm regiment as the Murkys and he and Baba Lala, his old friend, have had extensive discussions on the subject, he was again going to bring it up at the party tonight, and he, Kirit, yes, yes, he knew he was Kirit, need not fear any sort of reprisal from that skunk standing under that tree. The Dongs were working out something, he would just have to shift his treatment to a hospital in The Frontier under their trust, the air is fresh outside The City isn't it and the walk up and down would be good for his lungs, and he would no longer need to pay his medical fees.

Kirit nodded at Woegore on his way out and prepared himself for at least an hour's wait. His head was reeling from the implications of the judge's words which rather than simplifying his current predicament was going to increase his troubles. A hospital visit to The Frontier meant saying goodbye to a day's earning. It also meant paying for bus tickets. He looked out into the garden to see how the other man fared. From the distance he had seen the judge acknowledge Woegore's presence with the briefest of nods then set his head at a slant as if he had just developed a crick in his neck. Poor Woegore, he thought, and wandered off to sit under a tree. A few seconds later, he heard a shout. The judge had dropped the paper from his lap and was standing up brushing off something that seemed to have stuck to his cheek. Woegore's hands were on his hips, he was making no move to pick up his papers that had fallen out of his haversack. The papers lay strewn, he trampled over a few of them and was striding back across the garden.

"You coming?", he asked, looking at Kirit, his eyes flashing, but he wouldn't speak a word after that.

The two started walking toward. the corner of the boulevard between The Malacca and *The Meat* where Kirit hawked. The morning was gone, it was nearly noon. He didn't know about Woegore, but he needed a bite. Kirit broke the bun he had in his bag into two, handed Woegore a stool, borrowed from a neighbouring shop, and set the kettle to boil on his trivet. The boulevard was thick with people, buying, selling or simply gazing at items of daily use of which they probably had two at home. The trivet got knocked over more than once, the kettle spilled tea. But it was still enough for two cups and Kirit dipped his bread appreciatively in the warm liquid. His stomach was growling, he had better stand up and set his cart and start calling for customers. If you don't earn at least ten mukkas, Kirit, he told himself, your stomach's not eating tonight. Woegore still hadn't spoken a word, and was in fact, holding out his cup for more. Kirit put the kettle on boil again, when he was ready to pour, Woegore, he found, had crushed his cup, his eyes were streaming with unshed tears.

"That guy is really pushing me you know," he said. "He has asked me to meet him tomorrow afternoon, so I'll wait. I've given him something to think about, so let's see, after that, *he'll* see. Kirit, a year ago nobody knew who I was. Now they will."

20

The Night of the Hound

The phone rang in the empty room for a few frantic minutes and then fell silent. The approaching steps of a servant passing through the rooms caught its last trill; before he could speak into the cold receiver, someone coughed on the other side of the line and then put the receiver down. The servant, a boy not more than fifteen, looked around and then gave a few well-aimed kicks at the legs of the table, shut the door of the room and then slowly crossed a garden, muttering. May your roses stink and die, may your fountain be the perch of vultures, may the gypsies camp on your bed and never leave. Keeping a safe distance from the master, he mentioned the call.

"Who was it?" asked Baba Lala crossly.

"Don't know master, he wouldn't say."

"He must have said something."

The boy looked at him. Lala recognised that look. But you won't break me boy, you're not going to intimidate me with that look of infinite patience as if I am delaying your manhood with my questions. I only countenance such looks from my own boy, thought Lala, and he stopped himself from letting a smile spread across his face.

"He was *about* to say something but then he didn't. Coughed though."

"And you've come all the way to tell me that!"

"But he might call again, such people usually do. Shall I ask the cook to send you some tea here?"

"Yes, you do that, but pass me the shears on the ground, before you do," snapped Baba Lala, this boy was too clever by half, but with the elections coming he decided he would send him away from the house to stay at the Dong office to help. Let him do some work, he was always skulking around his living quarters. He would talk to Mangu and find more about him. He didn't want these Frontier boys, their heads all worked up with that Partisan shit, walking around the house making a mental note of what Polo had and what they did not. But where was Polo? He had heard some news a while ago that had made his hair stand on end. He hoped for both their sakes, that the news was wrong.

It wasn't, the boy impassively offered. He had often prepared the opium pipe himself, he said. "The addiction's not serious though. He's just about learned to draw.... Oh, there it rings again. Hurry master, do catch it this time!"

Charmis came on the line.

"It's about Polo."

"What about him? He's a good boy, judge. There's time, he'll get beaten into shape before the Plebiscite. I'm fielding him as the Dong's main hope. He'll surprise everybody, you'll see."

"Lala, I met a man today who said he had been hired to go after Polo. There are people who want him dead."

ON MANY of the city's new residential buildings yet to dry off the smell of paint, few could sit out the evening on their balconies that day. The wind was murderous, tossing in broken fingernails, ash, shards of glass, brick, blade, and there was a long queue at the chemists of maids whose mistresses had hurt their lips sitting on their balconies in imitation of their literary heroines. Who goes there? Who climbs the stairs? Who was that looking up—their heart was skipping to a mad beat, it was that kind of an evening. How the wind roared today! Even so, a few adventurous souls continued their watch, raising their tea cup to their faces like a rose, and cast their eyes down from the balcony, marvelling at the great height they were from the ground, stretching their hands to catch the wind in a touching gesture commonly seen in children, but they were now in The City and no one was going to stop them from trying anything new. The evening, in the meantime, was getting on and the street-bulbs had created pockets of white in the dark.

Mrs Mobilish, the wife of a senior postman, strained her eyes to scan the sidelanes of her flat, she could swear she had seen someone lurking at the cigarette shop around that corner looking up towards her window the other day. No, no one dare point at her, she and Mr Mobilish had nothing to do with either side, they may have come from The Frontier but they were nothing like *them*—now where was that lazy maid, was she buying up the chemist's shop? That fool she had brought with her from that godforsaken place did always pull her down! Look at her now running down the lane, just to catch that programme on the radio—but she doubted whether they would air it today. Since the afternoon, the radio had been full of dour messages. Every station had been repeating the same thing. Armed dacoit on the loose! Stay indoors! Stay indoors! Oh, we will, we will, kind sirs, we know all about dacoits, our maids are no less, but what does one do, we live with them, pay for their food and board, but we know how to lock our onions and tomatoes in the almirahs so that they can't reach them, but up on this verandah in this wonderful, wonderful air, they, the ladies, could pretend, could they not, that they were far away from such cares, that they were at the theatre, for down below was such an interesting scene.

A line of jeeps full of soldiers was curving out from the barracks and entering their lanes, their weapons jutting out of their sides like bagpipes. Mrs Mobilish's doorbell rang at this point and her girl came in pink-cheeked with excitement. Mrs Mobilish could guess what had brought that on. These girls make eyes at every passing flavour of the street, and with a jeep full of men, their day was made, you take the thin one, I'll take the one with the wart on the nose, oh they'd lie down with anyone who would buy them a ribbon every day. What's that fuss on the road, she nevertheless, asked coolly.

"Woegore, ma'm, they're looking for a Woegore—funny that they should think he was here!" she said rummaging through their shopping bags to produce the ointment, looking her mistress in the eye. "In these localities, where would such a man hide?"

"Your radio's full of him, but it has no details," said the

lady at which the maid hid her smile. My lady, she thought, knows well when to strike the intimate tone but knowing that the life of this moment was for a second, she struck her forehead in disgust to stretch the play. "Now that I did not ask! Should I go down and find out more? I also forgot to get the bread, I won't be a minute...." Mrs Mobilish wouldn't dream of saying no.

As the hours grew, the entire colony was on their balconies. Doors opened and banged. People went in and out to bunch up with their neighbours. No one set their tables. The jeeps had still not moved. Husbands and wives, daughters and sons who had gone out for work in the morning returned to find men in battle gear around their homes, crouching behind their flowerpots, popping out of open windows, pressing for the key to the terrace, why don't they go to The Frontier, perhaps their man was hiding there. But the soldiers had received no order to move, their man was still in The City, till found, he would have to be looked for, first in your lanes, then on your roofs, then under your beds, you have a sick mother, or your children are studying or you haven't cooked your dinner, oh we do apologise, not to worry, we won't leave anyone behind, we'll take everybody in, no one's a suspect yet, so everybody is.

But who is this Woegore, one soldier asked another, resting his rifle on the side of a water tank in a dark corner of a terrace as the evening turned to night. His colleague did not answer immediately, his rifle cocked up like an exclamation mark in the dark was now being raised to eye-level to point at the street. "I don't know what he's done", he said finally, "but that's the least of it, we don't even know what he looks like, there are two sets of sketches floating around with Saunders' office vouching for the authenticity of the first set, and Caelian Dado's the other, and the two sets of pictures having nothing in common."

"Look at the guy's nose in the first set," he said morosely pointing at the photograph and putting down the rifle. "They haven't got the nose right. It probably resembles my nose more than it resembles the one in the second photograph."

The other soldier took the photograph from his hand to look. "Mine too!" And both burst out laughing. A sound of gunfire in a lane nearby made them check the shells in their stack and crawl back to their old positions behind the tank.

"Well, whatever it is, this is the picture we've got and we've to work with it. We just have to get him," said the first man with a soldierly resolve brought on by the memory of an increased quota in meat and beans at last night's canteen, which he had been told would continue. "He's a threat to our way of life."

"In what way? And what , pray is our way of life? Getting up at cockcrow to jog around a field, turn our limbs left and right—I wouldn't complain to see that threatened! I mean what's this Woegore done to you or me?"

"What's come over you?" the first soldier shouted back and then remembered where they were. "All that I know is if the man comes in front of me I'll know what to do." He picked up his rifle and began to pace the terrace.

"We are a fine one to talk, we don't even know why we are looking for him!" the other one muttered, "these days with every man we go after, I feel I'm missing something, as if someone's holding a plate of food before me and to insult me says I can only take half of it. It feels as if I'm actually strengthening someone or something I should be killing—tell me, what's this Woegore done to you or me?"

The man answered with a shot. The bullet pierced a window on the opposite lane and loosened the square of glass. It fell on a child in his father's arms in the balcony below who watched the red dots spreading and then pouring down his daughter's face like paint in stunned silence—you are being naughty Mini this is not the time to sleep, wipe that colour off your face, you weren't born like that. It took another child to wail at the sight of his playmate from next door, bleeding, for the families on either side of the balcony to go and stay indoors. The lights went out in all the flats soon after, a few that had kept them on in one or two of the rooms, would regret their recklessness. Within minutes, it had drawn the sniper's attention, the bulbs in the kitchens were the first to go, and the man's exuberant whistles as he hit each target, shot their nerves to pieces. Dear lord, what had they done to deserve this? They praised the government, they praised their bosses, they kept their eyes to the ground, they kept the streets clean, they raised their kids and their kids' kids who praised the government, who praised their bosses—and there goes the second bulb! Soon enough, no window facing that terrace was left with glass. The panes, riddled with bullets, fell one after the other on the ground with a rude clatter. Where's the police, someone ring up the police, oh that's them outside it, then we'll just go very quiet and not disturb them and then they'll leave us alone, why don't they go elsewhere, but the very next moment, the shooter shredded the clothes left out on the balcony to dry, then he took out the streetlights busting the lamps till they cracked, shot at the dog cowering near a drain—and then put down his rifle to take a break. With the firing stopped, a few heads began to be seen once again in ones and twos by the windows but the whistling, now thin and whispery, went on—did it mean he wasn't done? He wasn't. It still hadn't been enough for him, spellbound as he was by his own scene and they saw him pick up his rifle again in pursuit, as it were, of a song he had left incomplete and he began to fire, again and again, as if he would fall apart if he removed his finger from around the trigger.

"Why beat up yourself—see! Take a few shots, you'll feel a lot better, after a while it's like aiming at a glass bottle during our training sessions. One goes down, another goes up, up down, up down. I got that window with my first shot—that's called marksmanship and why should I be surprised, I don't miss a session! Now you tell me, shouldn't a man earn his keep and look after his family with his skill?"

But the man, wouldn't speak or look at him any more, he was giving him the left profile as if he was going to be stuck on a coin, no sir, you haven't done anything worthwhile, I say go to hell, why did he always get paired with men like these he didn't know. When he did speak, it was to ask that same question he had got stuck on, but he had better be careful, somebody might have set him up to test *him*!

"What's this Woegore done to you or me or our children? I don't sleep easy, I just don't."

"Look, that's what the general will be telling the press

tomorrow. But if you can't sleep, don't sleep! Now man, take a deep breath, lift your rifle before it forgets how to fire, and focus, stop spoiling the whole thing, or because of you this will find its way into the Partisans' pamphlets somehow. Each time we do something big, they give it a spin and diminish it as if we work in the fire brigade, and not the army."

But the man next to him had turned into a block of stone. What was bringing it on—and this, even before he had fired a bullet! He was certainly going to bring it up with their superior and suggest that he not be posted on active duty, such men just know how to take the shine off the work for people who want to do it. He pulled the helmet down over his ears, he had had enough conversation, and raised himself slowly from behind the tank to gauge the scene on the street. A girl lay dead, next to a bag of groceries on the sidewalk—other than that the road had few distractions. The last vehicle was moving back to the barrack and a few people were being pushed inside a jeep but he could sense that it was nothing serious, they had not found their man, most of the soldiers had stayed where they were, they were not being called down from their posts. It was going to be a long night.

"No photograph has managed to capture the man," he said.

"And no photograph will," said the other man suddenly shaking his head, a hint of a smile around his lips, "if some day it's me on the run and you see my photograph, how will you find me if you don't know who I am? But if you did know, if you knew about my past I mean, or how I came to have such a past, what they did to my land or my father or my brother, and if you knew it, would you still hunt for me?"

"I signed up for the army and so did you. Now the gun is in your hand, the cartridges are in your pocket, you climbed the stairs to the terrace, but your brain's gone into your arse. You tell me what you think you are doing because I certainly don't understand it."

"Me? I'm thinking."

SIXTEEN MEN AND women were picked up all over The City that night and sent to the police station of Hardy Screw. Of the sixteen, not one had any lead to Woegore but as one officer, told Screw, they could not go around picking people up from their beds and then tell them they were innocent. They must have been upto something otherwise why would they have attracted a brother officer's attention—pigs always smell! The best thing to do was to ask them the officer suggested. People generally think they are to blame for something or the other and if they think you are asking them nicely, they may out of concern for their health, not waste their time. Screw, smarting under the fact, that the idea had not come out of his head, took his time to scratch his chin with the tip of his pen, to give the impression that he had better ideas to mull. He dispatched his junior to get him a file from his room upstairs and threw the man shivering before him in the basement the first question. The other fifteen were not packed off into a cell, they were made to watch the proceedings and draw whatever lessons they could from it.

"What do you think you are here for?"

"Last week, I wished my wife was dead...But every once in a while I'm sure she wishes me dead too."

"And this week you were going to act on it! And for that you hired a man called Woegore?"

"Honest sir, I didn't."

"What else? What else? Talk you crook, otherwise..."

Bendy Lulu, the officer sent out for the file had come in and seeing the investigation in progress, was waiting for permission to whisper in his ears. The expression on his face told Screw he was onto something. Screw nevertheless gave him a withering look to tell him he resented the interruption—let the boy stew, let him realise there were repercussions of speaking out of turn. After a few minutes, he called him over, to ask him what he had learnt. Lulu meticulously took out a sheaf of papers and dropped some in nervousness, and then found the right one to prompt his narration, but Screw did not soften. He gave the impression that he had followed the argument but was not in agreement with it. These boys, he thought, looking at the head now busy in clipping back the documents, think they are so clever, when what they really do is present ideas with an air of discovery, one had to be very careful around them so as not to be caught acting and reacting to their dual needs of being embraced by you, to begin with, and then their impatience to pull you down! Look, how he had humiliated him a few minutes back—thank god for small mercies that there had been few witnesses. But the information Lulu had extracted from the file was solid, he had to admit, and it had changed everything—it seemed he was no longer presiding over a routine enquiry over a robbery but a terror investigation! The man before him may not be Woegore or his relative but he was a Partisan, and he, Hardy Screw who had waited all his life to meet one, was going to catch one, even if they had nothing to do with the case! He looked up from the file at the man cowering before him with the love that butchers reserve for the day's first goat and decided to tell him as plainly as possible the facts of his life which it would do him good not to deny. He could, of course, deny it if he wished, but it would not sweeten his stay.

"The walls of your house are red! The flower pots as well! And the red hibiscus is the only flower you grow now that we have you rascal, you're going to tell me everything about the Partisans, otherwise I will tell you what you read, how you live, who you meet and that I'm the only one you are likely to keep meeting for the next 20 years as I'm going to keep you here for a very long time!"

With every accusation, the man grew more despondent, and then started to mewl. Screw was surprised—his first encounter with a Partisan and he had made him cry! He did wish the man wouldn't take it so hard—they hadn't hit him anywhere yet! "There, there!" he said in his best rallying tone: "We have a very nice garden in the jail and it's just lost its gardener, but no hibiscuses mind you."

The room erupted in laughter and at least ten men belched out sounds in imitation of low-paid stage villains. That there were so many officers in the room watching him conduct the investigation he had not realised, but Screw knew this was nothing new. Professional envy and camaraderie did exist side by side and he had been at the receiving end of both to know these were temporary knocks—take it on the chin, or give it back and move on. He turned around thinking he would join in the general cheer but a pair of still eyes paralysed his spine.

Caelian Dado was standing at his back ignoring the many minions requesting him to take their chairs to go through the file he had just abandoned, Bendy boy in attendance. Screw re-arranged his face and moved forward to greet him which he acknowledged without taking his eyes off the file. There would be hell to pay if there was some intelligence they had not spotted or worked on though everyone who had worked with Dado, said a marked change had come over him in the past one year. In the earlier days, Dado had been excitable, ready to go off the rails at the slightest deviation from his plans, but the medals they had stuck to his chest since that time, had cooled the furnace. But why was he here, Screw wondered. What had he been told? That they had caught Woegore? Even so, why would The Lambda's finest intelligence officer be sent to be an observer in a case about an armed robber? It was too minor an investigation for his intervention.

Or was it?

His head spun with the din of unanswered questions. Saunders' army, too, had been drafted in for the search last evening, he remembered. The boys in the field had begun to say that he and Dado were working at cross purposes but with Plebiscite around the corner, with power at a sniffing distance, there was bound to be various alliances and uncouplings. There were rumbles of a few generals being unhappy about handing The Lambda over—but that was probably nothing, you can't take back a house after the signatures are done or tell the new owners how to arrange their furniture. The meeting of The Partisans with the Fairlanders was another curious affair. Just a day or two away, there were no security arrangements being made at The Malacca where the meeting was to be held. It was as if no one was expecting them to eventually turn up... Lala's son Polo would represent the Dongs he had heard but the talk in town was he hadn't been seen for days... Anyway, all that's nothing to do with me, I'll get on with my work. What else does a policeman do but adjust his cap in the direction of the new masters, whoever they may be? Screw caught himself smiling in the glass of one of the room's almirahs, and quickly composed himself. He found he didn't know what to do with himself, or how to proceed with Dado in the room around whom worshipful islands of cops were forming in imitation of the other.

The story of Dado's rise was often told to promising juniors who wanted to quit the profession in order to retain them. Truly, what a meteoric rise the man has had! Caelian the Clown was now the model officer, he was loaned across all departments, coming in when an investigation was going nowhere to help rebuild it from scratch. There was, however, that unexplained case of that reporter from *The Meat* who had collapsed right outside the Fairlander jamboree last week and had not been heard of since. Dado, he found out later, was present on the spot. It was said that one of his operatives had brought the reporter in but it was still unclear as to what purpose—had he expected the reporter's capture to force the Partisan hand in some matter but they had not bitten that bait? Or had the reporter gone over to the other side and was hiding out in a cell with Danny the painter, another Partisan like him, whose escape and capture during his transfer from the barracks to the jail at about the same time when the reporter was just outside the jail was too perfect a coincidence to be true. Screw had heard the story from different sources, but he always felt no one had really got it right... Each time he had tried to work it out, the trail began with The Partisans but always led back to *The Meat*. Surprisingly, there had not even been a para in in the papers about these two incidents and none whatsoever in *The Meat*, the paper that employed them—but what if they didn't know, people disappear all the while, if I don't walk back here tomorrow, which motherfucker here would really care, so he might as well return to the crossexamination where, atleast he was asking all the questions. He took up the old thread—he wanted to bump off his wife did he, or didn't he?

The man lunged for his feet. Screw lifted him by the chin as if he were about to knight him and then crashed his face to the ground. The nose broke, blood spilled. Such moments tested Screw but then so what, he told himself, so had theorems, and for a second he led himself to pause one by one on the other terrors of his childhood, why what a day that had been when the bandicoot, big and hissing like a cat, had hidden in their kitchen and he had grown tall not by measure but by taking responsibility. On seeing his sisters howl, had he not picked up a jute bag and his mother's rolling pin and walked up to the creature, as if he had a club in his hand and had adopted the tone of voice he had used with vermins of all kind ever since, telling it, there was no need for things to get dirty, there was no need for its skull to crack under the club, that it should just climb onto the bag, surrender, leave their kitchen, find a home elsewhere, don't be seen in their parts—there, it had already made him feel better, so Screw saw no reason not to bear on the head of the unfortunate man in front of him all the hardness of which he was capable had not the sight of blood disturbed him for a few treacherous moments.

"Don't know Woegore! The man won't say anything else! If you don't know him—who does? I do? "

Of the sixteen people caught, thirteen were blind alleys. The first lot, those who were the first to claim that they were Partisans or seemed they were dying to be, changed their tune as soon as the first floggers were brought in through the door. One of them had been brought to the police station because his neighbour was convinced he had plans to burn the locality down on seeing him daily throw a cigarette butt into the hedge outside the flats at very late hours. He had been posting a letter to the department every other day urging action.

"Well, there were prices to pay of asking for public participation, but it had to be done, there was information coming in from all corners and not all's bogus, anyone here taking that attitude would be grossly wrong," said Dado with a nod taking in the room. "The public should feel we rely on them and are acting on their suggestions. Never laugh at somebody offering you information otherwise he won't inform you the next time." Besides, not all the arrests, he added, were a waste, a few of them were people in whom the radical germ was strong, and while they had begun to look for Woegore, there was no harm in cracking down on The City's Partisans.

Who knows they might have given Woegore refuge, termites nest with their like, and by the night was over he said he was depending on officers like them, mindful of the security of their old dame, The Lambda, and their buildings, their schools, their streets, their banks, their parks, to beat the shit out of The Partisans, to tell them they were wrong to dream of wanting to take them away. As to what was to be done with them, let the forceps, pliers and truncheons, first do their work, and then he would decide. No one spoke, in the presence of Dado it was unthinkable that anyone else would take that call.

As they took a break and everyone milled around Dado, someone ventured to ask him if he knew the future of The Murkys who often worked in tandem with them. Dado's answer was short. He didn't start it, he wasn't closing it down, it was time the force learnt new methods to do their job without sound or spectacle.

"The Lambda is going to be free. A policeman should be on school and housing committees and not get excited about march-pasts in the city. What is its use anyway? It bloody alerts everybody and makes us seem like invaders."

By the end of the night, every police station had been wired Dado's instructions. The time for deliberations was over; it was time to put the screws in place, the meeting with The Partisans wasn't until the day after tomorrow and they had to move in fast. At the police station of Hardy Screw, the fate of The Partisans was sealed, they were not going anywhere. Just because some of their leaders had been invited to a meeting in The City, it didn't mean they would be running around The City beating their drums. No newpaper was to be informed about the event, there was going to be no grand reception, they had been summoned and they were coming, and they had been told to be on time. The City's motor, when they arrived, would hum at the same rate as it did every day. The City's gate would open the inch it always did and not an inch more. They would be picked up at The Gate by police escort and led to The Malacca for their meeting. Dado picked up an artist sketch that had just come in of the woman who was leading The Partisans at the meeting with the general tomorrow. Hair falling from the crown like water on either side of rebellious eyes—the artist had let his sympathies show, who commissions these guys he wanted to know, get the bugger and gouge out his fingernails! Dado's eyes searched the room for Screw to shout at—the man had for long had it coming—but his face suddenly contracted in a grimace. Climbing the staircase up the basement, Dado suddenly felt short of air, his new office at *The Meat* had spoilt him. His lungs pumped gratefully as he came to stand out in the open outside the police station. If he didn't find Woegore before the meeting at The Malacca started, he had to know whom to blame.

21

Messages for Mir

How difficult it is to say I. How difficult can it be to say I? This is not the first time she has gone searching for it, but it has either waylaid her when she was deep in the company of others, men and women anxious to shed their own limbs so as to be part of a single forest, that there had been no time to trace the lines of her own hands, they were what they were only when they were joined to others and his. And what hands! Should he now be blamed that she had never left his side? He had uncupped her hands over her ears to let her bear the sound of her own screams, let her bones break as if it was a ritual to be followed before they could climb and fall off the same tree; made her look at the train come puffing from the factories as if they were coaches loaded with the world's riches; sat with her on the tracks as the soot of the engine sprayed their faces telling her this is how it was at festivals; It was difficult to say I, she now realised, now that the time had come. So when she set off tomorrow where they had agreed to meet, all the five, who had proposed their own names and volunteered to go together, it wouldn't be just her first chapter going out to meet her last chapter, should that happen, it wasn't just her story to make this decision, so let it not be said that Mir had sent Lavni for I am here with my own realisations but he is in me.

Mir had woken up and the cells of her veins were on alert, her breath held. She saw the chair in the corner pull over itself the white of the walls and disappear, then the table, then the window, till all that remained was the bed on which they had played like children the night before, willing fairytales to arrive out of nightmares, watching their limbs curl, hang from a hook, being pulled apart, then return to their bodies for a re-naming, then run without preamble outside, even though outside was no garden, get on the seesaw, jump from rock to rock, running, catching, grappling, pounding big stones and shells into little ones, till they built a ship, then a bridge, stood on a flight of stairs, then held basket, and the hours, like birds, flew a little around them.

I may halt in The City for a while, you understand, she said as he looked at her moving around the room touching and straightening a book or a chair that need not have been fixed, wondering why, now, she had to say such savage lies. I will be back in winter, the night after your first cough I'll get to know you'll see, and I'll be here. And if the winter is late and short? Then I will stay till spring. They got up, their eyes, elbows and shoulders, sitting up like scissors, refusing to touch, unless they could bruise the other—it was always like this before a parting, as if it had not been planned to the date and even the hour, and would invariably end in violent recriminations, You never loved me, I never had you.

The slow sounds of the afternoon grew around them. An entire shift in a nearby factory, brought down their hammers on sheets of metal with the force people reserve for the last blow before the bell for recess. Its gate cranked open with the sound of people momentarily free. The snack carts scratching the road came to a halt before them. The vendor greeted his daily customers warmly. The workers, at first, spoke little. After a bite or two, there were a few dry mutters, elbows were nursed, sores exclaimed over, knuckles cracked and the talk of double the wages in The City heard till the sound of the factory bell brought an end to all their talk. Atop their room, the crows scampered over the roof. The rats squeaked down the pipes. Mir left the bed to make tea. When he came to give Lavni a cup, he had something in his other hand, a tightly bound book—something Hog had sent word about, had asked for.

"Whose is it?" she said forcing a smile, neither of them she knew would give back a book.

"I've forgotten. But when you are back..."

"And if I'm not..." she said, but he wouldn't look at her so she moved towards the door telling him that she would be returning in a while, her hands swiftly patting down her hair into a coil and the gesture told him that no words had, that the time for words were over, that she would from then on collect herself, that she had work to do. And so did he.

Lavni walked on the pipes and bent in front of each window of the neighbouring hovels where a woman's face steamed in the smoke arising from the stoves. Over a pan too full of water in which a few tea leaves were swimming, they raised their hand in response to a greeting from the other side. At what time would she and the others start out, they asked, and for a while they discussed the night's journey in logistics. Yes, night was better they all agreed to start the journey, in The Frontier. They all started something new at that time didn't they and there was a silence in which they all dropped a prayer. Some raised their folded hands to Ai, Handsa-ai, and some, suspected Lavni, to the god of Horo asking them to spare their children over what had happened to Horo with no group telling the other who was praying to who. They still feel guilty about that! Horo or The Partisans—who had done more? Lavni looked at the bowed heads and the tense eyes with rising impatience.

When *our* book is closed, how will *we* appear, when they look at *us*, what do they really see, she wondered as their eyes opened and the women began to talk among themselves of a feast that had been planned at the foot of Ai's shrine later that night. Goats had been killed or were about to be killed; someone recalled the night they had taken down the temple and installed Ai, and that they had beheaded ten goats; when the last empress of China had died they had emptied the marshes of ducks and the smell of their roasting flesh had so perfumed the air for days that the poor of that country no longer felt the need to eat for days, or so the sailors of the ship that had just come in, said—the talk swung from here to there in tones of suppressed excitement, they had all but forgotten about Lavni standing in their midst the way they ran on like a river.

"A feast tonight? It isn't necessary," Lavni said brusquely, "I'm not going anywhere. If not tomorrow I will surely be back day after. We will all be back. What progress on the flags?" she said to change the topic.

"Did the dye on the flags dry?"

"It all depends which way the wind blows."

"Will atleast five be ready for the five of them?"

"Even if it isn't, you'll get one to hold."

"Dig up the road after we are gone just in case."

"Oh yes, we will get down on our knees and hands."

"They might send their hounds, their jeeps, their guns."

"Oh we know, we are prepared."

"There's a meeting in the evening before we go."

"In the evening we are going to the shrine, you go."

"Mir said it's important, he will be there."

"Why didn't you say so?"

The sudden burst of hostility—Lavni wasn't prepared for it, but she was unwilling to let go. She chided them on the work on the flags not being ready, but they would have none of it. Girl, they are sending a car for you, is it, their turn to change the topic, don't you take it, they said. They came on a car for that boy Danny—his sister sold herself to a City trader the other day only so that she could find out about the brother—and he never came back and now, neither will she. No harm will come on relying on one's arms and legs, said another, so you walk, but as you talk at the high table, be sure to mention us, freedom from pots and pans, onions and inconsiderate children, we should not have to cry in the new regime, and it had better be really new, a few said with a gurgle, and a few, gravely with a firm shake of their head as if they were already at the meeting. And if there were no chairs for them, they would sit down on their haunches if need be and dictate a constitution, and who said they couldn't. But why had they been really called for a meeting in The City by the Fairlanders? And why wasn't Mir going as well? Mir should go—at least Biran should, said some with a shrug, their eyes on her.

"They are calling. We are going to see what they have to say. The Plebsicite's around the corner they want to gauge where we stand, if we will boycott it or we won't, so hold your horses about a new regime, a new regime will mean a new king, new laws, what need have you for a new state, so long as we live the same reality?"* Mir or Biran—about that, Lavni wouldn't answer.

The group grew. The mood lightened. Women who had begun balancing their wide hips on their trunk-like legs, crammed against the walls of the hovels on the other side of the pipe. There was no room for anyone to move, or raise a hand to make a point, so they began to file out clutching each other to come and stand on the flat ground that, as they joked among themselves, had turned them into poets and rebels in the past one year. The Party had showed the way, it was true, but was it The Party alone that had used its imagination and showed that this could be a road? What a day to tell Lavni all this, muttered a woman and gave the other a hard nudge. Here, dear girl, I've brought you a few lemons, she said; take some puffed rice, said another; here, hold my child, sister, it's a mystery to me how a child in a home like ours has cheeks like this, all plumped up like a raisin; a handful of sugar from me, you can mix it with the lemons you just got from her, that's all I could give, sister, but do take it; nine bananas from me for the five of you as the men, they are sure to take two; here's my cat, Cairo, you have to have faith in her, even though she's begun to scratch, and the stars that were beginning to speckle The Frontier saw that Lavni's hands and eyes were full.

"Uma? I don't see Uma," Lavni said feebly and someone went looking for her, but some in the group seemed startled by the request. But they quickly recovered it seemed to Lavni, and understood it for what it was, this was no mere query, even though it was so expressed, and so they decided with no formal discussion to make the two estranged friends meet. Why wait, they would all go in the direction of Uma's house, they would meet her around the bend in case she was on her way. But if she was late in coming, after all Uma had to cross the railway line, after all her son Kanhu who had disappeared into The City for months was suddenly back home, they would call for her from the street, and she could come down or they could send Lavni up. There was no itinerary, no particular goal, though there should have been, hadn't they known such a night would come before The Partisans left for The City, but the hour was here as messily as an unplanned child and as they could do one thing well, and not two, the evening meal would have to wait or would have to get made by other hands, till the Partisans left, there was nothing else anyone was going to do tonight. The ground was wet, had it rained that heavily last night, but their feet left their mark and many of the men and women who came out of their houses in the hope of wishing the group farewell seeing that a group of women had just gone by and that Lavni was among them, saw those marks and drew their own conclusions. To some of them, the foot marks looked like fish walking about, the squall must have brought them in, so they hurried into their slippers to follow them in the hope of getting a share, the farewell could wait. But old Wodan raising his ribs from his cot had seen other signs. The Girl Walks Again, he whispered to his wife sitting on the floor blowing the stove with her mouth and the old couple who had seen enough reverses in life not to believe in magic, tottered out of their hut holding the hand of their granddaughter to give her the chance to believe in symbols. But they are not alone! Who else is hurrying by making a din, who goes beating a drum like that as if to awaken the dead this night? Who said there must be witnesses?

The ragtag group was soon followed by others, old people like Wodan himself who can neither sleep by night or noon; out of work mechanics, artisans, poets and minstrels–the gang among the first to join any procession, sure that if it was a procession, it was motivated by hunger and a little ahead there would be food, and once there was food, would there be no need for music? Look grandfather, so many feet, exclaimed the child; like every child born just a few years ago in The Frontier, she knew where all this might lead.

But the pace of the caravan with Wodan at their head was slow. The old man was stopping every now and then invoking The Girl but the crazed light in his eyes made it a case of private belief. Those who lost their nerve to pull on ahead was however pulled along by those who hadn't and they looked at the man with the flowing white hair and deeply lined face and decided to forgive him; his look and his locks were his own, they said, but there would be no place for prophets in The Frontier, so be careful old Wodan of what you say, here every man and woman keeps their own counsel. But the child he had brought with him, kept getting in between their legs and children in The Frontier were something else, their blood is asked for with as much seriousness as their elders, and they give it, so if a child was here who was stumbling as she walked, she had to be picked up without considering whose child she was.

What's your name kid, but she wouldn't answer and instead grew difficult by the minute kicking up her legs, then growing very still only to crane her neck till it seemed it would snap, so as to see, as it were, into the night, though what was there to see, everyone knew what came before and that what came after. Night here was unbroken, a black flag draped over their foreheads, they were a people written into the gloom, rising up with the risen and falling down to the ground when asked, oh Lord return to us so that we may begin to hope, so that we may recognise light as light, forgive us for placing someone just like us between us and you, we had done it before and we did it again, take us to a place, where no one leads us—and their noisy moans were raised to such a pitch that their ears echoed back their baroque tale of unbroken ruin, the bile poured down their throats, their hearts believed, and the doom that they had killed over many nights began to stir in the pit of their stomach saying with a great deal of sighing that their past vows to live to fight under the same flag could be overwritten by new vows.

A tall thin lad dark as coal joined the throng in the middle. They saw him come over from the direction of the flats by the station tucking his shirt in his trousers—must have left home in a hurry. He stood apart as the procession curved past the workshops of the masons and slowly lifted his young unsatisfied face towards the sky. His lips clamped over each other as if they were the gates to a new century, his eyes trawled up and down the crowd as if they were the only weapons he would rely on in the event of a battle, his hands he thrust into his pockets. But his chest was narrow, his arms were thin and they did not again want to linger on his face, that bad habit that was a step away in The Frontier of turning people into God. But they could not look away.

The lad had raised one thin hand to wave at some boys as old or a little younger than himself who emerged from the barber's shop on the other side, their faces contracted with anxiety. They were clearly going somewhere. Each of them had a bag in their hands which they would hang over their shoulders and put down on the ground the next minute. Perhaps there was more waiting to do, perhaps there were more of them to come. But the lad broke it up, the group hurriedly conferred, puffed a few cigarettes, slapped the back of the youngest, ruffled his hair, and then again resumed watching the clumps of people cluster, break cluster, then stumble along the general direction. Suddenly, a commotion tore up the already untidy assembly—the child who had now slipped down a benevolent shoulder was now running away from the procession moving her little feet and hands like the wheel of a cycle that is bent on an accident, nothing less would do. There were some loud whispers, it wasn't possible to catch all of them, every few minutes a new convulsion seized the mob and gave birth to new rumours, but there were a few remarks of how she seemed miraculously older than in the past one hour. The lad seemed to cheer and exchanged a few words with the others, whatever they were, a few more faces wore a smile. Had the Hittites thus smiled at the sack of Babylonia? But she had to be caught, there was no doubt about that, no girl or goat, could be allowed to run that free. A shout went up, with everyone asking everyone else to catch her, so when the lad placed himself in her path and stretched out his arms to her, she ran into them like the recognition of blood with the wound.

"Who's caught her? Who's that? Who's that with her?"

Some questions are answered in the walking of a road, they are not available at its beginning. The road may end or it may fork, but the question shouldn't. So it was with this caravan, how it would frame its future questions may be decided by what they will do when the answer emerges.

"Who's caught her? Who's that? Who's that with her?"

A thought crossed their minds which was passed down the column in an exchange of glances. Perhaps this was The Girl, Wodan was calling out to with his wild howl, and the throw of his voice, that had wandered in the gulleys ever since the first factory went up on his land in The Frontier now accosted them right where they stood in the shape of the child-woman to whom they had long surrendered—Ai! Handsa-ai! Is that you girl? Lead us! Tell us what we have to do!

A few shadows moved on top of a terrace on the same lane as the barber's shop. There was a huddle, there was some talk and some arriving at a conclusion. "It's Kanhu. So Kanhu's back —with one, two, four, eight, nine twelve of them," said two, looking down at the group standing aside from the stream of people gathered on the road. The news that he would be here had actually turned out right and so the message got relayed in a series of piercing whistles around The Frontier. But there were other imponderables, there had been too much clarity for a start. The accuracy of the details, the time of his coming, the size of his band, was a cause of suspicion, someone had tried too hard to win their trust, though it was true these things are not decided on the spur of the moment, so perhaps it was Kanhu himself who was making sure that the information of his coming would reach the right ears? They looked on as the lad bent down to pat the cheek of the girl, whisper a few words to her. The girl nodded. He heaved her up on his shoulder; with a movement of his arm he signalled the boys standing around him to join the throng that had organised itself into a column to go towards the shrine. As they left, their thin backs covered by the rucksack all of them were carrying, they saw him sling his bag across his chest, give his shoulder a bit of a jerk to balance the legs of the child, and set off in the direction of the mound disappeared by the dark in seconds. With no word of instruction, the group on the terrace kicked themselves, should they have let him go, should they have made contact, should some of them have followed him? There seemed nothing else to do but wait.

The man they were waiting for made his way from one of the factory gates, crossed the railway line, stopped for the train to pass bringing in men and women from the evening shift, raised his hand to them, refused an invitation for tea and walked towards the shop on the terrace. Kanhu is back, they shouted unable to wait for him to climb up the stairs. He halted their frenzy with an upraised palm, a veritable order for them to compose themselves, ascended the stairs, just one-up from the ground, washed his hands and legs, as they kept a distance, and walked over to where they stood. The news had reached him in the factory, he said and he said he was pleased.

"What now, Biran? What should we do next?" they asked crowding around him in the terrace.

Dusk had long gone but patches of purple were still visible in the east, that was enough light for anyone wanting to hit the road that hour. The blasted wind was keeping the night at bay, there was no turning away for their ashen-faced settlement from the circle of grey—a grey sea, the grey engine, grey days, grey time—but had it always been like this? From the grey they had all once beaten out iron, but Biran did not want to think about all that as he took the account of the day's happenings. The wind, said one of the boys, had blown the roofs of many of the houses, splintered the bulbs hanging from the fronts of butcher shops and smithys, a few rusty hammers and a few recalcitrant goats had gone missing but the no one, they reassured him, had raised a hue and cry. The Lambda was in control. But this evening, said another, men and women full of unexpressed desires were on the prowl, children were leading processions, the sea was hissing, the birds were home early, and we cannot meet anyone's eyes. But the talk returned once again to the thought uppermost in their minds.

"Kanhu is here. Will we just stand here? What should we do?"

"Nothing. We should do nothing," said Biran and watched the path to the mound light up with flames burning from each hand bearing a block of wood. Some ground soil would move under those feet, some old crabs would die tonight.

FROM UMA'S HOUSE the journey to the mound had taken all of them an hour. The women borrowed Uma's broom, the shrine had to be cleaned they said, fresh flowers to be placed at the rim of the blackened pot that was Handsa, the worm-eaten piece of wood that was Khandoba, her miller's stone to be washed and the quern to be read, would Ai not have left a message for them at this momentous hour? Let's not dally, let's be off, they said, the wind had been vile since morning, the sea was eating itself up, the water had to be separated from the pebbles flowing through the taps, there were scores of things to do while they were able. But come, let us first oil your hair, Lavni, let us line your eyes with kohl, and then after a dip we will go to Ai, at this hour every evening we've been going to meet our sad sister, but we've already told you that.... And so they went, past Horo's old house, now dismantled, his wooden furniture broken down to build a few benches; past the ship-breakers yard, past a few fishermen's sheds till they felt sand under their feet. The moon had just released the sickle into the sky.

"Don't mind me, you go ahead and take a dip," Lavni told Uma as the others looked on, "the time is near. I will soon have to be off." She hadn't expected them to agree, but they did. "Uma, you go with Lavni," they said and one by one, they saw the women walk towards the waters, their veils flapping behind them in the wind. Not a boat was at sea. Night had landed.

"It looks like they delivered me to you," said Lavni to Uma and both women, finally alone, laughed, their breath coming back in gasps; from the sea, the climb to the mound had taken another hour.

"You are here every evening—too?" she asked Uma, her mind racing ahead to think of the next question so that there were no awkward pauses, she wanted to be sure, she didn't want Uma to feel that she had been summoned, there was not much time to set things right. Time is so miserly when two people have a lot to talk, or have to apologise, make amends, present the past as witness, a witness with its own set of questions, but what we cannot ask each other is the biggest gulf of all and knowing that, what is left to talk about, but she would nevertheless try.

Lavni saw Uma bend down to pick the broom, now alone, it seemed difficult to speak sentences that would be comforting, or at the very least true. "They come here every evening to pay their respects, they said, but once here, look how they ran off to the sea," said Lavni once again. The swish of the broom fell harshly on her ears, but Uma did not reply.

Lavni walked over to the edge of the mound and looked around calculating its distance to The City. If they started out in the next one hour, by dusk they would have passed through its gates. By afternoon, she would have met Hog—Mir had wanted him to be at the meeting as well—no, in her heart she knew there had been no betrayal. She had given the same heart, the same worries, the same pain to one and the other. The air she had been choking on since the afternoon released. She was able to rouse herself. A little laugh bubbled to her lips—but she was not alone. The silence of the woman standing at a little distance from her brought her back with a wrench to other unresolved knots. It may have been due to the darkness but she would not have been able to spot the mound, she realised, had Uma not pointed it out. The mound where they now stood was now almost as tall as a building, almost head to head with Lala's horn factory and Zain Glassworks. This was the work of many months she realised—how was it possible that she or anyone else in The Party had not known? No one had brought it up either, surely someone must have known! The stone path carefully laid with pebbles brought from the sea to help reach the top of the mound was also a recent addition; the layers of mud and cement that were packed round and round the mound, that once used to be just a stump grown out of a pile of bush and earth just two feet off the ground, too, must have been dredged up from the sea. Now standing at its top, with the sea curling at her back, for the first time, she noticed the throng scrambling its way up towards it.

"Uma!" she called to point to the unbelievable sight but Uma's eyes were closed. Lavni smiled to herself. What a scene in front and to miss it! The entire Frontier seemed to be on their way to the mound! This was a felicitation, this was an embrace, they had all known she was being brought here all along, this was a planned farewell! A drum-beat rolled at the foot of the mound, looking down, it seemed to her that the air and the ground below were rising up towards her in sounds—cymbals, conches, the clatter of marching feet, the bleats of belled goats, this night they would let no one sleep, except for the woman half-standing next to her, her eyes in exile from her surroundings. She looked at Uma thoughtfully, her eyes were still closed and a sense of failure again began to creep up on Lavni. What was she doing up here? What had coming here accomplished with Uma? Friendships could not be resuscitated at tombstones. She decided to go down and join the crowd when Uma's hand stopped her, a stream of tears threatening to flood down her eyes.

"Why Uma! Don't cry, look everyone else is down below! But did you have something to say—is it about Kanhu? Look! He is back! There he is!"

And there he was mixed up with the mendicants, the singers, among the blacksmiths, among his boys—Kanhu, the master of the ceremony. With a woodcutter's swing the woodcutter brought down his axe on a pile of bramble. And there he was. The boys steadied the goats, the goats went under the axe. And there he was. Old Wodan left behind in the line, stumbled up and needed a hand and there he was. The boatmaker was readying the raft and there he was. The singers getting their cue bared their throats to sing and there he was. The women back from the sea asked where the saddle quern was, would somebody get down the miller's stone, and he was there.

"What would we have done tonight, without you boy?" a shout went up but he brushed it aside and put down the girl from his shoulder. Falling to the ground now like a bunch of flowers, the girl began to run towards the mound, clamber up a ladder that was rolling down, dislodging mud and soil with her fingernails, crumbling it, lathering the mound, as it were, all over herself, as if determined to change her shape, change the shape of both their beings. The entire caravan stood astounded for a while, then lifted its legs in a steady beat up the mound, its table-top now a few steps away, surprised by having come so far, no longer asking who was in charge, who was leading, when they were all headed, where would they return, who had the right to write an epic, who to read it, would tonight end, had tomorrow begun, is April here, is it April yet, what if there is no April... But at the top of the mound they found the two women but not the saddle quern or the miller's stone nor the cracked pot that was Ai or the worm-eaten shank of wood that was Khandoba.

Who had taken her? Where was she? Handsa would not be separated from them again! "Aieeee!" they shouted, "Where is Ai?" but the wind on top of the mound threatened to throw them off, the pressure of their feet began to dig holes on the ground, the structure they had built seemed ready to crumble, and old Wodan suddenly come out of his spell was insisting on grabbing the child and taking her back saying he had seen everything, but that girl, what's got into her, was kicking up her legs urging them now to move faster in one direction.

The minutes grew tongues, and in the hubbub, an hour passed. Down below, the goats had been bled, the old people and the children fed, the raft was ready and the wooden plank began to be lowered down the mound. All over The Frontier the night began to grow warm, the wind stopped its screech, the fires burned themselves out. Here and there a few children cried as if struck by a horrific vision, or simply now worn by the night asked to be returned home to bed. Kanhu watched as the boatmen loaded the plank onto the boat, the woodcutter held the nails in place, the carpenter drove them into the hull, the women pulled the gag out of the mouth of a half-crazed woman and freed the mouth of another who wouldn't let out a single cry. The girl now stepped forward. With a touch of her toe, she pushed the boat out to the sea.

The boys came to stand beside the lad, their lips dry. "And Mir? What do we tell Mir when he asks about Lavni?"

"That the boat has holes, it may yet find a country. Now let's get out of here. It's a long walk to The City."

"Can we go? Can we all go?"

"I don't know. You know. I didn't bring you here."

"But you will be coming with us otherwise who else will come with us?" they asked as they slowly started walking down towards the settlement, hit by the enormity of what they had done. A few of them tried to recover by blaming Mir, but Kanhu would have none of that. "Mir wasn't wrong," he said, "his ideas weren't becoming flesh. The movement cannot just be a word, what we do, must embody it. What we did today, even if no one understands it, Mir will. But somebody needs to be with him tonight. The rest of you must go to The City. Take everybody."

And because they wouldn't go without him, in the end, he went.

22

Operation Missing

The news leaked in the usual way—someone had said what he knew to someone else. From some shabby corner someone had spoken up, late, but someone did.

9:10 pm. The office of *The Meat* had been agog with the wildest rumours. Work stopped, then picked up, pragmatism won over emotion. A fleet of cars began to patrol the streets, plainclothes policemen began to appear in and around the newspaper buildings and checked at random the identity of people entering or leaving them. They didn't collar everybody, they let things loose, so that for every two people who had been heckled, there would be two more who would say that had not been their experience. Unable to hold himself back, Hog rushed to the centre of the newsroom, all quiet and tranquil as if it was a post-office in mid-afternoon. Except for the sounds of a few typewriters jamming, a few shouts of someone running out of ink, the habitual shouts of tea even without a desire for tea, reporters and editors were clicking their tongues at how best to announce the new developments in a headline that would dump criminality on the dead—when they died—and not on the government. A few huddled till Hog thrust himself in their middle. He urged them not to debate what they should be doing when people could be dying! But with Hog's entry, they felt exposed. They now advised him to be calm. A senior asked whether he would like him to intercede with Aristu on his behalf and plead Lavni's case who was leading, was she not, the Partisans into The City. Had The Partisans really believed the Fairlanders were calling them for a meeting, and what had they hoped to contribute?

10:10 pm. For the past one hour, ever since he had heard,

Hog had kept his fingers pressed into the phone dial ringing The Partisan office hoping for a ring back but no one answered the phone. Where was Mir? He scrammed down to the office lot where the scooters were parked and found Jirish there. They checked their watch. If the news of a regiment being out with shoot orders was true , on no account must The Partisans cross The Gate. They decided to speed the bike once out of the office gate but finding a squadron right outside, took a back alley out to take a longer route past The Malacca and Garrison Street to cross the last mile to The Gate. At The Malacca, they saw a white banner rolled down its turret announcing the meeting of the Fairlanders and Dongs but no mention of the Partisans. The Square was over-run with The Murks on their last assignment. A guard with Partisan sympathies, let them in through a side gate, hid their scooter and showed them the way to the north gate of the compound that was close to The Gate. As they came out, they were pulled into a waiting jeep that was seen going off towards the barracks.

10:17 pm. The Partisans reached The Gate and found it locked. They shook it till it broke, a sound that made the houses closeby, on reflex, turn off their radio and turn their thought to prayer. Dear God, they began, and beyond that were unable to proceed. A song had begun to break in the horizon. The song moved from lane to lane, ebbing to crest, crest to ebb, rise from strength to greater strength, with more feet, more lips, more mouths singing that song, till it seemed that everyone wherever they stood the song had placed them at its very centre, they no longer wanted to shut their windows to it, they couldn't open their doors fast enough. By the time the shots rang out, they had come to their senses. Those picked up by Dado's men on the suspicion of being a Partisan protested loudly for being clubbed with violators of public order. Why, they would have pointed out who the leaders were had they not disappeared.

10:45 pm. Five lads were picked up near the Black Quarters, three bags in their possession which they refused to hand over. They were paraded past the office of *The Meat*, no reporter came up to ask who they were or what their crime had been, perhaps it was dark, perhaps the hour was inconvenient, perhaps the news was inconvenient and inconvenient news die on a newspaper desk every day like autumn's old leaves.

11:15 pm. The police communique reached *The Meat* just in time for the last edition. With the least disturbance to the page, a box that had been kept ready to adjust the names of the dead was fitted in a fraction of a few seconds. There were a few tense seconds as the names they had been sent before were found somewhat changed—a subeditor insisted that the list they had been sent a week back had the name of the woman leading the Partisan assault on the City, and this one didn't, but perhaps she had given the police the slip. He was asked to let go, and he did. After all, it was the lead story The Lambda would be talking about tomorrow he wouldn't want to be held responsible for holding back the edition now would he when they had all worked so very hard on it.

Epilogue

Mrs Mobilish woke up early to begin her Sunday. The paper crackled in her hands as if it had been roasting in the oven. The headlines made her interrupt Mr Mobilish who was on a telephone call. Had he heard? He had heard. The bank they had invested their money in had been robbed last night! But it was all safe and secure. Five robbers from The Frontier who had been hiding in The City for months had been caught. One of them had lost his balance while standing at the edge of an open window on the third floor of the police barrack during questioning. Four others had killed each other in the lock-up in a brawl. Elsewhere in The City, the robber Woegore and his accomplice Kirit, had been chased to their hide-out and shot while running to flee. A former newsman, a proofreader, whose name had not been released, accused of selling his paper's news to another, had been caught while passing on the incriminating document to his handler. He, too, of course, had been caught. What a horrible night last night had been. She pulled the wrap close around her shoulders to shield herself from the vapours of others' sins. As for the biggest news of all, she would read that last. That Mr Mobilish—still on the phone call! Blast that man! Did he know that The Plebiscite was off! Baba Lala's son had been found in a bag! Lala had retired from politics! The police were closing in on The Frontier where The Partisans had escaped after vandalising their city following the murder. With Lala gone, Aristu Argot had been offered to take over the Dongs and assume control, the Fairlanders no longer wanted to run the government! But had Mr Mobilish heard? He had heard. So where did that leave ordinary folks like them? Free!

Mrs Mobilish folded the paper and went to stand on her

balcony to take in the new dawn. Her tuburosas red as pigeon blood were growing all around the verandah on stems as dry as matchsticks. She turned west, the sea was grey but calm. In the east they were dismantling The Gates, who knows if they would build others? The wind breathed on her cheek, the sun warmed her hair, she looked at her spotless hands, her pink toe-nails, and tried to gulp down the worms coming out of her mouth.

Footnotes

Chapter 1* A limerick, origin unknown, in which a man lands up in the office of a female officer, whom he feels he has to address as Sir-arass and accordingly, change the gender of the greeting 'good morning' to 'good mararass,' and tries to explain the reason for the absenteeism of his brother Madhu with a cock-and-bull story about hydrocele.

* ...One day, I will be what I want to be. One day, I will be a thought that no sword nor any book will bear to the wasteland...(Mural, Mahmoud Darwish).

Chapter 2 * Author unknown.

Chapter 4 *W.H. Auden's 'Epitaph for the Unknown Soldier'.

Chapter 7 * Taken from a poem, 'The Last Will', written by workers Nicola Sacco and Bartolomew Vanzetti in Boston, 1920, convicted for murders they did not commit and who died on the electric chair for their radical politics.

Chapter 10 * Hand-written poster mounted on the wall expressing protest and political opinion. The first dazibao came up on May 25, 1966 at Peking University. It said the university had became the hub of bourgeois anti-revolutionaries.

Chapter 11*Ai-mother.

Chapter 21* "Why do we need Narcissus as long we're Palestinians, and as long as we don't know the difference between the Jamé (mosque) and the Jame ah (university), both words having the same root? What need do we have for a state... as long as it is moving, along with the days, towards the same destiny?" *You as of now, are someone else*—Mahmoud Darwish.

Acknowledgements

Timir Basu, for being generous with his time and the permission to borrow from the *Frontier* archives.

RC Mody for the permission to borrow and alter his King George poem.

Sher Singh. Ashok Bhowmick, Irfan, Hilal Mir.